STATEN ISLAND NOIR

EDITED BY PATRICIA SMITH

This collection is comprised of works of fiction. All names, characters, places, and incidents are the product of the authors' imaginations. Any resemblance to real events or persons, living or dead, is entirely coincidental.

Published by Akashic Books
©2012 Akashic Books

Series concept by Tim McLoughlin and Johnny Temple
Staten Island map by Aaron Petrovich

Printed in Canada

ISBN-13: 978-1-61775-129-5
Library of Congress Control Number: 2012939266
All rights reserved

First printing

Akashic Books
PO Box 1456
New York, NY 10009
info@akashicbooks.com
www.akashicbooks.com

ALSO IN THE AKASHIC BOOKS NOIR SERIES

BALTIMORE NOIR, edited by LAURA LIPPMAN

BARCELONA NOIR (SPAIN), edited by ADRIANA V. LÓPEZ
& CARMEN OSPINA

BOSTON NOIR, edited by DENNIS LEHANE

BOSTON NOIR 2: THE CLASSICS, edited by
DENNIS LEHANE, JAIME CLARKE & MARY COTTON

BRONX NOIR, edited by S.J. ROZAN

BROOKLYN NOIR, edited by TIM McLOUGHLIN

BROOKLYN NOIR 2: THE CLASSICS, edited by
TIM McLOUGHLIN

BROOKLYN NOIR 3: NOTHING BUT THE TRUTH,
edited by TIM McLOUGHLIN & THOMAS ADCOCK

CAPE COD NOIR, edited by DAVID L. ULIN

CHICAGO NOIR, edited by NEAL POLLACK

COPENHAGEN NOIR (DENMARK), edited by
BO TAO MICHAËLIS

D.C. NOIR, edited by GEORGE PELECANOS

D.C. NOIR 2: THE CLASSICS, edited by GEORGE PELECANOS

DELHI NOIR (INDIA), edited by HIRSH SAWHNEY

DETROIT NOIR, edited by E.J. OLSEN & JOHN C. HOCKING

DUBLIN NOIR (IRELAND), edited by KEN BRUEN

HAITI NOIR, edited by EDWIDGE DANTICAT

HAVANA NOIR (CUBA), edited by ACHY OBEJAS

INDIAN COUNTRY NOIR, edited by SARAH CORTEZ
& LIZ MARTÍNEZ

ISTANBUL NOIR (TURKEY), edited by MUSTAFA ZIYALAN
& AMY SPANGLER

KANSAS CITY NOIR, edited by STEVE PAUL

KINGSTON NOIR (JAMAICA), edited by COLIN CHANNER

LAS VEGAS NOIR, edited by JARRET KEENE
& TODD JAMES PIERCE

LONDON NOIR (ENGLAND), edited by CATHI UNSWORTH

LONE STAR NOIR, edited by BOBBY BYRD & JOHNNY BYRD

LONG ISLAND NOIR, edited by KAYLIE JONES

LOS ANGELES NOIR, edited by DENISE HAMILTON

LOS ANGELES NOIR 2: THE CLASSICS, edited by
DENISE HAMILTON

MANHATTAN NOIR, edited by LAWRENCE BLOCK

MANHATTAN NOIR 2: THE CLASSICS, edited by
LAWRENCE BLOCK

MEXICO CITY NOIR (MEXICO), edited by PACO I. TAIBO II

MIAMI NOIR, edited by LES STANDIFORD

MOSCOW NOIR (RUSSIA), edited by NATALIA SMIRNOVA
& JULIA GOUMEN

MUMBAI NOIR (INDIA), edited by ALTAF TYREWALA

NEW JERSEY NOIR, edited by JOYCE CAROL OATES

NEW ORLEANS NOIR, edited by JULIE SMITH

ORANGE COUNTY NOIR, edited by GARY PHILLIPS

PARIS NOIR (FRANCE), edited by AURÉLIEN MASSON

PHILADELPHIA NOIR, edited by CARLIN ROMANO

PHOENIX NOIR, edited by PATRICK MILLIKIN

PITTSBURGH NOIR, edited by KATHLEEN GEORGE

PORTLAND NOIR, edited by KEVIN SAMPSELL

QUEENS NOIR, edited by ROBERT KNIGHTLY

RICHMOND NOIR, edited by ANDREW BLOSSOM,
BRIAN CASTLEBERRY & TOM DE HAVEN

ROME NOIR (ITALY), edited by CHIARA STANGALINO
& MAXIM JAKUBOWSKI

ST. PETERSBURG NOIR (RUSSIA), edited by
NATALIA SMIRNOVA & JULIA GOUMEN

SAN DIEGO NOIR, edited by MARYELIZABETH HART

SAN FRANCISCO NOIR, edited by PETER MARAVELIS

SAN FRANCISCO NOIR 2: THE CLASSICS, edited by
PETER MARAVELIS

SEATTLE NOIR, edited by CURT COLBERT

TORONTO NOIR (CANADA), edited by JANINE ARMIN
& NATHANIEL G. MOORE

TRINIDAD NOIR (TRINIDAD & TOBAGO), edited by
LISA ALLEN-AGOSTINI & JEANNE MASON

TWIN CITIES NOIR, edited by JULIE SCHAPER
& STEVEN HORWITZ

VENICE NOIR (ITALY), edited by MAXIM JAKUBOWSKI

WALL STREET NOIR, edited by PETER SPIEGELMAN

FORTHCOMING

BOGOTÁ NOIR (COLOMBIA), edited by ANDREA MONTEJO

BUFFALO NOIR, edited by BRIGID HUGHES & ED PARK

JERUSALEM NOIR, edited by SAYED KASHUA

LAGOS NOIR (NIGERIA), edited by CHRIS ABANI

MANILA NOIR (PHILIPPINES), edited by JESSICA HAGEDORN

SEOUL NOIR (KOREA), edited by BS PUBLISHING CO.

TEL AVIV NOIR (ISRAEL), edited by ETGAR KERET

New Jersey
New Jersey
New York
Freshkills Park
New Jersey
New York
Fresh Kills
Annadale
North Mount
Loretto State Forest
Lemon Creek
Park
Tottenville
Conference House Park

UPPER BAY

THE FERRY

ST. GEORGE

BAYONNE

PORT RICHMOND

TOMPKINSVILLE

STAPLETON

BAY RIDGE, BROOKLYN

GRYMES HILL

FOUR CORNERS

PARK HILL

VERRAZANO-NARROWS BRIDGE

GRAVESEND BAY

SOUTH BEACH

FRANKLIN D. ROOSEVELT BOARDWALK AND BEACH

GREAT KILLS

STATEN ISLAND

GREAT KILLS PARK

LOWER BAY

ELTINGVILLE

TABLE OF CONTENTS

11   *Introduction*

PART I: FAMILY AFFAIR

---

21   **BILL LOEHFELM**   Eltingville
        Snake Hill

40   **LOUISA ERMELINO**   Great Kills
        Sister-in-Law

51   **PATRICIA SMITH**   Port Richmond
        When They Are Done with Us

71   **TED ANTHONY**   Fresh Kills
        A User's Guide to Keeping Your Kills Fresh

90   **SHAY YOUNGBLOOD**   South Beach
        Dark Was the Night, Cold Was the Ground

PART II: FIGHT OR FLIGHT

---

107   **MICHAEL PENNCAVAGE**   The Ferry
        Mistakes

118   **BRUCE DESILVA**   Tompkinsville
        Abating a Nuisance

132   **MICHAEL LARGO**   Four Corners
        Paying the Tab

140   **BINNIE KIRSHENBAUM**   Grymes Hill
        Assistant Professor Lodge

PART III: BOROUGH OF BROKEN DREAMS

155 **TODD CRAIG**   Park Hill
     . . . spy verse spy . . .

175 **EDDIE JOYCE**   Annadale
     Before It Hardens

200 **LINDA NIEVES-POWELL**   Stapleton
     The Fly-Ass Puerto Girl from the Stapleton Projects

212 **ASHLEY DAWSON**   Tottenville
     Teenage Wasteland

233 **S.J. ROZAN**   St. George
     Lighthouse

254 **About the Contributors**

INTRODUCTION
AN ERRINGLY PERFECT LANDSCAPE

I n the always entertaining send-up known as the Urban Dictionary, "Staten Island" is defined as "a floating dump that sits in New York Harbor. Often mistaken for a populated borough." Alternate definitions include: "Brooklyn with parking," "recepticle [sic] of New York City's garbage—paper, plastic, and human," "where the hair is high and the IQ is low," and "name given to the small pile of gristle, burnt ends, and spit-out left on the edge of your plate at the end of a meal," as in:

Have you finished your dinner?
Yep.
What about that last mouthful?
Nah, that's just Staten Island.

Incensed? Insulted? Then you're probably not a native of the island. Some of Staten Island's most vocal detractors are those who grimly populate its clutter. They're the ones spewing expletives after a snowy-white Escalade or a tricked-out Camaro smushes them against the railing on the Outerbridge. They're growling because it's August and there's that certain fragrance wafting on the breeze. They're the ones who consider their entertainment options for the upcoming weekend and realize, once again, that the choices are 1) the mall; 2) the mall; or 3) hop the ferry and get the hell away from . . . the mall.

Next time you're on the island, slow your stroll and take a good long look at the oft-falling faces of its citizenry. There is very little veering toward glee. Sure, you can find giggling children romping in a kid-sized anthill at the Children's Museum or picture-book couples strolling hand-in-hand through the Greenbelt. There are raucous side streets that feel like a family reunion, with neighbors conversing from their stoops and a cool clash of salsa and Sinatra blaring from open windows. Indeed, there are sometimes whole gaggles of happy people doing apparently happy things and looking damned pleased to be living in . . . in . . . uh, that *other* borough.

But in front of, behind, and on either side of these perky few plods a Greek chorus on Thorazine, shuffling in the shadows and moaning a soundtrack of regional discontent. The tragic chorale seems to be made up mostly of my writing students at the College of Staten Island. When I ask them to write anything about where they live, they sigh and roll their eyes so dramatically they can see who's behind them without turning around.

Each semester I confront a different group of eye-rollers, but when the topic is Staten Island the consensus varies only slightly:

"Nothing *ever* happens."

"*Nothing* ever happens."

"Nothing ever *happens.*"

As a writer, I firmly believe that 1) there's nowhere where nothing ever happens; 2) something eventually happens everywhere, even nowhere; 3) everything is bound to happen somewhere; and 4) there's no such thing as nothing whenever you're somewhere.

Nothing ever happens on Staten Island?

Nothing happening on the glitzy Uggs-trodden paths of the Staten Island Mall, no steamy intrigue in Frederick's of Hollywood or in the cinnamon-dusted confines of Auntie Anne's?

No memorable drama on the relentless to-and-fro of the ferry? Nothing cool about the counter guy at the neighborhood bodega who always has a great story, or that gay club that opened up for a while then disappeared? How about intrigue in the lives of the dude and dudette of Staten Island stereotype—she orange-tinged, deftly manicured, and helplessly attached to her cell; he muscled, sticky-coiffed, and primping behind the wheel of that aforementioned Camaro?

Nothing interesting *at all*? I ask, and, after another round of eye-rolling, they're aching to elaborate.

"This place is too damned small."

"Everybody knows everybody else's business."

"Same people you grew up with, all the time. Never anybody new."

"There's no place to go but the mall."

"Being made fun of all the time gets tired real fast. I don't even tell anybody I'm from here."

And until I finally shut them up, all they do is continue to serve up more reasons why Staten Island is an erringly perfect landscape for noir, the ideal hangout for scoundrels, swindlers, liars, thieves, murderers, adulterous vixens, and assorted hooligans. Let's review:

1.

The place was too damned small. On all sides, water ate away at the island. Every day, the brick of the buildings inched closer to him, until Eddie could feel their soft scrape against his skin. Every street seemed to sweat, panting poisons through its many open mouths. There was no street he hadn't seen, no corner that didn't hiss his name. People walked toward him, through him, past him, all smirking on the edge of a smile. Laughing at him. But there it was, the sweet weight of the gun in his pocket. Soon he'd be able to breathe again. Eddie would blow a hole in the way the city touched him, and he'd climb through.

2.

"Everybody knows everybody else's business," Eddie spat, "and I don't want nobody knowin' mine." He held the bartender's wiggling little head in a vise grip until it stopped wiggling. He looked down, and the little guy's scalp was glowing red. Eddie got real pissed real fast because here it was, an interruption in his day, now he had to figure out if he felt like killing this guy. One minute, he's looking forward to the zarzuela and a nice chianti at Espana, now here's this loudmouth prick with his eyes popping out.

3.

Same people you grew up with, all the time. Never anybody new. Alexis could swear she said the words out loud, but there was Eddie, still asleep, snorting, his mouth open, his mountain of belly radiating heat. Just because their families had lived next to each other in New Dorp. Just because he'd given her that stupid ring in high school. Just because he was the first one to ask, she had to say yes, had to stand up in front of God and family and sign up for this? She sighed, fingered the little blade, studied his sweating pink neck.

4.

There's no place to go but the mall. There's no place to go but the mall, and there's no way to walk but in well-lit circles, then ride the escalator with its silver teeth, and the girls. There's no place to go but the mall, and the girls. Sheep boots and sequin skirts, low-cut tops, red-tipped nails, hair color of falling sun, skinny wrists, big perfect mouths, and the girls, swing purses, smack gum, talk the island, girls. Blindfold left pocket this time. Tape on the right. There's no place to go but the mall. There's nothing to do but wait.

5.

I don't even tell anybody I'm from here. I can hit Brooklyn or the Boogie B, sling it like I'm a gangsta, point my ride down the middle of the street. I can flash my piece, hold it against a throat, have a man whimpering my name. I can lay a woman down, then leave her, make her unknow my name if that's what I need. Then I get on that great big boat, and I'm gone. In the Bronx, some guy with a gun is searching the back alleys for me. Some big-hipped redhead in Brooklyn is aching to stake a claim. But I get home and the island closes around me, names me all over again. There's something about water. It cleans you.

So there.

Staten Island = 0 is a popular equation outside the confines of the borough. During Bouchercon, an annual national crime fiction convention, I sat fuming as a panel on "crime fiction set in New York" went on and on and on, with panelists bellowing darkly about nefarious goings-on and iconic characters in Manhattan, the Bronx, Queens, Brooklyn, and . . . and . . .

Finally, nudged by an irritated attendee who suddenly knew why her students didn't want to write about their home town, members of the panel acknowledged their omission with what amounted to, *Oh yeah, there's crime there too,* and went back to a spirited discussion of the Big Four.

Yep, there's crime here too. Good crime. Mystery. Dark, scary stuff. Big crime. The noir kind, without a good guy in sight. Just scan the headlines: *Skeleton in Staten Island Basement Points to Unsolved Murder; Staten Island Man Commits Murder after Victim Had Spit in Wife's Face.* Then there's the haunted Kreischer mansion on Arthur Kill Road. *Mob Wives,* for Chrissakes, with all that squalling, hair-pulling, and Botox. A recent spate of hate crimes against blacks, Mexicans, Muslims. Mist-shrouded abandoned psychiatric hospitals. Guys named Eddie. Underground caverns. Willowbrook. The ghostly ship grave-yard. The legend of Cropsey. That rolling landfill and all those secrets buried beneath it.

Even the one movie that was named after the borough got it exactly right. Here's the synopsis: *A Staten Island mob boss Parmie is robbed by septic tank cleaner Sully who has a pal Jasper, a deaf deli employee moonlighting as a corpse chopper.*

That's a damned sunshiny day on the island.

I'm not sure why Staten Island is the borough bringing up the rear in Akashic Books' Noir Series (okay, okay, yes I am), but here we are, the shiny coin in New York's back pocket. (You can't really buy anything with it, but throwing it away would definitely bring bad luck.) We will prove that SI is as rotten, vengeful, unforgiving, and badass as any one of its quartet of brothers.

This gang I've gathered is unrelenting. Among them is island native Bill Loehfelm, who crafts a stark and breathless character study on Snake Hill. In "A User's Guide to Keep-ing Your Kills Fresh," Ted Anthony chronicles the haphazard adventures of a murderous mob bungler. The blade-edged te-nets of street justice rule the day, and night, in Todd Craig's ". . . spy verse spy . . ." Michael Largo's "Paying the Tab" sits the reader on a barstool, then lifts you out of one world and into another. S.J. Rozan's "Lighthouse" moves with a chilling, elegant rhythm, and Linda Nieves-Powell arranges a jazzy in-troduction to the siren of the Stapleton projects. And lest you think that nefarious island hijinks are a recent development, Bruce DeSilva builds upon a true story of unbridled power and privilege, set in 1858.

That said, I'm slightly disappointed that there are no appearances by corpse choppers, which may be because it's become a perfectly respectable Staten Island job description. Nevertheless, I'd like to meet one.

Patricia Smith
July 2012

PART I

FAMILY AFFAIR

SNAKE HILL

BY BILL LOEHFELM

Eltingville

We came over the top of Snake Hill too fast, and started our drop down the other side at the same speed. My father's giant old station wagon slalomed deep into the snaky curves like a fat skier in wet snow. The tires didn't screech, but they squeaked now and again. Streetlamps were few and far between. The trees were black shadows on both sides, the foliage dense and dark, close to the roadside. I tried to keep the headlights focused on the winding double yellow lines in front of me, keep those lines centered in the crossed beams of light. I hoped to hell that no one was coming up the hill in the opposite lane.

My brother snored over on the passenger side of the wagon's big bench seat, having passed out sometime in the first three minutes after we left the Haunted Café back on Bay Street. I hadn't seen him put back more than two or three drinks, less than half of what I'd had, and I got that sick, nervous feeling in my stomach that had been coming on more and more lately, the feeling that he was messing with more powerful stuff than booze. Pills, maybe. Powders. He hadn't, I noticed with a quick glance, despite my insistence and his assurances, fastened his seat belt. Couldn't even do that for me. I wanted to slam on the brakes and bounce his head off the dashboard, just to make a point. But I didn't do it. I kept riding the sharp, blind curves in the road. He shifted in his seat with the back-and-forth motion of the car.

Why, I wondered again, tightening my grip on the steering wheel, was I driving like a maniac to get us home by curfew when there was so much more to worry about? Because, I reminded myself, curfew was what our folks cared about. Curfew and the car. They wouldn't ask what Danny was getting into, because they didn't want to know, and I sure wouldn't tell. Wouldn't say anything about a seventeen-year-old with a grown-up hangover. They never did anymore, not after the past two years in our house. We'd had all the bad news we could handle.

I looked over at my brother again. His forehead was pressed against his window. I couldn't see his face, but I knew he always smiled in his sleep—the benefits of an empty conscience. Another quick check of the road and I glanced at the dashboard clock. One fifteen in the a.m. Well, we'd blown curfew. That was a lost cause. Seemed I was losing causes by the minute. More important now was the matter of getting down the hill. If I couldn't deliver us home on time, I could at least deliver us home in one piece. That plan hit the skids, literally, barely a moment after I had that thought.

I don't know if it was oil, or gravel, or the greasy entrails of something dead and left to rot, but coming out of an especially sharp turn, the back end of the station wagon fishtailed hard left, as if God had flicked the ass-end of the car with his finger. I didn't panic. I didn't overcorrect. I didn't make a sound. I held steady and hit the brakes.

The back left corner of the station wagon slammed into the guardrail, the back tires sliding and scratching on some roadside gravel. A deep *thump* pulsed through the car on impact, as if someone had whacked an empty pot with a spoon and we were inside the pot. It wasn't that loud, considering, but it lingered in my ears for an extra second nonetheless. The chassis bounced once or twice and the car settled, still, on the side of the road like the collision had knocked the wind out of it. My brother groaned beside me. He touched his fingertips to his forehead. One eye was open, the other still closed. I guess he wanted to make sure the incident was worth the effort of opening both. I was glad he seemed okay. I grimaced in sympathy at the goose egg already rising over his right eye. Maybe that's why that left one had stayed closed.

"What the fuck, Kev?" he said. "We dead?"

"No," I said. "We're fine."

At least he knew we'd had an accident. He couldn't be that far gone.

He nodded as if I'd given him a lot of information to process. He squinted through the windshield with his one open eye then turned and did the same out the back window. He was looking, I realized, for the other car.

"Just us," I said. I turned around too. A cloud of thin gray dust hung suspended in the ruby-red glow of the brake lights. I realized I still had the brake pedal pinned. "I tagged the guardrail coming out of a curve. Too much of a rush, I guess."

"I don't know why you give a fuck about curfew anymore," he said, turning to me, both eyes open now, bewilderment all over his face. He sniffed. "You're the only one who does."

"Who do you hang out with?" I asked.

"You."

"And who else?"

"No one, really," my brother said.

"And how do we get around?"

"In Dad's car."

"Ask me again why I care about curfew."

My brother scoffed: "Dad'll let you have the car whenever

we hang out, especially *because* we hang out, whatever the fuck time we come home. What're you, dense?"

"And you're so wise on this how?"

Danny shrugged like the answer was so obvious he could barely speak it. "Dad thinks you look out for me. He thinks I'm safer when we're together. He wouldn't run the risk of separating us. Mom wouldn't let him."

"You saying you're not safer with me than you would be alone?" I swallowed hard. "Doing what you do these days?"

Danny turned one way in his seat, and then the other, glancing around us. "Didn't you just wreck the car?"

"I didn't wreck it," I said. I didn't know what part of my commentary his crack about the car had been meant to criticize. "Just dinged it up at most."

I decided I should get a look at how bad before I tried continuing the drive home, or continuing my attempt at a conversation with my younger brother about his growing drug problem. Just in case it was worse than I thought, worse than it had sounded. The car, I mean.

I opened the door, cool night air rushing into the car. I realized I'd been sweating, the breeze running up the sleeves of my T-shirt. I took a deep breath. When I turned to hang out the door and look, the seat belt caught. Danny stifled a giggle. I popped the belt free and leaned out of the car.

"You smell gas?" Danny asked.

"No." So far, so good. I hadn't even thought of that. Gas tank was on that side too. I heard the flick of a lighter and smelled cigarette smoke. Glad he was so confident. But things seemed okay. The back tire wasn't flat. I could see the hubcap. No dents that I could see in the back quarter panel, at least in the faint wash of the dome light from inside the car.

"Light me one," I told Danny. Without turning, I reached

my arm across the car for the cigarette. The lack of obvious damage had me feeling better, more and more confident that nothing was wrong that we couldn't play off as a parking lot accident and pin on some other idiot driver. Dad would grumble, but he'd forgive. And small dents he could pound out himself in the driveway. He was handy like that.

Danny slipped the cigarette into my fingers. I brought the smoke to my lips, tapped the brake pedal. The taillights ignited, a red burst off the back of the car washing over the wild green bushes and trunks of the trees. Still working, that was good. None of the telltale bright white gave away broken glass back there. Amazing, I thought, how bright those lights actually are. I tapped them again. And then I saw it. My throat went dry.

A shoe. One shoe.

A sneaker, really. A blue Ked, adult sized. The cheap kind you see lined up in flimsy cardboard boxes along those long rows of shelves at the K-Mart or the Korvettes. Like old people wore. No big deal, I told myself, a shoe by the side of the road. Except this shoe stood on its heel, tilted a little to the left. I could see a bony, hairless, blue-veined ankle, the cuff of a pajama leg. An old person. Some poor, senile, old bastard who'd probably wandered away from one of the estates on the hill.

My throat closed and my heart stopped, a fist reaching into my chest and squeezing my heart down to the size of a grape, strangling it.

Fuck me. I'd killed someone.

I heard Danny getting out of the car. Air exploded out of my chest and my heart started again. I lunged for Danny, locking onto his forearm. He glanced down at my hand, not looking all that surprised I'd grabbed ahold of him.

"Get back in the car," I said.

"Lemme go," he said. "I gotta take a piss. Since we're apparently camping out here for the night."

"Get in the car."

I did *not* want him seeing that body. And I didn't want anybody seeing us anywhere near it. I'd decided to run from the scene. I couldn't even remember making the decision. But I was totally sure of what I wanted to do.

"Dude, I gotta go," Danny said. "One sec."

"Wait till we get home."

"Who're you? Fucking Mom?"

"Someone could see us."

"I'll go back in the woods." He chuckled. "You already took care of the guardrail. Easy-peasy."

He tried to tug his arm free, half an effort because he expected me to let go. I didn't. He bristled, and for the first time since we'd stopped he looked a little angry.

"There's gotta be a car coming," I said, "either from ahead or behind us."

We'd settled to a stop on the wrong side of the road, facing into oncoming traffic, our headlights burning bright down the side of the hill. It was mid-spring, the trees had only half their leaves. Our car was blatantly visible from every direction. Our voices probably carried far in the quiet night. The sound of the station wagon slamming the guardrail certainly had. People did live up here. They lived nearby over on Todt Hill, and on Lighthouse Road too. The Hill people. Rich people. Rich people who didn't tolerate late-night, side-of-the-road bullshit, people who didn't come to see if you were all right, if there was anything they could do to help. They just called the cops and went back to bed and let the paid help deal with it. That could've happened already. The cops could be on their way up the hill as we sat there bickering like one of us had gotten more chocolate milk than the other at breakfast.

I didn't want to be dealt with. I wanted my brother back in the fucking car. And I wanted both of us home.

Danny settled on the edge of the front seat, one leg in and one leg out of the car, cigarette dangling from the corner of his mouth. He had his outside leg in the middle of the road. "What the fuck?" He reached under his seat, moving his hand around under it. "We don't have *any* beers left in here?"

I thought I saw headlights break through the trees below.

"We're in a hurry," I said, trying to keep my voice light, and failing. "Remember?"

I watched my brother for a reaction to my bullshit. Could I have made it any more obvious that there was something at the back of the car I didn't want him to see? I hoped my guilt and horror, not only over what I had done by accident but what I was now doing on purpose, amplified my fears, like that remorse-ridden lunatic in "The Tell-Tale Heart." I realized gratefully that Danny had most likely never read the story. I also realized I was glad and relieved he was high and therefore if not easily led at least leadable.

That thought made me feel like shit. It made me sick.

"We're going," I said, my voice a croak. "Now."

I braked as I put the car in drive, using the sideview mirror to look into the cloud of red light and exhaust behind us. I saw the second foot as we inched away from the shoulder. Though it tilted away from the first foot at the toes, the heels were nearly touching, the feet therefore making a V shape, like feet did when their owner was flat on their back. On the soles I could see the Rice Krispies patterns in the waxy, honey-colored rubber. Or maybe I was imagining that last part. Our grandfather had worn those same shoes in the last years of his life. Before he died after two long, long years of stomach cancer, calling out for morphine till the bitter end.

Back in brightly lit Eltingville, streetlights and porch lights everywhere, I parked the car a few houses down from ours. It annoyed the neighbors to no end, seeing my father's beat-to-hell, twelve-year-old, 1977 gray behemoth of an Impala wagon parked in "their" parking spot.

Back in the day, long before us, before he'd even met our mother, our father had been a brawler, and Danny and I desperately wanted, just once, to see him throw down on the neighbors we liked least. Like the 'roided-out dude from my high school who washed his Monte Carlo SS twice a week, shirtless and cranking shitty club music, like the whole island was his personal health club/coke den/dancehall. Or the old guy who lived alone on mental disability checks and never drove and so sat behind his living room curtains all day, even when the kids on the block were at school, the guy waiting for some Wiffle ball or street hockey ball to bounce onto his pristine lawn so he could crank the window and threaten to call the cops. Or, more specifically, his son, the cop, who we never saw, not once. But it never happened. Dad didn't fight anymore. At least not over parking spaces, and certainly not over the wiseassery of his silly sons.

After I turned off the engine, I sat behind the wheel for a few moments, a few breaths, willing myself to leave what I'd seen and done on the hill up there. I silently swore to never take that short cut again, curfew be damned. I had a brief, ridiculous thought that if we did get busted for hitting someone back on the hill, that we, that I, could somehow blame my father. If he hadn't been so anal about the curfew, I would never have been in such a hurry. That particular bizarre assemblage of necessary moments that led to me killing someone would never have coalesced and I would never have hit that person now lying there dead by the side of the road. My face got hot. Of all the rotten fucking luck. How many things had to go wrong for that person to be in that spot at that moment when the rear end of the Impala came smashing into them? If I'd tried to hit that person I never, ever could have done it. Not even head-on. What was that goddamn *idiot* doing wandering along a pitch-black road in the middle of the night? It had never entered my mind that there might be someone even more careless than me on that road. Certainly not someone I couldn't see coming. My head started to hurt. I had to stop thinking about it. Why was it so hot inside the car? I opened the door and stepped out into the street. Danny was already around the back of the car.

"Holy shit," I heard him say. It was an observation, not a weary summation of the night's adventures. That scared me. "Damn," he said.

A dent, probably. Maybe some torn-away piece of clothing. Blood, most likely. Worse, possibly. Body parts. I continued around the back of the car and saw what had arrested Danny's attention. The entire back bumper of the station wagon was missing. Gone. Shorn clean off when I'd fishtailed the Impala into the guardrail. And now lying by the side of the road at the scene of the accident. Could you trace a bumper back to the car from which it came? You could certainly get make and model and year. You could go around to body shops asking who'd come in for a replacement bumper for a '77 Impala station wagon. You could tell all your cop friends to keep an eye out for cars missing their rear bumpers. And then I realized no cop would even have to do that much work to find out what car had hit that dead person. Because, I realized, that bumper was lying there with the license plate still attached. I almost laughed.

I'd killed someone, fled the accident, and left the license plate at the scene. I was too dumb to be a character in a Poe story. What had Danny said about our dad trusting me to look out for him? Talk about misplaced trust. I thought for a moment about walking into the house, waking him, and spilling everything, putting everything in his hands. But I didn't want this on him, and I didn't really want him to handle it. I just wanted it to go away. Getting him involved wouldn't make that happen. Now was not the time for wishful thinking.

Danny had a fistful of hair at the top of his head. He was staring at the back of the station wagon. "Wow. I betcha that's hard to do. Dad's gonna fucking freak."

"We gotta go back," I said.

"We?"

"Yes, we," I said. "I'm gonna need your help."

"Dude, I'm tired. How heavy can a bumper be, right? Toss it in the back. We'll hit the body shop in the morning. I'm still suspended. I've got the time. I'll take it in."

"You don't have a license," I said. "You're not allowed to drive."

Danny laughed. "That's your best argument?"

"I need you to look for the bumper," I said. "I'm gonna be driving in the dark."

"Wait till morning."

"Dad's gonna walk right past here on his way to the train. He's gonna see it."

"Then let's move the car around the corner."

"Then how do we explain getting home without it?"

"Bus?"

"Fuck! Danny! C'mon!" I kicked at the space where the bumper had been. "Help me out here."

Danny started laughing. I could've strangled him right

there in the gutter. He'd played me right into a temper tantrum. He'd been doing it since we were little kids. I had a flash of us as eighty-year-old men, standing in this same street, me screaming at him, and him laughing. It would never end. He'd been willing to go back to Snake Hill from the moment I'd first asked. I should've known better. As if there had ever been a time when he'd rather go home and go to bed than traipse off on another adventure, no matter how minor. Well, this one wasn't as minor as he thought, but I saw no need to make him the wiser.

He walked to the passenger-side door, tried the handle, and found it locked. "We gonna go, or what?" He couldn't stop smiling. "I ain't got all night."

The words *accessory after the fact* scrolled across my brain. I tried to console myself with the fact that no cop, no court on earth, would believe Danny's denial that he knew nothing about the body. How would he defend himself? *Well, your honor, I was on the nod from a head full of backroom crank.* I told myself that in protecting myself I was protecting him too. And my father, whose name was on the registration attached to the wagon's license plate. Really, I was protecting the whole family by returning to the scene of the crime and cleaning it up.

I climbed into the driver's seat and started the car. *Maybe you should have thought about protecting the family*, a faint voice in the back of my head told me, *before you took Snake Hill at twice the advisable speed while six drinks deep on a weeknight.*

It's too late, I argued back as I pulled us away from the curb, *to do anything about those choices now.*

I took us back the way we came, the wide residential streets of our neighborhood narrowing into the older, winding commercial corridors of Amboy Road with its short canvas awnings hanging over the bricked storefronts, every building hugging the thin strip of sidewalk dividing it from the road. Coming around the curves, which I took slowly, it looked impossible to step out of the nail salon or the deli or the driving school and not walk right into oncoming traffic. At intersections, I lingered too long at green lights, petrified of committing some violation.

The streets we followed back onto Richmond Road were only one lane each way and usually bustled, jam packed with traffic in both directions, but at that late hour the streets were dead. We saw not a soul. And that fact only made me sure that Danny and I couldn't have looked more suspicious being out and about at that hour. Riding around in our damaged car couldn't help our image much. And should we get pulled over, how would we explain ourselves? Or the lack of a rear bumper, which was a great excuse to light us up in the first place. I wanted desperately to speed, to push our errand to its end. The knots in my stomach pulled tighter as we moved away from the homes and businesses and the road darkened.

We found the foot of Snake Hill and started our slow climb. I hoped we wouldn't encounter some version of my earlier, idiot self, careening down the hill road out of control at top speed.

"Think of it like this," Danny said. "Could've been worse. What if that guardrail wasn't there? Most of Snake Hill doesn't have any. We could've gone spinning off into the trees. Into God knows what else. What's the drop-off like over there?"

"I don't know."

"How steep you think it is?"

"I don't know that, either."

"Right," Danny said. "And now we don't have to."

"We should probably start looking for the bumper soon."

I slowed our progress to a crawl, barely enough for forward motion, and decided I'd move as far as I could onto the narrow shoulder should someone come up behind us. Danny kept a steady watch on the roadside. He was humoring me, as we still had a couple hundred yards to go before we came anywhere near where the collision had been. I was grateful. I needed him to be quiet so I could think. I needed to decide how much to tell him.

One of Danny's qualities that I most envied was his refusal to judge. I wondered if it was cynicism, optimism, or apathy that left him shrugging off every atrocity and most acts of kindness that he witnessed on the news or saw in the papers. He'd always viewed most of the world from a peaceful distance, and that was even before he found the drugs. Maybe that was what he liked about them. Maybe they made that distance deeper or safer or made it feel permanent and right. Maybe that distance got harder to maintain as he grew older. Or maybe it was Grandpa's death, or what it did to our mother, the way it stoked her hot tears and her raging temper, that made him want his boat to drift even farther from shore. The agony in our house certainly made the fight look futile, even I could see that, and I believed in heaven.

As we both peered into the roadside shadows, I found myself wishing I had left Danny home. Not that he would've stayed there if I'd told him to. He'd never have let me back out into the night alone.

I heard a sharp "A-ha" from Danny and turned to see him pointing dead ahead through the windshield. And there, in the middle of the road, in all its slightly tarnished glory, was the Impala's bumper. Intact and lying there like so much chrome road kill.

"Nicely done," I said, pulling the car over to the side of the road.

There wasn't much of a shoulder and half the wagon hung out into the traffic lane. We'd have fair warning about oncoming traffic from either direction, though, and the later it got, the smaller our chances of encountering another driver, anyway.

I threw the car in park, hit the hazards, and jumped out the door. I glanced into the woods, searching for the shoes in the weak glow of the Impala's dome light. I didn't see them, but I knew that didn't mean they weren't out there, or that Danny wasn't going to see them. Unless, of course, they'd never been there to begin with, something I could convince myself was true if I worked at it hard enough. I'd prefer having had a hallucination to the reality that I'd killed someone.

I heard a groan. A faint, B-movie zombie groan.

There was no way. The old man I'd hit had to be dead. I'd hit him with an out-of-control, two-thousand-pound automobile. Christ, I'd never considered the alternative. A fucking miracle.

Danny was out of the car, looking at me over the roof and waiting for instructions. I didn't think he'd heard the groan in the woods. Maybe I hadn't either. Then I heard it again.

"Fuck." I hung my head.

"Fuck what?" Danny said. "The bumper's right here on the shoulder. We're golden. Let's dump it in the car and get the hell outta here."

Another groan.

"Did you hear that?" Danny asked.

"It's nothing," I said. "Some animal in the woods."

Danny laughed. "This is Staten Island, for Chrissakes. *Animal in the woods*, like this is fucking upstate or something. Gimme a break. Somebody's out there."

We heard a faint rustling in the leaves. Faint enough that it could have been the wind.

"Fuck this," Danny said. He went back to the car, pulled

open the passenger-side door. He reached under the seat, and pulled out a gun from underneath it. A small black pistol.

I was shocked to see it. "What the fuck is that?"

"It's a Pez dispenser. What's it fucking look like?"

"Where did you get that?"

"I had it for a while, this dude at school bet me on the Jets game and didn't have the cash. What's it matter? You never saw it."

He walked around the back of the car, peering into the dark woods. He stepped to the edge of the trees, to where I'd taken out the guardrail with the car, the gun held loosely at his side. "Yo! Fucknuts! You ain't scarin' nobody."

Enough of this, I thought. I jogged over to the bumper, grabbed one end, started dragging it toward the car, the metal grinding on the asphalt.

"Help me with this, Danny. Put the gun away. It's somebody's old dog or something. Open the back of the car."

But Danny ignored me. He was staring into the dark woods, his head tilted to one side like a puppy that didn't understand a command. I stopped halfway to the car, bent over, panting, cradling one end of the bumper in my hands. I listened for what it was Danny heard. I heard it too. The old man's voice, a feeble attempt at words. Gibberish. Danny turned to me.

"There's somebody out there," he said, quieter this time, no aggression or defiance in his tone. "What the fuck?"

I set the bumper back down on the pavement. "I need your help. Me. Over here."

Danny looked at me for a long moment then he started into the woods, picking his way over the dead fallen branches and through the underbrush, sloughing his way across the carpet of dead leaves.

"Goddamnit, Danny."

I looked at the bumper at my feet, looked into the woods, where Danny was now a slow-moving shadow among the trees. He'd gone right by the spot where I knew the old man was lying. Danny was probably still drunk, I reminded myself. And still high, as well.

The battered gray hulk of the station wagon sat silent by the side of the road, the pulsing hazard lights making the car look like a UFO awaiting liftoff.

I wasn't a horrible person. I thought the guy was dead. I didn't see any benefit to anyone in confessing that I'd killed him. I'd get in trouble, as would Danny, who got in plenty without my help. I felt bad for the old man, bad for his family. He had people who loved him, though not enough to keep him from staggering along a dark road in the middle of the night. But why should two families suffer? It sucked that someone had lost their grandpa because I was a terrible drunk driver. Was it any worse than going by cancer? Any worse than a slow, awful death that traumatized your kid so bad that she traumatized her own? And why should my parents, one of whom had just lost her parent, lose their sons over the same accident, if they didn't have to? Nothing I did would bring him back to life.

But all that was moot now, I thought, because the old fucker wasn't dead.

I left the bumper where I'd dropped it and moved into the woods, making my way toward the shadow I knew was Danny. It got easier to find him when his disembodied face appeared in the golden glow of his lighter. He watched me the entire time I made my way to him. We'd ended up several yards deep in the woods. I'd thought the old man had been closer to the road. Then I figured it out. He'd crawled. Danny let the flame go out.

"Shit gets hot," Danny said. "Did you know about this? Is that why you were all fucking freaked?"

I said nothing. Hands on my knees, I bent over the old man, listening to his raspy breathing. How could he not be dead? I'd hit him with a fishtailing station wagon, flipping him over a guardrail. And yes, I'd left him there, broken and bleeding. Danny hit the lighter again.

The old man had gray eyes. They stared straight up. They stared past me and Danny, up into the night sky, maybe searching through the branches overhead for the stars. Maybe he saw something or someone coming for him. It did not appear that he saw me or my brother standing over him. I thought about how sad it would be if in his head, the last feeble circuits were firing and what he saw as the famed white light at the end of the tunnel was in reality just Danny's lighter, glowing there in the dark like the lantern on the ferryman's boat. No one would even look for him until the early morning. He wore thin blue pajamas and a ragged maroon robe that was thrown open, the top soaked dark purple with blood. His chest was caved in like someone had dropped a safe—or a station wagon—on him.

"This is a fucking mess," Danny said.

It was. The old man had misused the last of his strength crawling deeper into the woods and away from any chance of somebody seeing him in time to save him.

"We did this with the car, didn't we?" Danny asked. "You saw him, you knew he was here." He shook his head. "We gotta take care of him."

"Danny, listen. Look at him. He's got minutes left, tops. What're we gonna do? Drive all the way down the hill and find a pay phone somewhere? Nose-diving down this hill started all this. We gonna knock on doors up here on the hill? How do we explain how we found him? It ain't that tough to figure out he got hit by a car."

"I can't believe what I'm hearing. I never knew you could

think like this." He let the lighter go out. "What if he doesn't have minutes left, what if it's hours? He's hung on this long."

"I can't tell you what to do," I said. Fuck it. "We can carry him to the car maybe. You wanna take care of him, we'll take care of him."

Danny hit the lighter again. "That wasn't what I meant by take care of him." He held the gun out to me. "This is."

"Jesus, Danny. Are you serious? I don't think that's the right idea."

"You leave him here dying in the woods. Now you're squeamish? Look at the guy. We'd be doing him a favor." The lighter went out. "Remember how Grandpa hung on and hung on, for weeks, months after they gave him only days? You want that for this poor bastard? For his family? I wish somebody had come for Grandpa with a gun."

I looked back to the road, at the squat gray mass of the car. Its flashing lights seemed to mark the seconds passing us by, silently beating the time like a lit-up heart. We were really pushing our luck. Another car would come over the hill sooner or later. I appreciated my brother making a moral argument on my behalf, giving me an ethical parachute. He meant well. I was the good brother, after all, the one who, till tonight at least, concerned himself with such things. But if morals or ethics or right and wrong were really my worries, I'd never have left the old man there in the first place. I was learning fast what I really cared about. From the moment I saw him handing it my way in the lighter's glow, I'd had only one real concern about the gun.

"You misunderstood me," I said. "Somebody's gonna hear that gunshot. We can't have that."

We stood there in the dark, the old man at our feet, his weak scratchy breaths growing farther apart. I had the power to end it, his life, the whole fucked up episode I'd gotten myself and my brother into. All I had to do was accept the power, and not leave all our fates, as predictable as they may be considering where we lived, to other hands.

"Go back to the car," I said. "I'll meet you there in a minute."

"Fuck that."

"We can't leave him. We can't shoot him. Go. I'll take care of it."

"I got this," he said, kneeling down in the dead leaves. "*You* go back to the car. I'm much, much better at living with ugly shit than you are."

I kneeled across from him, speaking to him over the dying man. "Because it's only now that it's getting ugly?"

Danny crouched there, hands on his thighs, waiting, giving me time to make my case.

"You close and cover his mouth," I said. "And I'll pinch his nose shut. We'll carry it together. We'll never talk about it. Ever. That's my best offer."

"He's barely even here," Danny said, moving. "This shouldn't take long."

It didn't.

By the time Danny was halfway through his third whispered Hail Mary, the old man was dead. I hadn't thought to use the time to pray. And then we were done and everything would be like it had been from the beginning, an accident.

We stood, brushed the twigs and dead leaves from our pants, and crept out of the woods. We didn't speak. Danny helped me load the bumper into the back of the station wagon. It barely fit. As we drove home across the island, Danny helped me work up a story for our folks to explain what had happened—to the car. It was the only thing we talked about.

SISTER-IN-LAW

BY LOUISA ERMELINO

Great Kills

G et in the car.
I started to turn but there was a gun in my back or something pretending to be a gun. I faced forward. The voice was familiar, a woman's voice, a cigarette voice. Philip Morris unfiltered. I think that's the only way Philip Morris comes. Smoking them was a grand statement, too big for me, but if I was right about the voice then we'd shared a few together, she and I.

Angela?

Just get in the car. On your left.

She leaned over and opened the door and moved back. I got in. Her husband Joey was driving. He was a small guy and it was a big car. He looked like he was sitting in a hole. It was Buddy's car, a white Cadillac convertible with rocket fins, but the top was up, black and ominous.

Joey? I said.

Joey stared straight ahead, didn't even check me out in the rearview mirror. I was disappointed. I thought Joey liked me, but then I was always thinking people liked me when they really didn't give a shit. I felt better that I was in the backseat with Angela and not in the front with Joey. I knew about the piano wire around the neck, though this was no movie . . .

I actually felt bad. Until just now, Angela had treated me like family.

We were in the Village, on Barrow Street. I was on my way to meet Buddy at the gay club he used to own, before the feds subpoenaed him to testify. He said that was when he learned to sweat and gave up red silk lining in his custom-made suits. Maybe saying the club he used to *run* was a better way to put it. Only one group of people owned clubs in Greenwich Village, but it was undisclosed ownership. The State Liquor Authority kept close tabs on who got a liquor license.

Why did I know all this? I shouldn't have. My criminal involvement began and ended with my father's Prohibition bootlegging days and his stint as a bookkeeper for Tony Bender in the '30s. Good with numbers and honest, my father wasn't looking for power and glory, just enough money to start a legitimate business and buy a house. So how did I end up in a white Cadillac with rocket fins and this crazy bitch who was about to become my sister-in-law holding a gun on me?

I asked Angela where we were going. It was a legitimate question, I thought, under the circumstances.

Does it matter? she said.

I shrugged and she pulled my hair.

Staten Island? I said.

Bingo. She laughed.

My brother bragged how you were a college girl, Angela said. Me, I always thought you didn't have the brains God gave you. Angela really laughed when she said this. Hard to believe we grew up on the same street, she said to me.

I could have mentioned that she was a full ten years older than I was and her father wore overalls to work and gambled his paycheck before he got home Fridays, but her mouth was up close to my ear, her perfume was up my nose, and she was poking that gun hard in my ribs.

I met Buddy in Manhattan but he said he lived out on Staten Island. Right away I knew something was up. He'd grown up in the Village. Staten Island? For me, Staten Island was Middlin' Beach and my mother's stories about the rented summer bungalow thirteen blocks from the ocean her first married summer when she was twenty and had a newborn baby (not me). My father took the ferry out every weekend. My mother thought she'd died and went to heaven. Her eight brothers and sisters thought so too, and came out every chance they got. No screens, no plumbing. I don't remember the amusement park or my cousins making human pyramids on the beach for the camera but there was an old 16 mm movie of me in underpants licking the block of ice that sat on the porch.

What I'm saying is, that for me, Staten Island didn't conjure images of the high life. It was somewhere you went to if you were on the lam, it seemed that far away; where you went when you owed the wrong people money, the guys with the broken noses, Buddy called them, or when you couldn't go back to the neighborhood, like Angela, who needed a place to keep her husband straight after he got out of prison. Her mother watched the kids and the old man's insurance policy, which paid double after he was crushed between the ship and the pier, paid for the house on Florence Street that was a primo fixer-upper. Buddy said that when he came back from California after his marriage broke up, they were sitting on orange crates with candles stuck in cheap wine bottles.

We drove through the Midtown Tunnel and onto the BQE and I could see the Verrazano—for my money, the best thing about Staten Island. We turned left off the bridge and drove down what always felt to me like a country lane. The houses were old, the colors of old houses, green and brown. They had patches of grass in the front. Hylan Boulevard curved and looped before it straightened out and you hit the traffic and the

local guidos in muscle cars with music blasting, small strip malls
with the same three or four stores, Chinese restaurants that
would mix won ton and egg drop soup in one bowl, sandwich
shops called Angelo's and Gino's, an overstuffed sub painted
in primary colors on the plate glass window, bridal shops, ca-
tering halls, restaurants named Petruzzi's with lattice, cognac-
colored windows and endless parking. The Staten Islanders
loved outdoor parking. They loved parking lots better than
garages because in a parking lot everyone could admire your
good-looking, expensive car, and you could too.

Hylan Boulevard flooded in a sudden rain; it flooded bad.
The semi-attached condos that had been built on the grave-
yard of grand old houses flooded too, and the cars parked to
the sides of the front doors were moved to higher ground with
the first sprinkle.

Angela?

Shut up, she said.

I turned my head and she rammed the gun in my side.

Don't look at me.

Why? Because I might recognize you?

Funny. You think you're so funny. Watch me laugh. You
know, smarty pants, you should have just stayed where you belonged and away from Buddy. So now just shut your big mouth.

Someone should have warned me when I met Buddy that
his family was crazy, but who knew they were this crazy? And
let me tell you, when I met Buddy I wasn't planning on anything long term. All I wanted was a good time. And Buddy was
a lot of fun. He knew everybody and had all kinds of connec-
tions. We went to after-hours bars and gambling parlors, clubs
with private shows in back. We walked past velvet ropes and
got the best seats; drinks arrived at the table compliments of
the house. There were bear hugs and cheek kisses.

But honestly, did I need a guy who was broke and living with his mother, his two kids, his sister, and a brother-in-law who had five-to-ten in Dannemora under his belt? Living on Staten Island no less? Buddy was pretty quiet about the Staten Island piece and hinted that it wasn't so bad and maybe we could live out there after we got married. He was awful grateful to Angela for taking him in when the ex-wife grabbed the stash, dumped the kids, and went AWOL with a South American disco dancer named Chico.

We made the turn off the boulevard and onto Florence Street. I was starting to think Angela was really stupid. She kidnaps me at gunpoint and brings me to her house?

When Joey pulled into the driveway, I could see the television flickering with the kids planted in front of it. Angela and Joey had four kids of their own and they all watched television together and made popcorn on Saturday nights. The kind in the aluminum pan that you hold over the stove and the top blows up like a balloon.

Angela handed Joey the gun and he pointed it at my face. That was scary, the idea of taking a bullet to the face. I shut my eyes.

Joey, I said, did you ever shoot anyone?

I thought I told you to shut up, Angela said, which made me open my eyes.

She was digging in her huge black alligator satchel (which for sure had "fallen off a truck," but who am I to talk?). Before she'd turned nasty, Angela would throw things my way when they came in pairs. Shit, I was wearing an 18 karat gold Rolex that had actually been special order, serial number and everything, from some guy who worked in the factory and swiped a few selectively every month. I was one to talk. Thinking about my watch made me look down at my arm that Angela was trying to duct tape to my other arm. We both zeroed in on the watch at the same time and Angela ripped it off my wrist.

Last year, she said, this would have been mine. Buddy would have bought it for me, so I'll just take it now.

I saw this as an opportunity and gave her an elbow to the lip and a slap on the side of her head, right on her ear. I had nothing to lose. I had read about serial killers. Once they get you tied up, you're done for. If only . . . Angela pulled back and punched me so hard that if I'd been a cartoon, the whole strip would have been nothing but stars.

When I opened my eyes again, Angela had taped my wrists and tied me up. The rope was around my neck and connected to my duct-taped wrists, kind of a semi-hog-tie. A disgusting concept. I was hating Angela, not to mention Joey who was waving what I noticed was a very beautiful Beretta in my face. I recognized it as Buddy's gun. It was a pocket pistol—used, unfortunately. Buddy was going to give it to me—for protection, he said when he showed it to me. The only reason I didn't have it was that Buddy was waiting for a holster. Buddy liked everything just so.

Angela, I said, this is really stupid. What's going on? What do you want? For Chrissakes, I'm marrying your brother in six weeks. Take this shit off me!

She looked at her watch—I mean, my watch that seemed now to be hers.

We've got a lot of time, she said to Joey. Buddy doesn't get home for hours.

There she was right. Buddy had two jobs, one at a restaurant and the other at a mob-owned nightclub somewhere in the 70s in Manhattan where the boss had signed a half-dead Judy Garland while she was nodding off on pills. I was supposed to meet him when he got off at four a.m., which was hours and hours away.

Can I put down this goddamn gun, Angela? Joey said. And can we get moving? Would you quit yapping?

Okay, okay. I thought you were ready. You mixed the cement, no?

It's not just the cement. I gotta move the rocks. They gotta fit. I want it to look nice.

I could feel the blood in the back of my throat; she must have broken my nose, the crazy bitch. I imagined the mouse starting under my eye.

You know we're in Great Kills, she said to me. Great Kills, get it? You're gonna be great killed. Angela thought this was hilarious.

I wasn't feeling so cocky right about then, I have to admit. I thought I was better than Angela. I mean, comparing us was like apples and pears, but if you want to know the truth, while I appreciated her finer qualities, ultimately I did feel she was a creature below.

Angela, talk to me. Let's figure this thing out, I said.

It's easy, she said. You're a smart girl; you figure it out. But let me give you a hint. Buddy's got everything here. We take care of each other. We're family. What's he need you for? What's he got to go to Manhattan for? You wanna take the kids away from me? I love those kids . . . they call me Mama. They hug me so tight sometimes I can't breathe.

We can work something out, I told her. Maybe Buddy and I could live here. Maybe find a house nearby . . .

Buddy had hinted at this very plan and I had kiboshed it unequivocally. I'd lived in Rome and Paris and Bombay. I was going to live in Staten Island next to his sister?

Buddy told me he asked and you said no.

I didn't. I never said no.

Buddy's a liar?

No, he just doesn't listen. You know, Angela, how he doesn't listen. It could be great, all of us together.

She looked at me. I sensed that Joey was feeling bad for me. His hand wasn't shaking so much anymore. I willed him to put down the gun but he didn't. He just wasn't gripping it so tight that his hand shook.

Angela smiled. She was a beautiful girl. Black hair, skin like pearls dipped in milk. The first time I met her, she had on a one-shoulder dress and I swear I wanted to put my tongue against her skin and lick, it was that luscious.

I fell for that once, Angela said, with that other rat bastard. We were like sisters. Then look what I had to do. She took everything anyway, but at least we got the kids. Joey and I took care of her, didn't we, Joey? But just my luck, we get rid of one son of a bitch and Buddy finds another. He's a real pain in my ass sometimes, my brother.

Angela, be honest, Buddy's only here with you because—
Because what?

She didn't look so beautiful right now. I shut my mouth. Because he had nowhere else to go, I wanted to say.

Buddy's mother always said she was sorry she gave up the tenement apartment on Spring Street. She didn't call it a tenement, though. She called it her "nice apartment." From Buddy I knew it was three rooms in the back, facing the alley, tub in the kitchen, and everyone waiting in the hallway when one of them took a bath on Saturdays. Tenements weren't Buddy's style and neither was Florence Street, from what I could see. There were more trees on Spring Street.

Joey had been "fixing up" the house on Florence Street ever since he'd gotten out. Joey was handy, he had what they called "hands of gold," which he seemed to use for ripping things out and never putting them back, the bathroom on the second floor, for instance. We're getting a new bathroom, Angela had told me, but they'd been using the one in the basement for three years while Joey moved on to other projects, such as bust-ing up the stairs so everyone had to walk up a wooden ramp like the cart horses in the stable on Thompson Street.

And then there was Joey's wall. The first time Buddy took me to Florence Street, Joey was in the front yard mixing ce-ment. There were piles of boulders, different sizes, and Joey was using them to build a wall. The kids were carrying over the smaller ones and Joey was fitting them on top of one an-other and side by side and cementing them in place. The wall belonged on an English country estate. The wall belonged on meadows and hills and dales. The wall was beautiful and ri-diculous. The house was small and ugly and sat on a small and ugly lot, and then all around it, not more than ten feet out, was this magnificent stone wall that each time I visited got higher and higher, until it was starting to look like a rampart. Buddy laughed about it. He called it Joey's therapy. But I have to be honest, it gave me the creeps.

I'm tired of talking, Angela said to me. Get out of the car.

No, no, Leave her in the car until I'm ready, Joey said.

We can't leave her in the car. We'll put her in the basement while you set things up.

The basement? Did you ever carry dead weight up stairs? Joey said. I'm no Hercules and for sure, she ain't no lightweight.

I let the insult pass. I'm always surprised when people say mean things about me. As I said, I was always thinking people liked me when they really didn't give a shit. But all that aside, what the hell were they talking about?

I pulled at my wrists, but when I did, the rope tightened around my neck. I was afraid I would pee myself. I thought I'd bring up using the bathroom but I wanted to wait for the right time. Maybe I could get away then, make a noise, maybe I had a chance. The kids would hear, the old lady, deaf as she was, the dog, the neighbors not twenty feet away, someone.

Angela smiled. She can walk, she said. She can walk up the basement stairs. It'll be dark.

You're kidding me, Joey said.

I always believed in you, Joey. Even with that crazy wall. I always believed in you. That's why I stuck, through thick and thin.

I have to go to the bathroom, I said.

You wanna take her? Joey said.

Let her piss herself, Angela told him. She looked me straight in the face. Whatta we care?

Can you guess the rest? Joey put the gun to my temple. Angela duct-taped my mouth. She checked the rope around my wrist and my neck. She pulled me out of the car and down the basement steps. Joey wanted to put out a mat so I could lie down. Angela said no. I'd piss on it, remember I had asked to go to the bathroom? And then she'd have to throw it out and Clorox the place. She'll be lying down forever, Angela said. Just like the other one.

In the end, they put some blankets on the floor and pushed me down. I could smell dog on the wool but I was glad just to lie there and close my eyes. I heard them leave. I watched the light go away as the sun went down. I heard the scrape of the trowel. I heard one of Buddy's kids call out to Joey, asking him why he was working on the wall, it was nighttime. I think I slept. And then they were pulling me up. Angela and Joey. And walking me up the stairs.

There was no moon. I wondered what Buddy would think—if he would think that, like his first wife, I had just up and disappeared. Gotten cold feet? Left him at the altar? And the kids

. . . would they feel abandoned again? Miss me? I noticed when I got close to the wall how wide it was, wide enough to lie down on. The wall was different heights in different parts. I wondered how high it would go in the end. I realized I would never know.

Angela took my arm and walked me to a place where the wall was low, maybe four feet, and she made me lie down. I felt the stones that jutted through the layer of cement hard against my back, my shoulders, my head, and then she picked up a boulder, so big that it blocked my vision. It would have blocked out the moon if there had been one in the sky, and she brought it down with all her strength.

Buddy came home early the next morning. When he woke up, he took his coffee into the yard where Joey was working on the wall. The kids were rolling stones. They were still in their pajamas.

It's really coming along, Buddy said. This wall is going to be here after we're all dead, Joey. It's like the goddamn Colosseum.

The phone rang and someone inside picked it up. Is that for me? Buddy shouted.

You expecting a call? Joey said.

I thought it might be Ruby. She never showed up last night.

She ever done that before?

No, Buddy said. Never.

WHEN THEY ARE DONE WITH US

BY PATRICIA SMITH

Port Richmond

M aury's eyes were crazy wide, staring right into the camera, just like they were on yesterday's show and the show before that. His hand rested on the shoulder of some blubbering white girl, Keisha or Kiara something, her hair all hard-curled and greased up into those stiff-sprayed rings, smeared black circling her eyes, greening gold Nefertitis swinging from her ears, more faux preciousness twinkling from her left nostril. Seems like K or K's baby daddy could be any one of the fidgeting young black men and—surprise!—she kinda didn't know which one.

The contestants were all sloe-eyed, corkscrew braids, double negative, mad for no reason except that they had been identified on national television as fools who didn't give a damn where their dicks went. It was time, once again, for the paternity test and Maury's dramatic slicing open of that manila envelope. For some reason, the prospect of finally knowing whose seed had taken hold reduced Kiara or Keisha to unbridled bawling and a snorting of snot.

Jo had the show on more for background than anything, but she stopped for a closer look at the little nasty who'd opened her legs and been done in. It amazed her how anybody, let alone a white girl, could look at any one of those sadsacks and feel bad enough about herself to fuck him. "I ain't never been, or ain't never gonna be, that damned horny," she said out loud, just as Tyrell, sloe-eyed and corkscrewed, was revealed to be the father of the squirming little bastard in question.

"I'm gon' take care of my 'sponsibility," he monotoned, a semi-earnest declaration which was greeted by wild hooting and hand-clapping from Maury's drama-drunk studio audience. Even after receiving the sudden blessing of papahood, Tyrell avoided looking at or touching the mother of his child. Kiara or Keisha stood, shivering in a whorish skirt and halter top, in dire need of at least an orchestrated hug. She continued to keen.

I cannot watch this shit, Jo thought, just after thinking, *Where did she find an actual halter top in 2010?* Although she made a move to punch the television off, she didn't do it. Instead she lowered the volume so the string of skewed urban vignettes could still distract her from what she really needed to be doing. Maybe the next segment would feature some tooth-challenged redneck hurling a chair across the stage upon discovering, after a week or so of sweaty carnal acrobatics, that the he he thought was a she was really a he fervently embracing his she-ness.

Jo revisited her mental to-do. Last night's crusted dishes, still "soaking." A mountain of undies and towels, waiting to be lugged to the Bright Star laundromat, where the guy who guarded the dollar changers—to make damned sure that no "nonlaunderers" used them—never missed an opportunity to converse with her tits. Oh, and she'd skipped breakfast again. After her last tangle with an oil-slick omelet at The New Dinette, a succession of Dunkin's dry toasted things, and her own ambitious attempts to get healthy and choke down oatmeal, the idea of a morning meal had lost its appeal. By three p.m. she'd be trolling Port Richmond Avenue, inhaling a loaded slice or two at Denino's or resigning herself to The New's lunch menu and one of their huge, dizzying burgers.

There wasn't much in the fridge—various leftover pastas curling in Tupperware and cold cuts she could practically hear expiring. Ravenous, she spotted the pack of Luckies on the edge of the dinette table, and her whole mouth tingled with crave. Although the pack was half-empty, she didn't remember buying it. *Just one*, she thought. Just one, and maybe a little drinkie to follow. Instead she closed her eyes and took a deep breath, shutting it out, and did what Katie had told her to do. She said the word "poem" out loud.

That's it, she thought, scrambling for her wire-bound notebook and new pen. I'm going to write me a poem. From the flickering Panasonic, Maury asked, *When did you first suspect that Aurelio was sleeping with your mother?*

Poetry was Jo's new medicine. During her last trip to the university hospital's emergency room, her vague complaint that she had been "sleeping too long and smoking too much and maybe drinking a little harder and my kid is driving me crazy" earned her a useless nicotine patch and the advice of Katie McMahon, a perky community counselor, who suggested she put little bits of her life into lines. Rhyme or not, no matter. About anything she wanted it to be about. "If you call it a poem, then it is," Katie had said.

Surprisingly, the little scrawlings helped. She'd written more than a few choice lines about Al, the ex-cop who showed up with his monthly hard-on to pound her into the mattress with something he called love. She wasted whole pages on Charlie, who'd inhabited her womb for nine months, and now had no patience for her "stupid fuckin' rules." He dropped by occasionally to pilfer weed money from her wallet, gobble the contents of the refrigerator, or sleep off an encounter with too many shots of Jäger. On good days—or when she needed to remember that there had actually *been* good days—she wrote all pretty about a moment when she was full of light, strolling over the Bayonne Bridge like she was walking on water. From up there the island magically shed its dingy and became more than gossip, stench, and regret. The key to happiness on Staten Island, she decided, was to get as close as you could to the sky and make the assholes as small as possible.

Flipping to a fresh page in the notebook, she clicked the top of her pen and licked the point the way she'd seen real writers do before they—

A key rattled in the lock and the front door was flung open with such force that it banged into the wall, knocking more mint-green chips from the plaster. Jo felt her heart go large and stone.

"Hey, what the hell is up, Jo?"

He refused to call her *Mom*. Or *Mother*. Sixteen years old, six-feet-two inches of swaggering explosive. Her son.

"It's hot as shit out there. What's in this place to eat?"

"I think there's some ham in the—"

"The same ham as last time? That shit's old. Ain't nuthin' cooked in this bitch?"

Jo steeled herself. "Charlie, I told you not to come in here—"

"Cursing? Hungry? And you gon' do *what*?"

Jo knew the answer. Nothing. She had never not been terrified of her son. Charlie had ripped her open at birth, glared at her as he bit her breast to demand milk, pinched and pummeled his kindergarten classmates, set fire to wastebaskets in school restrooms, been suspended from sixth grade for showing up plastered on a vile mix of Kool-Aid and vodka, and greeted all attempts to control and educate with a raised middle finger. He strutted and primped in Day-Glo Jordans, a too-big Yankees cap twisted sideways on his head, pants two-sizes-too-wrong pulled down so far the waistband backed his ass. He adopted the lyric swagger of black boys, taking on their nuance and rhythms while hissing about "niggers" in the circle of his crew. While Jo watched in horror, Charlie grew as wide and high as a wall. He arced over her when she dared make mama noises, and huffed in her face with dead breath, which stank of cheap tobacco.

His eyes looked like someone had died behind them.

She wasn't sure what he did during the day. It wasn't school. She'd gotten letters and phone calls from Port Richmond High attesting to his continued absence. "He's a dropout," she finally blurted to one well-meaning guidance counselor, before hanging up the phone.

There were even rumors that Charlie had managed to father a child. Sometimes, when she closed her eyes, Jo could see him snarling, fully erect, a gum-cracking girl laid wide and waiting. His lovemaking would be thrust and spit. When she thought of a child built of Charlie and air, a thick shudder ripped through her.

"Did you hear me? Food! I'm fuckin' hungry! I swear, Jo, don't make me have to—"

She sprang from her chair and bolted for the kitchen with no idea what she would do once she got there.

He'd only hit her once.

One clouded August night, a week after Charlie turned sixteen, Jo saw him on the street just after finishing her part-time job at Bloomy Rose, a florist in Midland Beach. She'd worked late that night, helping with a huge order for the funeral of a local politician. As she wound her way toward her bus stop, a fierce rain needled her cheeks. Assuming the rain had driven everyone inside, she was surprised to see a dark human huddle on Father Capodanno Boulevard just before Midland Avenue, and even more surprised to see her son at its edges.

But there he was, hanging on yet another corner with Bennie Mahoney, a no-gooder from New Dorp, and two other boys she didn't know. Their backs were hunched against the downpour, and she saw the orange flare of cigarettes. She wanted and didn't want to know what they were up to.

The sign on the nearest building on Midland read Q.S.I.N.Y., and she could hear the guttural thump of dance music from inside. The letters made no sense to her until she realized where she'd seen them before. The island's first openly gay club had launched on the Fourth of July weekend to much fanfare and trepidation. Staten Island wasn't known for its tolerance, and there were worries that the patrons of the club would become targets for ham-handed haters.

The letters stood for Queer Staten Island New York.

Jo felt an ominous drop in her belly.

Charlie's views on all things gay were well known and frequently bellowed. While Jo admitted a cringe when she thought about man-on-man, and a starkly uncomfortable curiosity when she considered girl-on-girl, Charlie's florid vocabulary was peppered with references to "fuckin' fags," "cocklickers," and "turd burglars." Jo remembered a bespectacled whisperer from their block who had packed up and hightailed it off the island with his family after being on the receiving end of a vicious beatdown. He never identified his attackers, but Jo remembered how he would practically shrivel when he passed Charlie on the street.

The Charlie who now, for no good reason, was in the middle of a meeting outside a gay dance club. Afraid of what he might be planning, and before she thought about the consequences of doing so, Jo shouted his name.

The group stopped its conspiratorial grumbling. All eyes snapped to her, standing across the street from them, the wind crimping her cheap umbrella, her cotton blouse plastered to her breasts and darkening with rain.

Her son's eyes bored holes into her. He did not move.

Bennie punched Charlie's shoulder hard, and laughed. "Hey, it's your fuckin' *mommy*." The two other boys joined in the merriment. But Charles Liam Mulroy, his steel-gray eyes locked to his mother's, did not speak. Jo couldn't bring herself to utter his name again.

They stood that way, three of the young men snickering, one son motionless and burning, one drenched mother craving the world of ten minutes ago. Finally, Jo spotted the approaching bus spewing puddles. She scurried to the stop and boarded, never looking back.

Late that night, she woke from a fitful sleep to an angry wall in her room, a wall dripping rain and hissing through its teeth. After two deep glasses of screw-top wine, gulped to calm her nerves, Jo hadn't heard Charlie come in.

"Don't you ever fuckin' do that again. You wanna be somebody's mother, get your ass a dog. Don't you ever admit you even fuckin' know me. Not in front of my crew. You see me, you don't say shit. You lucky I didn't lay your bitch ass flat right there on the street."

She didn't realize she was holding her breath until her head began to pound. Charlie was panting, fists clenched, backlit and glowing in the moonwash. She was just beginning to think how oddly beautiful the image was when it grabbed a fistful of pink pajama top, pulled her up from the pillow, and then knocked her back down with a slap that rattled her teeth.

"Don't. You. *Ever*. Fuckin'. Embarrass. Me. Again."

He dropped his body down on the side of the bed, waiting for Jo to meet his eyes. She couldn't. She lay with her head flattened to the left, the way it had fallen after the slap. She felt his hard gaze. After a wet intake of breath, he slowly lifted the pajama top and clamped her bare right breast with a huge, calloused hand. Jo silently willed her spirit out of the room. Charlie squeezed rough, then pinched the tip of her nipple so hard she whimpered.

He laughed. "This some sick shit. Wow. Man. You done got my cock hard in this bitch."

He popped up and strutted out of the bedroom, leaving behind the dead green smell of bad weather.

They never talked about it. She never called anyone, never thought about reporting him, never even mentioned it to Al, the ex-cop. From that day on, she never acknowledged him in public, no matter what he was doing, who he was with, where he was. And she stopped remembering the thick smear of blood she'd see on his skinned knuckles that night. She stopped wondering whose it was.

"I am fuckin' starvin' up in this bitch!" Charlie screamed again.

Jo clawed through cabinets and the fridge, searching for something, anything, that wasn't the same old ham. In the front room, Maury had probably morphed into another screechfest. She wanted to be back in that room, opening her notebook, finding that empty page, picking up her pen . . .

"Ooooohhhhh, godDAMN! What is *this* shit?"

Jo bolted for the living room and swallowed hard at the sight of Charlie holding the purple notebook, starkly focused on a particular page.

"Give that to me," she said, as calmly as she could manage. "That's mine."

"Oh, hell no. I'm seeing *my* name, so this shit is *my* business. I already read the one about you gettin' naked and fuckin' that cop. Mama's a muthafuckin' freak."

His eyes scanned the page, and she saw it all take turns in his face—confusion, anger, embarrassment, confusion, realization, anger again. She wondered what poem he'd found. She wondered what she'd pay for writing it.

Charlie started reading, his voice all exaggerated white:

Charlie is not a son, not a boy, not a man
He is the way a day turns toward a storm
He is a star that screams before disappearing
He is night without a bottom
I can't wake up from him, can't give
him back, can't even give him away,
can't think of anyone who would even want
that kind of exploding. I can't even say his
name without my heart stopping. I wish I
could remember giving him a home
in my body. I wonder if it would just
be easier to stop stop stop loving him
as easy as it was to stop loving me

Hearing the poem out loud, Jo couldn't help noticing that she was using the word "even" too much. Concentrating on that kept her from focusing on the ominous silence that followed Charlie's booming of the word "me."

The silence was broken by a laughter Jo had never heard before. Charlie threw back his head and opened so wide she could see the collapsed gray teeth at the back of his mouth. He laughed so hard he sputtered, and when he could manage it, he spat out snippets of her poem. "*Not a son! Give him back! Give him away! Home in your body! Stop, stop, stop!*" He laughed until there were tears in his eyes. "*Stop!*"

Still snorting, he pushed past her into the kitchen, waving

the notebook over his head. He slapped it flat on a burner of the gas stove and held Jo at arm's length while he turned the knob up far as it would go. Flames leapt up around the notebook and burrowed toward its heart. The smoke alarm started thin, warbled, then blared. Above the din, Charlie laughed maniacally.

As Jo's poetry flared and sizzled, all those words she had scraped directly from the surface of her skin, Charlie turned the water on full blast in the kitchen sink, where last night's dinner dishes were still soaking. With a pair of metal salad tongs, he lifted the blazing notebook and tossed it under the running water. Jo could swear she heard it moan.

"You are such a sensitive bitch," a suddenly solemn Charlie hissed. "*Getting in touch with your feeeeeelings.* Grow some fuckin' balls."

Jo fell to her knees on the tile and felt the day collapse around her. Before she could scream, she heard the front door squeal on its hinges and bang shut, so hard the smoke alarm hiccupped and died. And the laughter stopped.

No, it didn't.

That night, Jo woke to the sound of shouts and sirens outside her bedroom window. That wasn't unusual for Port Richmond, but there was something jagged about it this time. For a moment, she was disoriented. She had fallen asleep in her clothes, so tangled in her bedsheets that she couldn't move right away. She smelled liquor somewhere—on her pillow? in her hair?—and remembered swilling Jack Daniel's after Charlie stormed out, hoping to drop the curtain on one bitch of a day. She felt bleary. Her eyes opened behind a cloud. She peered at her alarm clock. Four fifteen a.m.

Jo imagined that an acrid whisper of smoke was the dying breath of her poetry, still floating in the kitchen sink. Until now, she hadn't realized how important the pages had become to her, and nothing in the notebook could be salvaged. The heavy thought of beginning again made her head drop to the pillow, to the left, the way it had when her son slapped her. She wanted sleep to pull her under again. But the street noise grew louder and more insistent, the stench more disturbing than the island's usual garbage-tinged funk.

Jo freed her legs from the sheets and lumbered to her window. Number 302, directly across Nicholas, was burning. Had burned. The two windows on the top floor were soft-sputtering black and orange. Her mouth hung open, torn between awe and panic. She'd slept through a damned fire? Had there been people inside? Were they okay? Why couldn't she picture the people who lived there? Were they black or white? After all, they were right across the street. She must have seen them hundreds of times. Were there kids?

Where was Charlie?

The weight of the question sickened her. Was she concerned about the safety of her son, or worried that he could somehow be responsible for the blaze?

Jo pulled on her old CSI sweats and a T-shirt, slipped into her sneakers without tying the laces, and ran outside, careful to lock the door behind her.

Nicholas was clogged with fire trucks, firefighters, and people spilling excitedly from two-flats. Jo's eyes darted wildly, searching the crowd for Charlie's sneer, his chopped reddish hair. She wanted to cover her ears against the *Oh my God, oh Jesus, Dios mío* babble of panic. All those upturned faces, the shouting, the questions, that bladed smell.

And the screeching woman, suddenly flailing, throwing her body against a knot of people determined to hold her back.

Grim-faced firemen hauling four body bags out of the still-smoking building. More screaming.

Jo squeezed her eyes shut then, and she saw them clearly, the people who lived on the second floor. A smiling black woman holding the hands of a toddler and a little girl. An older girl. A teenage boy trailing behind, lugging those light-blue plastic bags from the Port Richmond market. She saw them stop to climb the stairs at 302 Nicholas.

But the screeching was not that woman.

The screeching woman was the mother of the woman who died, the grandmother of the four children who died.

Jo found that out during breakfast at The New Dinette. Exhausted and shell-shocked, her clothes smelling vaguely of smoke, she gnawed a slice of bacon and slurped peppered eggs while listening to tragedy's hum. No one could talk about anything but. She half-expected to hear her son's name.

The woman Jo had seen behind her closed eyes was dead. So were the two boys, the two girls. They had all died, but it wasn't the fire that killed them.

"That boy killed his brother and his sisters and his mama," Marla, a waitress, said to everyone who would listen, and to a few people who wouldn't. "Slit they throats, set that fire, then killed hisself."

Jo hovered over days of congealing breakfasts at The New long enough to hear different versions of the same story, which meant it must be true. Or, most of it. Melonie, seven, her throat sliced open, dead. Brittney, ten, throat slit, dead. The mother, Leisa, her throat not slit, smoke exploding her chest. The little one, Jermaine, still whole and unbloodied, clung to a chance but lost his fight at Richmond University Hospital. The fire had loved him so hard that when he first reached the emergency room, no one was sure if he was a girl or a boy.

Then there was C.J., manchild at fourteen, collapsed in a river of blood, an old-fashioned straight razor under his body. His own throat slit. The whisper was that he had a history of setting small fires. His charred note nearby: *am sorry.*

Jo couldn't grasp the mathematics of it, the impossibility of killing your family then sliding a blade across your own throat. She had seen that boy. She had seen him laughing, bouncing his little brother on his shoulders. She had seen him watching his sisters ride their bikes, barking like a big brother when they veered too close to the street. She had . . .

Charlie setting fires in the boys' room.

Charlie burning the words that wondered what he was.

But C.J. wasn't Charlie. Thank God. Her son hadn't gone that far, hadn't burned that house down, hadn't killed anyone.

Then her next thought, before she could stop it: *But if he had, someone would have come for him. Someone would have taken him away.*

Charlie and Bennie, smelling like men, sat on the couch half-watching the Red Sox beat the Yankees. The two of them overwhelmed the room. Their flopping arms and spread-eagle. Their vile mouths, open and chewing. Their uproarious stink.

Jo's son was on full blast: "Man, you hear about that crazy nigger killed his mother? And his sisters? With a razor, *then* burned them up. Nigga got some balls though. Cut this *own* throat too. Gotta give him credit for going out tough like that. Musta not liked his mama. Bitch musta been ridin' his fuckin' nerves. He took her *out.*"

Bennie snorted as Charlie pointedly met his mother's eyes and grinned. He raised a dirty glass of something clear.

Whenever he was home now, which was less and less, Jo folded herself into the smallest corner of the place, stitched her lips shut, and learned to nod. She fried huge slabs of fatty meat, mashed mounds of potatoes, and became a regular at Mexico Supermarket. (She couldn't shop at the Port Richmond store anymore because of the light-blue bags.) She crammed her basket with honey buns, jalapeño chips, taquitos, powdered donuts, Red Bull, ice cream, cigarettes, pork rinds, and moon pies, then slathered everything with butter and served it up to her ravenous ass of a son.

She wouldn't give him time or room to want for anything. She didn't want him to realize that she'd already served her purpose. She wouldn't give him reason to open her throat, burn her down.

All Charlie did was eat, sleep off highs, and grow taller and wider. His pores leaked poison and stained the walls. Jo cooked and nodded, answered promptly to "Hey, bitch," and hid her new notebook, a smaller one, behind a row of vases on a high shelf in her room. When she was sure that Charlie was out, she wrote poems to her new dead friend Leisa, who had a son who killed her.

When they are done with us
When they are done with us
When there is no longer a road
From our blood to theirs
All we do is remind them
of need
And it is us who taught them
never to need

anything
Suddenly there is no river deep enough
for us
No fire blue enough to strain for our bone
No love
at all

Jo tried not to imagine what Charlie would do if he found this notebook, if he saw how she held whole conversations with a woman she did not know. She had lived for years just across the street. Jo wished she had spoken to her past the occasional nod, wished she hadn't assumed they'd have nothing in common because the woman was black and Jo was white.

No. Not *the woman*. Leisa.

They could have shopped together at the market, waddling home laden with light-blue plastic bags filled with cans of tuna, spongy white bread, brown fruit. And when the moment was right, Jo could have taken Leisa's hand and said, gently, *Describe your son's eyes.*

They could have saved each other.

One morning Jo copied a poem she'd worked on the whole day before, trying to make it perfect.

Leisa, it is hard to admit
the poison that burned through our bodies
and became them
Hard to recite this crooked alphabet
Hard to know we can no longer
circle them with our arms
and contain their whole lives
Their horrible secret is how they

burst like flowers from our bodies
They damn us for remembering
They damn us for wanting
to sing
that story

It still wasn't perfect, but there was something Jo felt she needed to do.

She pulled the page carefully from the notebook, folded it four times, and wrote *Leisa* in her best flowing cursive. Then she crossed the street to the makeshift altar, a raggedy explosion of blooms and mildewing stuffed animals in front of 302 Richmond's scarred shell. There had been people milling around the altar every day, but now there was no one. She studied it for a minute, then tucked the poem beneath a bug-eyed duck. She whispered a run-on sentence that may have been prayer.

Then she walked down to the bodega to pick up coffee and copies of the *Advance* and the *Post*. Reading both the Staten Island and NYC papers was her entertainment, akin to watching *Maury* and *Springer* in the mornings. Wallowing in the grime and drama, she was reminded that she lived both in, and close to, a cesspool.

The place was packed with people, which was unusual for the hour. There was that tragic hum again, that sad tangle of different languages in stages of disbelief. Jo wondered if something had happened during the night.

At the newspaper rack, she read the headline and the first graph of the *Post*'s front-page story before she even picked it up.

IT WAS MOM IN STATEN ISLAND
MASSACRE HORROR:
The mother did it. The horrific murder-suicide that ended in

*an arson on Staten Island was committed by the deranged
mom, who slit three of her kids' throats before she killed
herself and her baby in the blaze, law-enforcement sources
said yesterday.*

Autopsies showed that C.J., Melonie, and Brittney had pills
in their stomachs. They were dead before the fire. They hadn't
just lined up and waited to be killed. They'd been drugged first.

And the note: they'd found Leisa's diary and compared the
handwriting. *She* had written *am sorry. She* had left the note
close to her son's body, which was like putting a smoking gun
in his hand.

Jo felt a needle traveling in her blood. She picked up the
paper and left, without talking to anyone, without paying. She
didn't remember her walk back home, but when she looked up,
she was there. And so was Al, the ex-cop, hovering around her
door, grinning like a Cheshire and, as always, leading with his
zipper.

"Hey, Jo-bean," he hissed. "Been thinkin' about you like
craaaazzy. Came by as soon as I got a break." His chapped
lips brushed the side of her face, then his tongue touched. Jo
thought maybe the heat of another body would burn away the
rest of the day. Wordlessly, she let him in. Then, as soon as the
door was closed, she blurted her usual fears, the fears a man
was supposed to take care of. The fears were Charlie, Charlie,
Charlie.

"You know, that kid needs a father to keep his ass in line."
That was always Al the ex-cop's first suggestion, although he
never hinted at who that father might be. "You want, I'll have
some of the guys pick him up, scare the shit out of him."

Al seemed to have forgotten again that he was an *ex*-cop
for a reason. Al seemed to have forgotten that once, sick with

drink and aimlessly speeding in his cruiser, he'd scraped a sizable stretch of concrete barrier along the entry ramp from 440 to 278, stopped, and was promptly hit from behind by a grandmother in a Subaru station wagon. Two squad cars showed up to sort through the mess. They secured the silence of the terrified granny, scrubbed the scene clear of Al's airplane miniatures, and concocted a cover-up tale that would move a hardened judge to tears.

But later, when Al was oh-so-vaguely pressed on the details, he caved and admitted—well, everything. Swilling in his cruiser. Shooting sparks as he hugged the barrier. Getting rammed from behind. And being helped by his pals in blue. Babbling, he even named the pals.

Of course, he was fired. Even cooled his heels in the slammer for a bit.

So none of "the guys" he spoke of so lovingly would be inclined to do any favors for good ol' Al. Jo didn't bother reminding him about the circumstances of his ex-ness. He liked playing cop, so she let him.

He even fucked like one. Like he was alone. Everything he said to Jo—*at* Jo—was addressed to Al, the ex-cop: "Oh, you're hitting that pussy today, boy." "She's gonna remember this." "She's gon' be calling your name for days."

Jo had hoped that a body against hers would blur the day, dim the smell of fire. But not this body.

When he left, her room smelled like his deluded monologue, his miserable spurt. The newspaper sat on the bedside table. *The mother did it.* Leisa had killed herself and her children. *Tell me why*, Jo tried to beg her dead friend. But what came out was: *Tell me how.*

Maybe the smiling C.J. she'd seen playing with his siblings and lugging home groceries was just another kind of Charlie, one who'd learned to paint his snarling face with light. Maybe Leisa was crazy, out of her mind, her head crammed with the kind of wounding Jo was beginning to know.

Jo started to cry. She wept from bone, from memory, from loss. She wept for Leisa, for C.J., for the stranger who'd escaped her body and named her *Bitch*. She wept from lack of love, unleashed wracking sobs that hung wet in the air. She wept for the shadows that were Staten Island, the prison she lived in. She wept past the pushing open of her bedroom door, the brash boy who suddenly stood there.

"Fuck you cryin' for?"

Jo's head drooped as Charlie filled the door, swaying, smelling like he'd drank something with blades. "It smells like ass in here," he slurred. "Like your ass mixed with somebody else's ass." He laughed then. "Was the dick that good? It made you cry? Hell, if it wasn't nasty sick, I'd hit that. Make you call *my* name. Give you some shit to cry about."

He lumbered off. Jo heard him fall into bed in the other bedroom, still laughing, snorting. Soon he would rock the house with snotty snores. He would sleep deep into the night as poison spilled from his pores. He would wake up hungry, snarling, looking to be fed *up in this bitch*.

She pulled the notebook down from its hiding place, found her pen, and wrote another poem for Leisa, the mother, the murderer.

Where did it seep into you,
the ghost of the only answer?
How did you pull it in,
breathe it in, own it?
How did you find the teeth
you needed to take back your

own body, to build a revolution
in darkness? And how brave
of you

to take all of them
with you

There was more she wanted to say, but Jo was afraid that writing more would lead her to a road she couldn't travel. *Not the why, but the how.* She craved Leisa's strength *(the how)* not her weakness *(the why)*.

She went to the kitchen and pulled down a note Charlie had written and taped to the fridge months ago: *DAMN GO BY SOME FOOD*. Already, she could hear his drunken snoring. She took the note back to her room, sat down, and began her work.

Going back and forth between her son's scrawled note and a page in her notebook, she worked for hours to get it right. The fat O. The swirl of the S. The strangely elegant Y. She felt Leisa gently guiding her hand as she traced the letters, traced the letters, mirrored the letters.

Down the hall, Charlie sang razors. But in Jo's room, he was writing an apology for what he was about to do. He was saying, *I'm sorry*, finishing with that strangely elegant Y.

This time, the dead boy would sign his name.

A USER'S GUIDE
TO KEEPING YOUR KILLS FRESH
BY TED ANTHONY
Fresh Kills

NEW YORK NEWSDAY
Wednesday, April 11, 2001

3 CORPSES IN L.I. CAR TRUNK
Authorities Unsure How Long Ago Deaths of Men, Woman Occurred
By Silvia D. Bruce, Staff Writer
The bodies of two men and a woman were found yesterday in the
trunk of a Chevy Impala in Captree State Park in Suffolk County,
and authorities said the deaths may not have been recent. A source
said the case may have a connection to Staten Island . . .

N ow and then, there are moments in a man's life that offer up complete clarity. They're rare, and rarer still is the ability to recognize them. It is only the truly intelligent, self-aware man who finds himself in a moment of clarity and actually sees it for what it is—and moves forward in a productive way.

Manny Antonio was not that kind of man.

If complete clarity sidled up to Manny in a tube top and fishnets and offered him a freebie, no strings attached, he would bitch-slap it and choose the company of his right hand and some Jergens instead. If complete clarity were an all-you-can-eat buffet of Chinese food, Manny would ask for the menu and order the chicken and broccoli. That's just Manny.

Or, I should say, that *was* Manny. Because all of Manoel Antonio's verbs got turned into the past tense on Staten Island exactly ten years ago today. It was ugly, it was messy, and it was—what are the exact right words here?—fucking hilarious. And it was precisely because Manny didn't know the moment of clarity when it came rushing toward him like a steroid-addled fullback.

I. MANNY'S PROBLEM

That would be Josephine and Conrad Spencer, late of Ho-Ho-Kus, New Jersey (what's with those dashes, anyway?). They weren't a bad sort, really. Their problem was that they loved to redecorate. Obsessively. Couldn't stop, in fact. Did up the living room in a South Pacific tiki theme for thirty grand, then redid the den in midcentury modern. Eames chairs and clean lines. That was another forty-five grand.

They borrowed big time from Marine Midland for those two rooms. Then they wanted to remodel some more. I mean, you and I may not like our kitchens to look like a warehouse from the 1930s, but to each his own. They wanted to borrow 50K more, but Marine Midland was wising up to them, and the loan officer told them to talk to the hand. So they looked for other, more . . . creative, shall we say, options.

Long story short, those informal solutions got mad when the repayments weren't happening on schedule. They turned to their own informal solutions, things got ugly, and the conundrum finally made its way down the food chain to Manny.

Manny Antonio was what Sergeant Joe Friday would have called "a small-time hood turned contract killer," a Portuguese thug who was a bad seed from the get-go. When he was a kid, at a neighbor's sixth birthday party, he popped all the balloons with a paring knife and pulled both claws off the birthday boy's pet crawfish. Blame the parents, if you must—divorced, addled by pills, dogged by anger-management issues before those words were ever invented—but if you ask me, Manny Antonio was born bad.

And even in that, he kind of sucked. I once had a basketball coach who said the wisest words a thirteen-year-old can hear: "If you're going to do something, be good at it. If you're going to chase pussy for a living, that's a choice—but be good at it." Manny wasn't even good at being bad. The best you could say about him was that he was very average at being very average.

Which was why he was a forgettable thug, the kind of scrub who gets the job done eventually, without any great panache. He inspired no emotion in anyone whatsoever. Remember Duffy Dyer, that second-string catcher from the early 1970s? What he was to the Mets in those days, Manny Antonio was to the people in the tri-state area who needed some thumping and killing done.

That points us back to Conrad and Josephine. She was the kind of woman who, when you see her berating the Acme cashier about the price of Shedd's Spread or complaining about the pepperoncini in the endless salad at the Olive Garden, you're glad she isn't your next-door neighbor. So when the informal loan outfit starts getting increasingly persistent in recovering its investment, she makes the tactical error, in an unfortunately aggressive phone call, of telling its duly appointed agents to take a hike.

Predictably, the duly appointed agents are not thrilled with this turn of events. They are particularly agitated about the part where Josephine implies that if the pressure does not abate, the involvement of local law enforcement might ensue. Namely the detectives of the Ho-Ho-Kus Police Department. "And don't think I won't do it. We have rights!" Josephine Spencer yells over the phone.

So the duly appointed agents, realizing the potential calamities associated with imminent police intervention, decide to schedule a visit to offer more personal customer service.

As you may be aware from the movies, these kinds of duly appointed agents rarely choose to undertake such visits on their own behalves. So they duly appoint their own agent. That is Manny.

I will pause at this point to say that the unfortunate breakage of an $8,500 original Eames Lounge Chair was not intentional on Manny's part. Though I will say also that Manny has no idea what an Eames Lounge Chair is as he breaks Josephine Spencer's neck across its armrest. He does, in passing, note the comfort of the vintage piece a few minutes later when he reclines in it briefly while using his boot-clad right foot to kick the supine Conrad Spencer's Men's Wearhouse-panted ballsack.

I doubt any other of Charles and Ray Eames's creations have witnessed such an assortment of unpleasantness—particularly to the soundtrack of a small-time hood humming Alan O'Day's forgotten 1977 pop anthem "Undercover Angel" while occasionally interrupting himself to growl at his victims, "Fuck you, you fucking fuck."

But I digress.

With the Spencers appropriately lifeless, Manny sets to getting their bodies into the Impala he has rented the night before, under an assumed name, from the Avis in Weehawken. It is past ten p.m. on a Wednesday night, so he is able to roll them up in two throw rugs (certainly not from the midcentury modern den; that is, of course, hardwood flooring) and, with some exertion, get them into the car without, he thinks, anyone getting a glimpse of his activities. He then sets out for his favorite dumping ground.

That is where the trouble that ended Manny really begins.

II. FRESH KILLS

I knew Manny pretty well. I was there at the beginning, and I was there at the end. I made the effort to get what he was about, even when it was clear there was not much there to be got. So here's how I think it went from his point of view at this juncture.

Manny crosses the Goethals, which he hasn't done in a while. He hates the Goethals. He hates all bridges. What if you stall on a bridge? What if you get a flat? You're a sitting duck, and if there's a body in the trunk, much less two, you're totally and completely fucked. Mister State Trooper, please don't stop me.

What's more, the Goethals is vertigo-inducing, and Manny has vertigo bad. Don't even talk to him about crossing the Verrazano or the GW. They're much longer and higher, and that would just be too much. He's also claustrophobic, so no Lincoln or Holland. Good thing he never needs to get to Long Island.

Fresh Kills is his go-to dumping ground. It's huge—things can get lost there with very little effort—and it's actually hard to get caught disposing of a body as long as you stay near the edges. If you get into the belly, you either get lost or get accosted. So far, unbelievably, neither has ever happened to Manny. At age thirty-seven, he's dumped about two bodies in Fresh Kills for each year of his life.

It's not as if he has any other choice. Manny used to go in-land for his body-disposal needs, but inland New Jersey was the purview of the Chinese syndicate down in Metuchen. Nobody dared get anywhere near the Meadowlands; that had belonged to the Italians since Eisenhower. And the Pine Barrens has become entirely Eastern European territory; if the Russians don't cut off your balls for using it for corpse disposal, the Serbs or the Ukranians will. All of them know Manny for trying to litter his hits in their territory. All despise him with that dull, unmotivated disdain that means he can probably stay alive as long as he doesn't actually get in their way too much.

Those nuances haven't really mattered much lately, though. Business has been slow for Manny, as it often is for mediocre people who do things mediocrely, particularly contract killing. He hasn't even been to Staten Island for eighteen months, not since that date with the Vietnamese chick who worked at the nail salon on Richmond Avenue. Like most of his dates, that one hadn't gone well for Manny. He was hoping the evening would end with her on her back saying, "Fuck me." Instead, it ended with her on her high horse saying, "Fuck you."

"Fuck you too," Manny replied. He hasn't had a date since.

Manny makes it off the Goethals and eventually exits onto 440 South, careful to put the Impala's turn signal on at exactly the appropriate points. No sense in getting stopped for a stupid traffic violation.

For the next few minutes, he takes a series of narrow back roads to the edge of the landfill, to an access road that leads to a stone hut, inside of which is Manny's guy. By that I mean the watchman Manny pays to look the other way while he goes into the landfill to get rid of what he needs to get rid of, no questions asked.

Imagine a landscape brimming to the horizon with garbage. You saw that Pixar movie WALL·E, with the robot scampering around in a future America that has been turned into a giant garbage dump? That's sort of what it used to look like in big chunks of—well, big chunks of New York City, frankly.

These days it's difficult to imagine what it used to be like around here. You drive around now and see mostly rolling hills of green with roads gently snaking through them, and they're turning the whole thing into reclaimed wetlands and a giant park. Hard to believe that the detritus of our parents and grand-parents lurks underneath, entombed for generations. Probably until the end of the planet itself. If the aliens ever land, they'll be able to learn a lot from the Clorox bottles of the Beat Generation, I'm sure.

That night, though, it had been just a few weeks since something game-changing had happened, something Manny—moron that he was—had no idea about. Fifty-three years after Robert Moses created it, the Fresh Kills Landfill had closed for business. Giuliani and Pataki had been on hand that day to watch the last barge, with a huge sign on it that said, *LAST BARGE*, chug to the dock. All that meant one thing: Manny was about to be royally screwed.

He thinks it's business as usual, though, as he pulls up and climbs through a hole in the razor-wired fence to get to the door of the hut. It is dark, but that's not odd. His guy is often asleep at the switch.

"Yo. Rodrigo." Manny dry heaves a couple times. The humidity is ugly for early April, and the place stinks to high heaven.

Nothing.

"Rodrigo! Manny! Manny Antonio! Got some transacting to do! I need the digger!" Manny bangs on the door of the hut. Silence. Another minute passes. Finally, Manny leans in and shines his pocket Maglite on the window part of the door and sees the sign:

FRESH KILLS LANDFILL
CLOSED PERMANENTLY 3/22/01
CONTACT DEPT OF SANITATION
NO TRESPASSING

"Fuck," Manny says to no one in particular. "Goddamn-fuckingshitcocksuckerfuckfuckfuck." Manny's command of English, not exactly Wordsworth even on the best of days, falls apart completely when he's stressed.

Manny pulls a map of Staten Island from his back pocket and is gazing at it with the flashlight in his mouth when he sees a light in the distance. A car approaches. There's a flashing light. It's a cop—no, wait. It's some sanitation patrol truck. It pulls up, sees a human being in its headlights, and screeches to a halt, kicking up the dust of a billion spent Marlboro butts and empty dishwashing liquid bottles and discarded maxipads.

"Sir, can I help you? What are you doing here? You're not authorized to be here." The guy is about twenty-three, scarfing fast food and dripping melty drive-thru cheese onto a uniform that, if it weren't khaki, would look like a mall cop's. He seems utterly bewildered that Manny is standing in front of him.

"Don't worry," Manny says. "Just tying up some loose ends." He puts on his best I'm-in-control voice.

The rent-a-cop sighs, puts down his Arby's, and starts to get out of the car. "I'm going to need to see some—"

At that moment Manny does the last rational thing he will do on the final night of his life. With his Maglite still chomped in his teeth like a panatela, he pulls his Kel-Tec P-11 out of his waistband and shoots the guy between the eyes. The report rings out, echoing across the trash-saturated emptiness. Inertia keeps the guy standing up for a second, dead on his feet. Then a dark stain starts to spread around his khaki crotch. His ears twitch and he collapses with a dull thump.

"GodDAMNit!" Manny has no idea what to do.

He stands there for what feels to him like hours but is probably more like five minutes, wondering if rent-a-cop reinforcements are on the way. He searches the body and the car; no sign of a walkie-talkie. Maybe the guy wasn't in communication with base, or whatever.

So what does he do next, the dumbshit? Well, he says to himself, I gotta get rid of this body, and I might as well get rid of the van too, so—and this is the logic of a lifelong dullard—he sets the van on fire with the rent-a-cop's body in it. It promptly catches the gas tank and, as Manny hurries off, the whole thing explodes, taking the hut and a pile of garbage with it. A huge plume of smoke and orange flame claws into the air.

Manny floors the Impala, banking off a pile of old kitchen appliances and skidding along the dark dirt road as he tries to regain control of the wheel. Behind him, everything is fire and thick soot.

As he gets back onto the West Shore Expressway a few minutes later, he hears sirens in the distance. He diligently uses his turn signal to get back onto I-278.

Manny is crossing the Goethals for the second time in an hour when he notices that something is caught in the passenger-side windshield wiper of the Impala. He can't quite see what it is, so he turns on the wipers. The only thing that tells him what he's looking at is the Dole sticker. It is an old banana peel, decayed beyond recognition.

Nervously, Manny starts singing underneath his breath: "*Undercover angel . . . midnight fantasy . . . I've never had a dream that made sweet love to me . . .*"

In the trunk, the Spencers do not hear him. They are, after all, dead.

III. MEANWHILE

Two days pass.

No one hears from Manny.

Multiple police departments are sniffing around.

The disappearance of the Spencers after what looks like a violent struggle has made the *Bergen Record*. On the radio, 1010 WINS is calling it a possible home invasion by a stranger and telling people in North Jersey to lock their doors.

The rent-a-cop's murder has made the *Advance*, the *Daily News*, the *Post*, and even the *New York Times*.

The informal loan outfit is not happy. Which means the duly appointed agents are not happy.

Phone calls are made. Arrangements are set up. Money changes hands.

Another day passes.

IV. THE END, MY ONLY FRIEND

I had always liked Manny despite his shortcomings. But the world has to evolve. Hopey I don't know about, but we definitely have to be changey. The trouble with Manny was that he couldn't change. He got stuck in his own rut and created his own feedback loop.

So here's how it ended, ten years ago today:

Three days have passed. The cops in Ho-Ho-Kus have cordoned off the Spencer home and started an investigation. Neighbors are worried. One reports she saw a guy carrying carpets out to the trunk of some Chevy. A Lumina, she thinks it might have been.

On Staten Island, the rent-a-cop's murder is being investigated as some kind of mob hit. Turns out the kid, who had the job only because someone's uncle's cousin's brother-in-law got him on the books, was linked to some crime family down in Philly. His name was Pascale. He was studying computer science.

Manny has not called in to the duly appointed agents. The cops find his StarTAC in the parking lot of the Showplace bowling alley, and find it has a lot of calls to numbers that are entirely too close for comfort if you happen to be one of the aforementioned agents.

In fact, Manny is on hour seventy-five of a full-on, tri-state panic attack. He has driven from Staten Island to Watchung, from Totowa to New Haven, trying to figure out what the fuck to do with the bodies in the Impala's trunk. He considers briefly dumping them in the water in Bridgeport, but the docks are too well patrolled. He even starts heading, via back roads, to Rhode Island, where he thinks he can dump them in the salt marshes on the coast. But, in quick succession:

He overheats his engine heading east on I-95.

He (you'll love this one) flags down an AAA truck for help.

He manages, somehow, to keep the AAA guys out of the trunk. They fix things and go on their way.

He turns around, heads back toward Jersey, makes it to Secaucus, where he buys a disposable cell phone. Then he thinks: I'll go back to Staten Island. I'll just sneak into the landfill from another direction and dump the bodies. Brilliant.

He is panicking. He hasn't showered in four days, hasn't eaten in two. He's surviving on Jolt and NoDoz. The ticking clock is haunting him, floating above him in his mind like it used to in those 1950s noir flicks that starred actors like Edmond O'Brien. He actually thinks he can see the clock in the sky as he crosses the Goethals yet again, cursing the Spencers and the duly appointed agents and Goethals himself, whoever the fuck he was.

Manny approaches Fresh Kills again. It's about one a.m. on Saturday, and nature, as it will forever do, is reasserting itself. Like the garbage that encircles them for acres upon acres, Josephine and Conrad Spencer are starting to putrefy.

In the driver's seat, with the air-conditioning on, Manny can't really smell them. But the moment he gets out of the Impala, the odor that envelops it is almost intolerable. This makes him very paranoid at red lights. What's worse, the remnants of Josephine's Dior Poison, freshly applied to the nape of her neck only ninety minutes before Manny cracked it over the Eames armrest, is still a potent ingredient in the olfactory mix. It's as if hell were slow-roasting a pork shoulder one evening and trying to cover up the scent with some demonic Glade Solid.

Manny has nowhere to go, no place left to turn. So he does what he's always done in these dead-end situations, where there are no more options: he calls me.

"I'm fucked," he says. "I need help. This job's gone way bad."

He knows I'll come. I always do. I'm his big brother, after all.

I'm the reason he's so mediocre, or so he likes to tell me. I'm the educated one, the one who (according to Manny) got spoiled and sent to college or (according to me) did the work that pushed me forward. I'm the one our parents had the foresight to send away to my aunt's when they started fighting and having the drug problems. They kept him with them in North Jersey as they fell deeper into their slow slide, through the Nixon and Ford administrations and well into Carter. Talk about general malaise.

I was, of course, expecting his call. See, there's something Manny doesn't know about the whole situation, and it's the key bit of information: Yes, I'm going to help him out if at all possible. But I'm also probably going to end up killing him too.

The informal loan outfit, it seems, has given up on the duly appointed agents. One of the "loan officers" is an old crew buddy of mine and knows that I, like my brother, supplement my legit income with occasional freelance dirty work. He knows that the guy his outfit is trying to track down is my brother. He also knows, and I won't get into why here, that at heart I'm an amoral prick who would do anything for money. He's mostly right.

"Make your brother disappear," my crew buddy tells me. "I don't care how, I don't care where. I don't care if he's dead or living on an estate in the Falkland Islands. Just. Get. Him. Out. Of. Our. Hair."

For that he offers me $11,000. I accept.

That's where my head is when I pull up to a remote corner of the Fresh Kills Landfill, not far from the South Mound, at 2:46 a.m. on Saturday, April 7, 2001. I am going to tell my brother that he has to leave the United States of America for the rest of his life, and that I will give him $8,000 with which to do so, and that we will never see each other again. And that if he comes back to this country and I find out about it, I will kill him.

You may notice that $3,000 of my fee is unaccounted for in my plan. Hey, every job has expenses.

I see Manny lurking in the dark, right where he said he'd be when he called from the pay phone on Forest Avenue. I pop in two sticks of Doublemint and get out of my car. I am driving a gray 1983 Chevy Citation, which I got for $700 from some guy named Honest Achmed in Yonkers. It's the perfect kind of car for this line of work: just old and cheap enough to be ignored, not old enough to be considered classic yet. And easily disposable.

"Thanks for coming." Manny is wired. His voice is pulled taut.

"No problem. Tell me about the last three days." Frantically, kinetically, he recounts the saga from his point of view, leaving nothing out. I am amazed that he can still think coherently, but his tale makes sense. And, from what I know from my employers, it's all true.

I look at him, trying to keep a poker face. "So what are we

going to do about this situation?" I am calm, and he sees it. That makes him more tense. He always hated that I knew how to keep my cool when he didn't.

"Do you think I fucking know? Why the fuck do you think I called you?"

"Manny—"

"Don't *Manny* me, dickhead. Just help me." He is trying to be menacing, which he knows doesn't work with me. He just sounds pathetic.

I lay it out for him. Leave the United States, go somewhere, don't come back. Or choose what's behind Door Number 2, which will only end badly.

"Wait. What?" The realization is dawning for my dimbulb brother. "You're working for the fucks who are coming after me?"

"Yeah, Manny, and if it were anyone else working for those fucks you'd be lying on the ground already with a bullet in your brain."

"Fuck you."

"Fuck you. You want a chance to get out of this alive?"

"Lemme get this straight," Manny says. "They hired you to kill me? You took a job to kill your own brother?"

"It doesn't have to be this way. Just say yes. Just walk away. This is the moment where you get to change things. You can do anything you want. You just can't stay here. Don't be a dumbshit. Just this once, don't be the dumbshit you've always been."

"No," he says. "Fuckfuckfuckfuck. They send my own big brother to kill me." He is flop-sweating, almost crying. I notice that he is wearing a Members Only jacket. I thought those disappeared around the time the first George Bush was elected president.

"Look, Manny. You're a cocksucker. You've always been a

cocksucker. I can't say I love you, but we have a lot of history and a lot of blood. You're my brother. Let's at least try—"

That's when things go south. Something changes. Manny stands up straighter. I know this moment. It's the one where people realize the end is racing toward them, so they have nothing to lose. This is the about-to-die version of beer muscles.

Manny reaches into his waistband and pulls out his gun. "I'm not going anywhere, motherfucker. But you are." He aims the Kel-Tec at me. "Later," he says, and fires.

Fuck, I think to myself. I'm smarter than this. I can't believe it.

His shot misses. To this day, I have no idea how.

I move quickly, instinctively. I leap at Manny, punch him in the throat even as I bring my steel-toed boot down on his left ankle. The gun bounces away. He goes down instantly, gasping. I marvel at how much his face looks like my own, but without the intelligence. It's like he's a clay dummy molded and sculpted and fired in the kiln to resemble me, but without any of the life. I think of when I was nine and he was five and we slept in the woods behind the house one night. I tried to protect him by beating a rabid squirrel dead with a tree branch. He asked me, eyes shining, if we could find another squirrel and do it again.

I head butt him. His eyes, decidedly not shining, loll and sink back into his head. I kick him in the nuts. I hear a sound like a beach ball deflating. He waves his arms, lashing out in semiconsciousness, and connects with my left ear. I go down and see stars, my mouth open against the ground. Stuff goes into it, and I taste the garbage of New Yorkers in my mouth. I spit frantically, crawl to my knees, and go right back at him.

Fuck you, you fucking spoiled brat, I think to myself. I've been putting up with this for too damn long. I lean down, head butt him again, and then bite off his right ear. I spit it out in his face. I realize I am crying.

I also realize, through my haze of anger and tears, that the Rubicon has been crossed. There is no going back.

My baby brother is still gurgling when I take a decaying single-serving milk carton off the ground, crumple it up in my hand, and shove it into his mouth. I grab his chin and ram it upward into his skull repeatedly, which has the odd effect of making him look like some Warner Bros. cartoon character chewing a particularly recalcitrant piece of beef jerky. I can hear his jawbone squeaking. Inside his mouth, lit by the moon, I can see the words 2% *milkfat*.

Manny strains to breathe. I am picturing, in my mind, Joe Pesci's final scene in *Casino*, when he is buried alive in the desert. Manny and I watched that movie on video the last time we hung out a few months back.

I spit out my wad of Doublemint, pull it into two pieces, and shove one up each of his nostrils. That does the trick. Airflow is now nonexistent. As he pushes to clear the airway and take in oxygen, his face turns red, then purple. His left eye blows out and goes dim, taking on the look of a built-in eye patch. Arrrrr, I think to myself, making the pirate noise in my head.

Like I said: fucking hilarious.

I spot the Kel-Tec on the ground a yard or two away. I grab it, anchor my heel, and fire down at him. His head explodes at my feet. Brain on my boots. The shot has knocked the gum out of his nose, and he makes one final, inadvertent exhale.

"You asshole!" I yell, spitting in what's left of his face. "Couldn't you have just this once listened to me? Couldn't you have just fucking said yes?"

No one hears me. I have just killed my brother. I feel . . . nothing. I feel absolutely nothing.

I black out. When I wake up, it is thirty-five minutes later. It is still dark in the landfill. It still smells. My brother is still dead, lying next to me.

I climb to my feet, reach into Manny's pocket and take out the key to the rental car. I shamble over and open the trunk of Manny's Impala. Josephine and Conrad Spencer stare up at me with unknowing eyes, supine, the lump of the spare tire under rough felt between them. The smell is almost unbearable.

I lift up Manny's body, carry it to the trunk, and place it between the two people he killed. I do so gingerly; he is, after all, my brother.

Turns out I was Manny's moment of clarity, and he chose the hand and the lotion. Offered the grand buffet, he went with the chicken and broccoli. Maybe it was gonna be this way no matter what. Maybe my parents just did him too much damage. Maybe it's true what they say: garbage in, garbage out.

I, however, am still alive. And I need to get out of the country's biggest dump and deal with the mess that my brother made and that I have to clean up.

That I can do. I know what Manny does not—that when it comes to dumping bodies, Suffolk County is the new black. In the new millennium, everyone who's anyone is getting rid of their dead people there.

How could Manny have known? He was too phobic to take the tunnels into Manhattan and Long Island, too stupid to even consider there might be a new frontier beyond the ones he spent his life haunting. The closed-minded fuck couldn't even consider there might be another way to do things. Just like Dad. "Oh, I couldn't possibly stop taking the pills. There's no other way, boy." Assholes.

I park the Citation where it won't be seen and wipe the

steering wheel and driver's area free of any prints. I get into the Impala and make my way to Richmond Avenue, then I-278 East and the Verrazano-Narrows Bridge beyond. I am careful to use my turn signal and not speed; no sense getting nailed on something stupid at this point in the game. Dawn is starting to break. I love the Verrazano and the chance to see lower Manhattan at dawn. The Twin Towers are always so beautiful just before the sun starts to rise.

I pass through Brooklyn, pass through Queens. I get on the Utopia Parkway and hit the gas on Manny's rented Impala, humming "Undercover Angel" as I drive east toward Suffolk County. Maybe I'll stop in and see my big sister in Yaphank while I'm out here. She and I have always been close.

V. ME, HAPPILY EVER AFTER

I can't believe my brother is dead ten years. Seems like yesterday. I have lots of fond memories when I think of him, ones that predate the day I pocketed the money that finished him off. Family's like that, though. No matter what, in the end you still feel connected. Nothing feels better than blood on blood.

These days, I run a legit business—data processing for corporations that need to outsource it. It's pretty good—I have twenty-three employees who call me boss—yet I sometimes miss the roll-up-your-sleeves-and-get-dirty flavor of my former job. But being a thug for hire is, I suppose, a game for the young.

Funny thing, though: the money I got from getting Manny out of the way started me down this path. After that I got better at killing, more nimble, and I really started to rake in the cash. I innovated. Within months, I was the first in the business to use a GPS to plot the distance between burial sites, the first to use tasers for more efficient and cleaner torture, the first to understand how the Internet can be used to mine data and make contract killing more efficient. Change is everywhere these days, and people who don't adapt will die. Figuratively speaking.

I got out in 2004 when I met the woman who would become my bride. She has no idea what I used to do for a living. Today we live on Staten Island, on a little hill where you can see the bottom of Manhattan. The Towers are gone from the view, of course, but still—I can't imagine being anywhere else. It's right in the middle of things, but it's remote too. We have two boys, six and two, the same age difference as me and Manny. They're good kids, but sometimes they fight. I hate when brothers fight.

I do think this park they're building where the landfill once stood will be cool. I'll probably even take my kids there. History is history, even when you can't talk about it. Even when it involves fratricide. I like to think that I did Manny a favor, got him out of an unresolvable situation—and a life—that he simply couldn't handle. This is rationalization, I know. But that's what killers do. We rationalize. It allows us to pretend we're regular members of society. I've just managed to do it longer than most.

You could argue that people never change. I would disagree. Because the day I killed Manny changed my life. I didn't know it then, but I know it now. It was a horrible thing that taught me how to improve myself. These days, I almost never feel like a killer anymore. I owe that all to Manny.

Now and then, there are moments in a man's life that offer up complete clarity. They're rare, and rarer still is the ability to recognize them. It is only the truly intelligent, self-aware man who finds himself in a moment of clarity and actually sees it for what it is—and moves forward in a productive way.

I am that kind of man. My brother, as I stated earlier, was not.

DARK WAS THE NIGHT, COLD WAS THE GROUND

BY SHAY YOUNGBLOOD

South Beach

T he sound was soft at first, a scratching that seemed to be part of the hip-hop song blasting from the open windows of the vintage bronze Mercedes as it pulled up next to the white Lincoln I was sitting in.

An unnaturally tan, pear-shaped man, wearing a plaid golf hat and sunglasses, stepped gingerly onto the gas station's oil-stained concrete in a pair of shiny penny loafers. He wheezed as if he had asthma and tucked the tail of a pink, buttoned-down shirt into the waistband of a pair of gray sweatpants, which were stained at the knees. I saw that the muffler of the wide four-door model car was almost touching the ground.

The man grunted and stretched his arms out as if he'd been driving for a long time. He turned in my direction and sniffed the air with a grimace. The wind had shifted and the aroma from the nearby Fresh Kills Landfill, also known as "the dump," wafted over the top of a long line of leafy green trees, cleverly planted to camouflage the rolling hills of garbage facing the Staten Island Mall. The man slammed his car door shut, turned on his heels with a military twist, and marched into the store. Although there was a driving boom box beat thumping out of the windows, I was sure now of a dissonant muffled tapping coming from the sagging trunk of the Mercedes.

It was club night and my new friend Francesca "Frankie"

Dacosta had stopped at the gas station near her house on the western shore of Staten Island to buy a six-pack of peach wine coolers and a bag of ice. I had met Frankie a few days before, at the grocery store on Forest Avenue. I was standing in the produce aisle holding a large bunch of collard greens. My fingers felt the leaves as if they were braille, as if some message decoded along the thick stems and fine veins could explain why Raymond, my husband of forty-two years, was gone. It was so unfair. He had been hammering a nail into the wall so we could hang the framed photo of our last trip to the Grand Canyon when he fell to the floor. The doctor said a blood vessel had burst in his head. Six months and one day after we both retired from thirty-seven years of teaching in the New York City public school system, we thought our lives were just beginning.

I sat up night after night for two weeks listening to Blind Willie Johnson's sorrowful blues, a moan accompanied by bottleneck guitar, raw emotion that echoed my grief, *Dark was the night, cold was the ground* . . . I didn't want to die, but living without my Raymond took the sweet out of everything.

Frankie turned a corner in the supermarket and saw me standing in the produce section holding the collard greens like a wedding bouquet. Silent tears poured down my face onto the front of a red silk blouse that had been my husband's favorite.

"I wanted to take a picture, but my good sense took over and I gave you a pack of tissues and took you home with me," Frankie told me later.

I opened the passenger door of the Lincoln and was about to get closer to the sound when Frankie came flying from the store like she was being chased by demons out of hell. The loose black shift she wore was hiked up above her pale knees and she pressed the sack of wine coolers to her chest. She tossed the bag of ice onto the backseat, barely missing my head.

"Get in! Lock the doors!" She barked commands and I followed orders. Frankie jumped in the car and hit the power lock three times. She pressed another button and the windows rolled up at lightning speed.

"You're sweating. What's going on?"

"There's a really creepy guy in there. He's trying to get the attendant to give him half a gallon of gas in a mayonnaise jar, thirteen matches, and six yards of silver masking tape."

"Sounds like he's making a recipe or something."

"Or something." Frankie wiped sweat off her upper lip with a handkerchief.

"I think there's a body in the trunk." I rolled the window down a few inches. "Listen."

"That's crappy music." She waved the handkerchief in front of her face.

"Listen," I shushed her. We both heard a loud thump.

Just then the driver of the Mercedes strolled out of the store cursing the gas attendant's mother. I rolled up the window and looked over at Frankie. Then my head snapped back toward the Mercedes when I heard a crash. The man had thrown the empty mayonnaise jar against the side of the building before getting back in his car. The Mercedes took off, leaving behind a trail of smoke, the smell of burning rubber, and the echo of screeching tires.

"He's headed toward the dump. Should we . . ."

Frankie pressed her lips together and shook her head. "Marie, honey, this is Staten Island. We should be blind, deaf, and dumb." She brought two fingers to her lips, closed her eyes, and pressed her other hand to her ear.

"Maybe it was a big dog," I said, sure it wasn't.

"Yeah, and maybe it won't snow this December," Frankie countered, pulling into Friday evening traffic on Richmond Avenue.

"What if it's somebody you know?"

"I don't know the kind of people who'd be locked up in the trunk of a car, do you?"

"He was acting so crazy. I just know he's going off to do something bad."

"He's a bad man. What do you want to do about it, Marie?"

"We didn't do it already, so I guess we leave it alone."

"Thank you. Enough already about that bum."

We stopped talking about the guy, but I couldn't stop thinking about him.

We took the long way to Frankie's house. She liked driving through Todt Hill where the wealthy lived. Frankie said Paul Castellano of the Gambino crime family had lived in a house that was an exact replica of the White House, down to the flagpole flying both the American and Italian flags. I read somewhere that Todt was a Dutch word for *dead*. There was a large cemetery nearby and I also took note that there were no sidewalks or public transportation in the neighborhood.

On the day we met, Frankie invited me to her South Beach home and a meeting of the Staten Island Ward Widows of America. After her husband Ignacio died, Frankie had painted every room in her house bright yellow—with the exception of the bedroom, which she painted red velvet. Frankie had a sweet tooth, and sleeping alone for seven years hadn't made her any less lonely for companionship, or desserts. Although the widows took turns making dessert, Frankie had a great recipe for cannoli, which was to die for.

"Marie," she said, "for you, I'm making cannoli. I want to bring some sweetness back into your life."

She worked real hard to make me smile again.

Making the cannoli was an all-day affair. The recipe had been given to her by her mother-in-law, along with the responsibility to pass it on to the women in the family. When Ignacio died of a heart attack on his job as an electrician for the city, Frankie had been inconsolable for months. She read an article in the *New York Times* about a group of widows who met every month for dinner and companionship. Those were the things she missed most, and so for the past seven years she and her friends had been meeting monthly in each other's homes to eat together and put some sweetness in their lives.

Frankie, Olympia, Celia, Theresa, and Angelina were well into their sixties, and all but Angelina were either widowed or divorced. At first the women eyed me a little suspiciously. It was rare to see a black woman in this part of Staten Island—especially in this famously clannish Italian stretch of Hickory Boulevard—although I had recently learned that in the seventeenth century early settlers on the island had been French Huguenots and freed slaves. I didn't say much at that first meeting, and after brief introductions the conversations started in as if I weren't even there.

Today the women arrived at the front door of Frankie's home within minutes of each other. Celia was the first. Frankie had invited her after months of listening to her complaints about being a jailhouse widow. Although Celia's husband wasn't dead, she was hoping he'd die in prison where he had been for the past three years serving time for bigamy. His wife in Ireland showed up on their doorstep one day demanding back-child support for a teenager he claimed to know nothing about.

"Excuse my French, ladies, but that Irish fucker ruined my

retirement. I'm supposed to be lounging on a beach in the Bahamas with a cold cocktail in my hand."

Angelina, still as thin and girlish as she was in high school, had a bum for a husband. Tito had terrorized her from the moment she met him in high school, bullying her into marriage at sixteen and getting her pregnant every ten months for the next six years. She finally had her tubes tied after saying a few dozen Hail Marys. She wasn't a widow, but she dreamed about it. She was an honorary member of the club and a portion of every meeting was dedicated to exploring ways to kill Tito. They had poisoned him, hired someone else to kill him, put a spell on him, and each month looked forward to concocting the most creative murder so that Angelina would be eligible for his pension. Tito had left the family years ago, so in a way Angelina was living like a widow, but without the pension. She earned income as a wedding seamstress and had a team of well-behaved children who helped make her home business a success.

Olympia, loudmouthed and vain, divorced her husband thirteen years ago, but she still cooked him dinner every night and delivered it to him in the basement of his Kensington Street home, where he'd lived since the young secretary he left her for left him when he ran out of money. His business failed and his hair fell out. Still, he was the father of her two daughters and she was grateful for that, but was hoping he'd die soon and put everyone out of their misery.

That day she wore a bejeweled patch over her left eye because her recent self-improvement had been laser surgery so she wouldn't have to wear trifocals. She had a tall weave of teased hair that fluffed around her face like blond cotton candy; Frankie said she looked like a disco pirate and I had to agree. The only thing missing was a parrot on her shoulder and a cutlass in her hand.

After Theresa's first husband died in a mysterious fire, she got involved with a married man who strung her along for ten years before marrying her. She was still mourning her dead husband while trying to keep the new one interested.

"Come on, Frankie, give me the recipe. Bennie would buy me a fur coat if I made cannoli like this," Theresa said.

Requests for Frankie's secret cannoli recipe were always appreciated, but she declined with her usual answer: "If I told you the recipe I'd have to kill you. This one goes with me to my grave, ladies, since it looks like neither one of my sons want to make me a grandmother."

"What's the matter with your Gianni? He's a handsome guy, got a good job in the city," said Angelina, already a little tipsy from her second glass of chianti.

"Too damn picky, my Gianni. He's thirty-five years old and still no wife." Frankie dabbed at her mouth with a linen napkin.

"You should've left him in Sicily with your brothers for a few years."

"My brothers would've killed him. He likes to read books. They're fishermen, they gut fish for fun. Gianni hates fish. He barely lasted a week every other summer. One good thing came out of it, though. He speaks perfect Italian."

"Theresa, you got anybody for Gianni? Is your youngest married yet?"

Theresa was well respected as a matchmaker since she had miraculously married off her homely thirty-year-old niece to a retired boat captain in Sardinia and successfully introduced a young cousin with a limp to a cab driver who lived in Sunnyside.

"My Sheila's married three times already. The oldest is married to her job. Works for a lawyer in Bay Ridge but she spends most of her time in the city. She seems to have a taste for married men," Theresa complained.

"Just like her mother." Olympia poured more chianti into my glass.

"What do you mean, Olympia? Ben was almost divorced when I met him. We got married right after his divorce was final."

"Ten years later, wasn't it?" Olympia smiled at me and winked.

"Olympia, I swear I'll put your other eye out and it won't be temporary."

"Frankie, your son Charlie, he's connected, isn't he?" Olympia changed the subject.

Frankie's look could have sliced through the Italian marble fireplace. Her voice was cold and dropped to a whisper: "My son Cicero is in construction like his father. He's a legitimate businessman."

"I didn't mean anything . . ."

"Cicero's a good boy. He brings me a box of assorted from Alfonso's Bakery every Sunday, and my Gianni, he works with me in my garden. He bought me a Madonna to put in the backyard. He'll help me install it before the ground freezes. Gianni, he's a good boy. A little queer with the books and all, but I couldn't be more proud of him. He teaches English at a private school on the Upper East Side."

"My Nardo saw him coming out of a double feature at the mall last week," Celia offered.

"Was he with somebody?" Angelina asked.

"All alone. So sad. He's so good-looking." Celia picked up the framed photo of Frankie's youngest son from the buffet.

"Movie-star handsome," Olympia said, passing his photograph around the dining room table.

"I know I can find somebody for him," Theresa insisted.

"Staten Island is like a village. Everybody knows your freak-ing business and thinks they can improve it." Olympia adjusted her eye patch.

"So, girls, how we gonna kill Angelina's husband this week?" Frankie asked, passing the dish of cannoli around a second time.

"What about poisoning his favorite dessert?" I suggested.

The women all laughed. "We tried that years ago. Don't you watch *CSI: NY*? It's got to look like an accident."

"Tito didn't come for dinner. The kids called him a dozen times, but he won't answer. It's not like him."

"Do you think he's gambling again?" Olympia asked.

"Maybe. Some fat guy driving a Mercedes came by the house looking for him. He reeked. Who wears Old Spice anymore?"

I glanced over at Frankie.

"Debt collectors," Frankie said, smiling.

A week before Christmas, Frankie invited me to stay the week at her house after I confessed that all I did was listen to the blues and cry into several glasses of red wine every night. Neither of us felt like traveling during the holidays and we didn't want to be alone. Her sons worked on the holidays and at most dropped by for a glass of wine and a quick meal. My husband and I were both orphans and never had children. I felt so alone in the world without him. We made a few friends over the years among our colleagues, but they were all couples.

Frankie was surprised when her son Gianni called to say he wanted her to meet his girlfriend. She invited them over for cannoli and coffee the day I arrived.

When Gianni told his mother his girlfriend's name, Luzette, she thought the girl was French. He didn't tell her she was black.

"Nice to meet you, Mrs. Dacosta, Mrs. Greene," the petite caramel-colored girl whispered.

"Mrs. Dacosta was my mother-in-law. Francesca was my mother's little girl. Call me Frankie and speak up."

"*Ma!* A pleasure, Mrs. Greene," Gianni said, shaking my hand and grinning like he'd won the lottery as he looked back and forth between me and his mother. The ladies were right, he was movie-star handsome and the young lady he brought home looked like a model. I felt sorry for that pretty little whispery girl, not because Frankie was mean but because it couldn't have been easy meeting the mother of a man who was so clearly a mama's boy. Gianni hung their coats and scarves on a hook by the front door.

Frankie led us into the dining room we had spent all day decorating with garlands of fake holly and bowls of silver balls. She picked up the platter and offered Luzette a cannoli. The girl took a small bite.

"The cannoli . . . It's . . ."

"I know. Pretty good, huh?" Gianni mumbled through a mouthful.

"I don't think I've ever tasted anything so good. How do you make them?"

"I'd have to—"

"Ma, let's install the Madonna," Gianni cut in before his mother could threaten the life of his beloved.

"Tonight? It'll be dark soon."

"I know, but let's do it now. You know I don't have much time during the week, and weekends . . ."

"Yeah, I can see you've been busy." Frankie eyed the girl up and down.

"Ma, do you mind if I check the scores?"

"No, the remote is on the shelf behind the TV."

"Why do you put it there?"

"I get exercise when I change the channels."

Gianni turned on the TV, then flipped through the channels. He didn't seem to find what he was looking for.

"I'm getting you a satellite dish for Christmas," he said.

"Get yourself a—" Frankie's mouth opened, eyes wide. She stared at the TV as if the Holy Mother herself had appeared on the screen.

"The body of a man missing since late fall was found at the Staten Island dump this morning. He allegedly fell asleep in a dumpster and was crushed nearly beyond recognition by the industrial compactor at the Fresh Kills Landfill. The body has been identified as Tito . . ."

"Angelina's Christmas present!" Frankie exclaimed, then powered off the TV.

At that moment the kitchen phone rang. Gianni practically ran to answer it. A few minutes later he came back into the dining room buttoning up his coat.

"Ma, we gotta go. Cicero's truck broke down on the Verrazano Bridge. We'll be back in a flash. Nice to meet you, Mrs. Greene." He grabbed their coats and Luzette's hand and they disappeared into the night laughing like young people should when they're in love.

There was an awkward silence after they left.

"He never brought a girl home before. I thought he was gay."

"So, what did you think?"

"Can I be honest here? I always thought black was beautiful, before it was a popular opinion. Beautiful, yes, but not one of us. She must be pretty special for him to bring her home."

"I must be pretty special too."

"You're black?" Frankie laughed, and so did I. "Do you know how they met? Gianni said she was an angel of mercy.

She took care of him after the ferry crashed back in October. I thought she was a nurse."

"A French nurse." I smiled.

"We should call Angelina, congratulate her." Frankie started putting away the cannoli.

"I knew it wasn't really a dog in the trunk of that car."

"Oh yes he was," Frankie said, biting into another cannoli.

We put on our coats, heavy gloves, and snow boots, and trudged out into the backyard. The ground was frozen, but there we were at dusk with a shovel and a pick ax in thirty-degree weather digging a hole for the white marble Madonna statue her son had given her. Unstoppable, Frankie went into the garage and came back with a lit propane torch. She handled it like a professional and passed it over a large square of earth. Tossing me a shovel, she took up a pick ax and we went to work.

"You know what brought me to New York? A man who lied to me, cheated on me, then dumped me. Before I met my husband I didn't think I would ever be able to trust anybody again. His friends didn't approve of us because I wasn't Jewish. Raymond saved my life." A flood of tears cooled my cheeks.

"My cannoli never had this effect on anyone before."

"Frankie, you don't have to love that girl, but she loves him and he loves you."

"It's okay by me if Gianni and that young lady want to have some café con leche babies so I won't have to take the cannoli recipe with me to my grave. I'll show her how to make gravy."

"What kind of gravy? The kind you put on biscuits?"

"Madonna! Have you got a lot to learn, Cookie." She wiped the tears from my eyes.

"I never had a nickname before."

"Well, Cookie, it suits you."

We had been digging for about twenty minutes when I heard Frankie let out a low moan.

"Madonna!"

I looked down into the hole and saw the skull. There was a dirty Dodger's baseball cap on the ground beside her feet.

"You bastard!" Frankie spat the words.

"Is that your husband?" I whispered in the dark.

"Are you nuts? That's Jackie Domino. He lived next door."

"How do you know it's him?"

"He wore that Dodgers cap like a flag."

"What's he doing in your backyard?"

"How the hell should I know? That dirty pile of bones kissed me at his sister's wedding, then bragged about it to some of his friends. I told my husband what really happened. A few days later Jackie told everyone he was taking a vacation in Florida. I never saw him again. His daughter sold the house not long after that and moved to the city."

"Frankie, we have to call the police."

"Not gonna happen, Marie."

"Did you give him your cannoli recipe?"

"Wasn't me, if that's what you're thinking. Jackie Domino was not a nice man. No class. Could've been anybody. His ex-wife, she was paying him alimony for the pleasure of not being married to him. He was a big gambler, liked to play the ponies, it could've been his bookie. He was a bully. His kids hated him too."

"What about your husband?"

"Ignacio? He was no saint, but I don't think he'd have killed Jackie over a kiss. Rough him up a little, no doubt, but he wouldn't have risked making me a jailhouse widow over this worthless pile of bones."

She picked up the Dodgers hat and turned it over like she was searching for clues, then kept her head down and wept. I put my arms around her and hummed that blues song I held onto in my cloudiest hours.

Dark was the night, cold was the ground . . .

Without speaking another word we worked for the next several hours in the growing darkness, mixing concrete, covering up old secrets, installing the Madonna, and whispering prayers of forgiveness.

"There are friends and there are friends who'll help you get rid of a body. Cookie, you're all right," Frankie said, biting into her third cannoli.

She reached over and held the hand that only a few hours before had touched the bones of Jackie Domino.

PART II

FIGHT OR FLIGHT

MISTAKES

BY MICHAEL PENNCAVAGE

The Ferry

In life sometimes the tiniest mistakes have the greatest consequences. That's the problem with mistakes. You can't control them. You can't prevent them.

They just happen.

Like this one.

You're at a bar over in SoHo. It's one of the nice ones. You know the type. Smoking isn't allowed but it's got a huge outdoor terrace. Palm trees and tropical plants sway in the warm night breeze. Inside, scented oxygenated air runs through the ventilation system to make you feel invigorated and get you in a drinking mood. The employees have wide smiles and can-do attitudes. This isn't one of those joints with the dollar drink specials. And you would never *ever* think of venturing inside. Well, maybe in the past. When you were younger and looking to see just what this town had to offer. Maybe even prove yourself a little.

But not anymore.

Tonight is Ben's bachelor party. He's the first of you to get hitched. Maybe someday when more of you are married, bachelor parties will be occasions of dullness and drudgery. But not now. Not this one. The way everyone is acting, it's like you are all getting married in three Sundays.

There's eight of you celebrating. It's a small group but large enough to be noticed. Everyone is dressed to impress. Everyone is dressed to kill. You've hired a stretch limousine and it makes everyone feel like a celebrity. You tipped the driver generously earlier in the night and he's now at your beck and call.

This is the fourth bar you're hitting tonight. Or maybe it's the fifth. They're beginning to blend together. But the sun hasn't risen yet so it can't be *that* late.

There's a boxing match on the television above the bar. A title belt is being decided. A small crowd is watching it intently. You catch the bartender slip a Benjamin into a money pouch and you realize he's taking side bets. You watch the fight until the round ends. Harold, one of the guys in the bachelor party, glances over at you. "What do you think?"

You shrug your shoulders. "Not bad."

"I bet you could whip either of their asses." He takes a swig of beer and staggers back one step.

"You're drunk."

"You want to place a bet?"

"No."

"Fine. I will then. Who's your money on?"

"I'm not sure."

"Don't bullshit me. You know who's going to win."

"Is that right?" You fold your arms. With each bar Harold has become more irritating. He can't hold his alcohol worth a damn.

Ben walks over to the group. He's beaming. "I have a confession to make. I've known the owner of this place for a few years."

"So?"

"He's given us an invitation into the back room. They got a craps table back there."

"Are you out of your mind?" one the group says.

"It's my bachelor party. Come on. It'll be fun. Just a few tosses of the dice. That's all I'm asking."

The group argues this for another minute before Ben wins out. After all, it's his night.

You all dutifully follow through the security checkpoints. They check IDs and pat down each of you for weapons. You've made it this far without getting separated. No sense in starting now.

The back room is small. A craps table is in the center, surrounded by a pair of poker and roulette tables. Security is everywhere and the pit boss warily keeps an eye on both the players and the observers. How this place hasn't been busted is a complete mystery. You guess the room can be broken down and the machines removed in minutes if the owners feel the Heat coming down.

The table bet is so steep it's criminal. Mark pulls two hundred from his wallet and the croupier slides over a feeble stack of chips. There's some serious money at play. A woman has on a diamond necklace worth more than an average person's house. She's got three stacks of chips so tall they'd knock someone out if they fell over. A man standing across from you is wearing a suit worth two week's pay. He tosses a small stack of Benjamins toward the croupier as an afterthought.

You look around in amazement, not believing that places like this actually exist. You are in a different world. The people in here are out of your league. Way out of your league.

Someone hands Ben the dice. He takes a generous sip of scotch for good luck and gives the two six-siders a whirl. They come up with a five and a six. Money all around. A few claps come from the crowd. He gives the dice a second roll. Similar results. Folks at the table emit a small whoop of joy. The man standing to Ben's left is wearing the largest Stetson you've ever seen. He pats Ben on the shoulder. With a flick of the wrist the stickman slides the dice across the green felt table.

Ben grabs the pair, blows some warm air into his fist, and lets them fly. They bounce off the bumpers and start heading back to him. They stop after a few turns. For a moment the crowd is speechless. "Yo-leven," replies one of the croupiers. Ben takes a short bow and the crowd erupts. Passersby stop, snared by the commotion. The house begins distributing winnings across the table.

Three more tosses of the dice and you're amazed at how quickly fortunes have turned. The table is packed now. Others want in on the action. You take a step back so they can join in. It's a half-step, really. But it's enough to knock into the person passing behind. It feels like your shoulder has struck a concrete brick. Manners have always been your strong suit and you quickly turn to apologize.

The man isn't big. He's immense. At least six foot six and probably twice your weight. He's got an entourage and you're suddenly staring up at what looks like the defensive unit of a football team.

There's a large red stain on the man's white suit jacket. A stain you suspect you're responsible for. The man looks down at his chest. His upper lip begins to curl, like a dog whose tail you just stepped on. Veins pop out on his brow and across the sides of his shaved head. He looks like someone just shot his mother.

"I'm really sorry about that," you stammer. "My fault completely."

The man flicks his hand at his chest as if expecting to whisk away the spot. "You're damn straight it's your fault. This jacket set me back eight hundred dollars." Baldy is quickly flanked by two of his crew, making him look like the runt of the litter. One of them peers over his shoulder. His eyes narrow. Disgust is in his voice. "Man. That suit is fucked up. You might as well go throw it away."

You look into the guy's eyes. You've seen this before. A sinking feeling settles into the pit of your stomach. Things are rapidly deteriorating. "You can send me the cleaning bill. I'd be more than happy to pay it."

"What the hell good is that going to do me now? Me and my boys were going to hit some more clubs and score some ass. Can't do that if I'm smelling like shit."

Harold walks up alongside of you, as does the rest of your group. Mark has handed off the dice and grabbed his winnings. For a moment the two groups stare one another down. Sweat forms on your brow.

Baldy mutters something under his breath and turns to go. You sigh with relief. He's leaving.

"Pussy."

The comment comes from Harold. He's the biggest guy in your group—as tall as Baldy, but at least fifty pounds lighter.

Baldy's antennae catch the signal. He whirls around, teeth clenched, face red. He points a finger at you. "You're a dead man." You open your mouth to say that it's a misunderstanding. That Harold has had at least six gin and tonics too many. But Baldy and his posse are gone.

You look over at Harold. He's already moved on. You realize he probably doesn't even remember what he just said.

Ben walks over and slaps you on the back. "You okay?"

"Sure. No problem."

"Don't worry about those meatheads. A few more drinks in them and they'll lose whatever brain cells they have left." He thumbs back over to the craps table. "You want to have another whirl with me? I'm hot tonight, baby! Hot!"

You shake your head. "I'm going to get a drink."

You leave the gambling room and head over to the bar. A band is playing on a small elevated stage. The lead singer, a woman in her late twenties with short, jet-black hair, isn't half bad. She's belting out an INXS song.

The bartender serves up a seltzer with a splash of cranberry. You used to drink. Heavily. But that was during the *Foolish Days*, as you now refer them to. These days you know better. You know *much* better.

Three songs in and you're starting to feel a little more relaxed, a little more at ease. The singer has moved on to some Rolling Stones and the replay of the Yankees game is going your way.

"Sympathy for the Devil" is being belted out when you roll your neck to work out a small cramp. You notice Baldy talking to one of his friends at the far corner of the bar. Things go from bad to worse when you realize that two more of his goon squad are at a table to your right. Their beers are evaporating faster than they are drinking them. They're trying their best to look disinterested in you but are failing miserably.

You wonder where your friends are right now. The club is mammoth. You consider texting Ben but reconsider. They're all three sheets to the wind by now. That would just make things worse. You don't need a riot on your hands.

Baldy is staring straight at you. Fury is in his face. There's no mistaking it. You've seen it many times before. He's going to make his move. You glance at your watch. It's really late. Dawn is fast approaching. You can try to wait him out in hopes the alcohol will cause him to lose interest.

Five minutes pass and your patience begins to wear thin. You look around but your bachelor party is nowhere to be seen. Have they left without you? You glance at your watch. You came in on the ferry. The next one leaves in about thirty minutes.

You drop some bills on the bar, grab your jacket, and leave.

* * *

There's a slight breeze in the night air. It's been a long day and it's refreshing. The ferry terminal is about twenty blocks away. If you pace yourself you can get there in time. A taxi speeds by. You consider hailing it but you need the exercise.

You get to Whitehall Terminal with a few minutes to spare. Above the entranceway, the ten-foot-tall, blue-block letters spelling out *Staten Island Ferry* feel like they are inviting you in. The terminal is apocalyptically empty, which makes it feel even larger than usual. The only people around are those passed out on the floor who don't know or care that their way off Manhattan is leaving soon, stranding them for another hour.

You pass through the waiting area, pass beneath the yellow LED sign telling you to *Have a nice day*, and make your way onto the ferry.

The metal and wood bench seats are hard and uncomfortable but they do the job of keeping you awake. The ferry, like the terminal, is eerily quiet. The overhead lighting is glaringly bright when compared to the outside darkness.

The engines roar to life and the ferry captain slowly guides the boat away from the pier. The floorboards begin to vibrate. Even the windows rattle. You wonder how the boat hasn't sunk to the bottom of the harbor by now. Shouts of alarm can be heard outside as the ferry pulls away. Someone is being yelled at. The distance between you and the dock quickly widens.

A few weary souls are peppered throughout the deck. The vessel is emptier than you've ever seen it. But then again, it'll be dawn soon.

You'll be in Staten Island in twenty-five minutes, but between the walk and long night of numerous seltzer waters, your bladder demands attention. Reluctantly, you decide to hunt out the men's room.

The stench hits you even before you reach the door. For a

moment you contemplate trying to find another one. Maybe it'll be more sanitary. But you *really* have to go, so you begin breathing through your mouth and hope that it looks better than it smells.

Inside, from the way the floor is rattling, you would think the engine room is right below your feet. You pick the cleanest stall and hope you don't come down with a case of shy-bladder syndrome. The boat is swaying more than usual and you clutch the stall railing as if you were riding a bronco.

Once you've finished, you unlock and open the stall door. Immediately you wish that you hadn't.

Baldy is leaning against the sink, his arms crossed. He takes the toothpick out of his mouth and flicks it onto the floor. For a moment you think it's an illusion. But then the illusion starts to talk.

"That was pretty tricky of you, trying to give me the slip. But I found out which direction you were heading." He sneers. "And you were dressed like someone who lives on Staten Island. Jumped onto the boat just as it was sliding away from the dock." He cracks his knuckles. "You have no idea how long it's been since I did some ass-kicking." He ponders that for a moment. "At least five weeks, I think."

You look to the exit door. His buddies aren't there.

"Don't worry about us being interrupted. I've got a janitor's cart blocking the doorway. We should have enough *alone time* before anyone gets curious."

"I'm sorry for the misunderstanding. I promise to get that shirt dry-cleaned."

"Jacket. You fucked up my jacket."

"Hey. No problem. I'll dry-clean them both."

"Shut up. You sound pathetic."

"I'm really not looking for any trouble."

"Well, you certainly found it." He steps a little closer and you can smell the reek of alcohol on his breath. There's not going to be any reasoning with him.

Baldy cracks his knuckles again, forms two fists, and you think, *How did it come to this?*

He takes another step forward. His massive frame blocks out the sink lights behind him. You take a step backward. Take another and you'll find yourself back inside the stall. You consider that for a moment, but it would only provide a barrier for a minute at most, before he rips the door off the hinges. You look to the ceiling. There're security cameras on the ferry, but none in here.

Baldy brings his pair of sledgehammers into view. His left is above his right. You take him for a southpaw. He swings. You duck and he slams his fist into the stall door, shaking it violently. This serves to enrage him even more.

He shoots out a left hook. You spin sideways and it passes by your ear. The move has boxed you in somewhat and reflexes kick in. You throw a hard right jab. Nothing fancy, but you put your weight behind it and twist your hips and remember to retract it a little, just like you were trained.

Or at least that's the plan.

As your punch is unleashed, Baldy makes an unexpected move. He steps in closer, thinking he can hit you better. It's something an amateur or a drunk would do. During your days in the ring, you would *never* expect someone to do that. Certainly not at the beginning of a bout when the fighter still has his wits about him.

There's nothing you can do. It's too late. It all happens in slow motion. Your fist connects against the top of Baldy's nose. A loud crack echoes through the bathroom. Cartilage snaps. But that's not what concerns you. You hear bones break. From the neck. Just below the occipital. Baldy stares at you for a moment before his eyes roll back into his head. He lets out a short gasp and his body spasms, causing him to spin around and collapse face first against the countertop. Even before he strikes the surface you know he's already dead.

His head hits the edge of the chrome sink at the exact spot that your fist connected. A loud *gong* is heard as the wash basin is shaken from its mooring and hops up into the air.

Baldy collapses onto the metal floor and doesn't move. There's blood everywhere. Time grinds to a halt. You don't even hear the boat's engines anymore.

You stare at yourself in the mirror. Calmly, but quickly, you straighten your clothes and smooth your hair. None of Baldy's blood is on you. You steady your breathing just as if you were in the ring. You compose yourself one final time and open the bathroom door. There's no one in the corridor outside.

You slip out of the bathroom and quietly slide the janitor's cart back in front of the door. You make your way to the outside of the ship.

The night air over the water has grown cold, but it feels good. The waves crash against the bow and the smell of salt hangs heavy in the air. You sit down on an orange metal bench and stare out at the far shore. The lights from the St. George Ferry Terminal are faintly visible in the distance.

The boat lurches as it strikes a swell. Sweat beads on your brow. Nausea begins to overtake you. You try to clear your head, but it's not working. Your hands are shaking just like they did when you first started using the heavy bag. You clench them into fists and jam them into your pockets.

The area is empty. At least you think it is. A drunk college kid stumbles over and slumps down on the bench near you.

"Goddamn, it's cold out here!" he shouts, and then laughs at himself in amusement. He looks over at you. "You cold there, bro?"

"I'm fine."

"You don't look fine. You look sick. You know, I should be the one who's going to be sick." He begins to detail how many shots of Absolut he's had. You're not responding and he scratches his head, peering at you intently. He says you look familiar. Has he seen you before? Maybe on television? Are you some sort of actor? You shake your head. *No*, you answer, looking out over the water. The sky is now a gun-metal gray but the water remains ink black. Sorry to disappoint, you tell him, but he's mistaken.

You're no one special.

It takes two days for the incident to hit the local paper. It's on the bottom of page eight next to an article about a dentist in Castleton Corners expanding his practice. The reporter explains how Baldy, a.k.a. Lloyd Peterson, blood alcohol level of 0.15, passed out on the Staten Island Ferry and broke his neck against the bathroom sink. It turns out that Lloyd had done two years in Altona Correctional Facility for aggravated assault. The funeral is on Tuesday.

You're about to toss the paper into recycling when you spot an article about the boxing match you saw on television at the club. The fighter you thought was going to win did so. It turns out he's undefeated. The reporter is comparing him to another boxer, Louis Cartwright. They wonder if this fight will make Cartwright come out of retirement to defend his title. Apparently he lives in the paradisiacal neighborhood of Emerson Hill.

You walk outside onto the porch and look up and then down the street. The birds are chirping. A slight breeze blows through your hair.

It's nice. Real nice.

But paradisiacal?

ABATING A NUISANCE

BY BRUCE DESILVA

Tompkinsville

The *Suzanne*, under the command of Captain Robert Beveridge, sailed from the Cuban port of Mataznas on April 20, 1858, bound for Liverpool with a rich cargo of sugar. Two days out, the captain died of yellow fever. The following night the disease took the cook and the cabin boy. The next day five seamen, too ill for duty, shivered in their sweat-drenched hammocks.

The first mate steered the ship toward New York City and dropped anchor in the lower bay. Surviving crew members were loaded into a smaller boat named the *Cinderella* for a short sail against the tide to the northeastern tip of Staten Island. There they were stripped naked, and their clothes were burned. Then they were wrapped in thin blankets and carted into the New York Marine Hospital, more commonly known as the Quarantine.

Soon, they would have company.

By August 16, forty-one barks, brigs, sloops, and schooners lay at anchor in the lower bay, all of them banned from putting in at the Port of New York. Their colors had been struck and replaced with the flag that inspired more terror than the Jolly Roger ever had.

The Yellow Jack.

From the library on the second floor of his fine house atop Staten Island's Fort Hill, Dr. Frederick Hollick studied the harbor through his spyglass. He counted thirty-four ships at anchor beyond the four piers that jutted from the grounds of the Quarantine. Each vessel had arrived packed stern to bow with riffraff from Ireland and Germany, all of them exposed to—or already deathly ill with—typhus, cholera, and smallpox. The forty-one yellow fever ships, the ones that frightened the good doctor the most, were too far out for him to see, but he knew they were there. He'd read all about it in the New York City newspapers.

Dr. Hollick panned his glass across the rolling thirty-acre grounds of the Quarantine: St. Nicholas Hospital, a huge, hotel-like redbrick structure where the disease-carrying first-class passengers were housed. The old, ramshackle Smallpox Hospital. The two-story Female Hospital. The squat brick dormitories for the boatmen who ferried passengers from infected ships. The eight wooden typhus shanties that were home both to diseased steerage passengers and to the stevedores who had the filthy job of unloading contaminated cargo. The wooden offices, stables, barns, coal houses, storerooms, and outhouses. The three fine doctors' residences. The vegetable gardens. And the cemeteries where one out of every six persons who entered the Quarantine would spend eternity.

When the state of New York first located the Quarantine here in 1799, it seemed to make sense, Dr. Hollick had to admit. The island was lightly populated by farmers and clam diggers, most of them living miles away along the island's south shore. But then a landing for the ferry from Manhattan was built beside the hospital. And well-off city dwellers seeking a few days in the countryside began to arrive. And hotels to serve them were constructed near the landing. And the villages of Tompkinsville, Castleton Corners, Clifton, Stapleton, New Brighton, and South Beach just grew and grew. There was industry here now: breweries, brickmakers, the Dejon Paper Company, New York Dying and Printing, and Crabtree & Wilkinson—makers of brightly colored head scarves that the servant girls favored.

Now more than 20,000 people lived on the island, most within a morning's walk of the Quarantine. In Tompkinsville, where the good doctor resided, wood-frame houses, general stores, tobacconists, saloons, and hotels stood directly across the road from the six-foot brick wall surrounding the pestilent hospital grounds.

And every year, people of Staten Island fell ill.

The worst was 1848, when one hundred and fifty islanders contracted yellow fever, and thirty of them perished. The rest of the populace fled in terror. That summer and fall, vegetables rotted in untended gardens. Unpicked fruit dried to husks in apple and pear orchards. Hotels and stores stood empty, and grass grew in the streets.

Every year since then, there'd been smaller outbreaks of smallpox, cholera, and yellow fever; and this year, the situation was becoming grave. Something had to be done. Dr. Hollick put down his spyglass, sat behind his desk, took up pen and paper, and began to write.

Three days later, the local worthies who had received Dr. Hollick's written invitations filed into his drawing room and settled into his upholstered, Empire-style furniture:

John C. Thompson, the general store owner known as Honest John—not so much for his business practices as for his rants against political corruption.

Ray Tompkins, whose family owned much of the empty land south of the Quarantine, and whose ancestors had given Tompkinsville its name.

Thomas Burns, the leader of Neptune Fire Engine Company Number 9, and owner of Nautilus Hall, a hotel and saloon located directly across from the Quarantine's main gate.

Henry B. Metcalf, the county judge.

And Dr. Westervelt, Hollick's neighbor from the foot of Fort Hill.

Two latecomers, Attorney William Henry Atherton and real estate agent John Simonson, had to settle for hard-backed chairs dragged in from the dining room.

All sat in grim silence, waiting for Dr. Hollick to start the proceedings.

He began by reading the roll of the summer's yellow fever victims.

"Mr. Kramer, who was employed by the Quarantine to burn infected bedding, took sick at his residence in mid-July and died soon thereafter. A few days hence, his wife succumbed. The German tailor and his son, who lived at the end of Minthorn, just one hundred feet from the Kramers, were the next to contract the disease. By the grace of God, they have recovered. Mrs. Neil, wife of one of the hospital's stevedores, was not so blessed. She died at home at the end of July. Then Mrs. Halladay, who owned the house occupied by Mrs. Neil, fell ill and died. Her boy also sickened, but he has recovered. In the first week of August, Mr. Young and his daughter came down with the fever, as did Mrs. Finnerty, who lives on the same block. They appear to be recovering, but their neighbor, Mrs. Holland, has perished. Mrs. Cross and her servant fell ill two weeks ago, and both died last week. Mrs. Quinn, who lives between Townsend's Dock and the gas works, took sick last week, and I do not expect her to survive."

When Dr. Hollick was finished, Dr. Westervelt added more bad news: "Mr. Block, who lives at the corner of Jersey Street and Richmond Terrace, died of the fever this morning, and his widow has taken to her bed with it."

"I hadn't heard that," Dr. Hollick said.

"It is an outrage," Thompson sputtered. "The Quarantine does little to confine the disease within its walls. Some of its nurses and orderlies are permitted to reside in the village of Stapleton. They pass by my door every day, spreading disease among us as they go to and from work. Others who live and work on the grounds venture out to trade, mainly in establishments that deal in spirituous liquors."

"Of late, patients are also roaming free," Simonson, the real estate agent, said. "Under cover of darkness, they scale the walls and wander aimlessly through the town, horrifying the good people of Tompkinsville with their indecency and filth. And stevedores in the Quarantine's employ loot cargo from infected ships and peddle it on our streets."

"And now that the cemeteries on the grounds have filled," Attorney Atherton added, "the dead cart rolls out of the gates at twilight two or three times a week, spreading disease as it makes its way to the new cemetery north of town. Three nights past, the cart broke down; a corpse lay in the road for nearly an hour before a relief cart was brought out."

Dr. Hollick knew this was not how yellow fever was spread. The disease lurked in the miasma that drifted from open hospital windows and rose from the holds of infected ships. Winds swept the foul air through the town, putting everyone at peril. That was why, even in the heat of summer, the doctor kept his windows closed. But this was not the time, he decided, for a science lesson.

"This is all terribly bad for business," Burns broke in. "The guests in my hotel can look out and see right into the windows of the hospital wards. At night, they hear the cries of suffering. It is no wonder that so few of my patrons book a return visit."

"The very existence of the Quarantine is injurious to property values," said Tompkins, who stood to make a fortune from his holdings if the Quarantine could be made to magically disappear. "It has created a prejudice against the entire island."

Burns and Tompkins could always be counted on to bring any discussion around to money. That wasn't Dr. Hollick's main concern, but he held his tongue. He'd take his allies where he could find them.

"So, my friends," he said. "What are we prepared to do about it?"

"Perhaps we might make another appeal to the state legislature," Judge Metcalf suggested.

"Not this time, Henry," Dr. Hollick replied. "We've petitioned Albany for more than a decade, but our pleas for relief have gone unheeded. The time for action has come."

With that, Judge Metcalf rose to leave. "Perhaps it would be best if I remain ignorant of your intentions," he said. "I fear you may all be appearing before me before the month is out."

A few days later, under cover of darkness, a wagon rolled up Fort Hill toward Dr. Hollick's residence. It drew to a stop beside his fence, and its contents were hastily unloaded. The following evening, the same wagon trundled through Dr. Westervelt's gate and continued to the rear of his holdings, which abutted the northern boundary of the Quarantine. There, its cargo was stacked against the hospital's six-foot-high brick wall.

Shortly after eight p.m. on the evening of September 1, a red signal lantern was hung from the branch of a tree on Fort Hill. Thirty of the area's leading citizens, four of them carrying muskets and two with pistols in their belts, gathered in its glow to hear Dr. Hollick read three resolutions from the Board of Heath of Castleton, the largest town in the area. As some of those present surmised, the good doctor had composed the words himself. He had secured the board's official blessing that very afternoon.

> Resolved: that the whole Quarantine establishment, located as it is in the midst of a dense population, has become a nuisance of the most odious character, bringing death and desolation to the very doors of Castleton and Southfield.
>
> Resolved: that it is a nuisance too intolerable to be borne by the citizens of these towns any longer.
>
> Resolved: that this board recommends the citizens of this county protect themselves by abating this abominable nuisance without delay.

The men let loose with three huzzahs. Then they gathered up the goods that the wagon had dropped off three days before: ten boxes of wooden matches, twenty-five bundles of straw, and twenty quart bottles of camphene.

With Thompson and Tompkins in the lead, the group proceeded down the hill. Dr. Hollick, however, withdrew to his home to observe the evening's festivities from his library window. Arson, he told himself, was a job best left to younger men.

At the foot of the hill, the men crossed a dirt road and approached the gate to Dr. Westervelt's property. Normally it was locked, but on this evening it had been left open. The men walked across an unmowed hayfield to the north wall of the Quarantine, set down their loads, and hefted what had been left there for them: four wooden beams, each affixed with handles.

The men grunted as they swung the battering rams against the brick. In minutes, they reduced an eight-foot section of wall to rubble.

In Manhattan, five miles across the harbor, the shops were bedecked with placards and ribbons celebrating the completion of the Ocean Telegraph, over two thousand miles of cable that connected New York with London. A torchlight fireman's parade marched through the city. Fireworks bloomed in the night sky.

The men in Staten Island gathered up the matches, straw, and camphene, and streamed through the gap they had made.

They came first to the wooden typhus shanties, assembled before one of them, and hesitated—as if suddenly realizing the enormity of what they were about to do. Then Thompson raised a bottle of camphene over his head and smashed it against the side of the building. Tompkins struck a match and tossed it.

Whoosh! The men heard the rush of oxygen as the front of the shanty exploded in flames. Inside, someone shouted: "What in God's name was that?"

Red tongues leaped up the dry shiplap siding and licked the tar-paper roof. Oily black smoke billowed into the overhanging oaks. Inside the shanty, the patients began to scream.

A nearby sentry sounded the alarm. Stevedores raced out of their dormitories. Thompson and the rest of the townsmen stood by and watched them run into the burning shanty and stagger out with invalids in their arms. The stevedores laid the patients in the grass and covered them with blankets. Then they grabbed more blankets from a nearby storeroom and tried to beat out the fire.

As smoke and embers spiraled into the night sky, Dr. Daniel H. Bissell, the hospital superintendent, dashed from his residence with a musket in his hands. At the burning shanty, he confronted Thompson and ordered him and his men to leave the premises.

"We shall not do so," Thompson replied. "It is our duty to help put out this fire."

"This shanty is lost," Bissell said. "Help us pull it down, and perhaps we can prevent the flames from spreading to the others."

Instead, Thompson and Tompkins led the men to the adjoining shanties. They streamed inside, dragged out straw mattresses, set them ablaze, and tossed them back in. Bissell confronted Thompson again, brandishing his musket. Thompson wrenched it from his hands and clubbed him in the head with it.

Bissell fell. In the flickering firelight, his blood looked black as it leaked onto the grass. He clutched at his wound and moaned.

The townsmen took up a chant: "Kill him! Kill him!"

They might well have done so if Tompkins had not intervened. "We are not murderers, my friends," he said. "But we shall complete the job we have come to do."

While the shanties burned, the townsmen roamed across the grounds, setting fire to the coal houses, barns, and stables. Panicked carriage horses burst out and galloped off into the night. The men torched the ramshackle smallpox hospital and broke into one of the physicians' residences to loot the liquor cabinets. Then they tossed camphene bottles through the windows and tossed in matches.

A few minutes later, Michael McCabe, a Quarantine watchman, discovered several men stuffing bundles of straw in the doorways and stairwells of St. Nicholas Hospital. He ordered them to stop. They ignored him and set the straw on fire. The building's patients, most of them ambulatory, streamed out of the doorways in their nightclothes.

Outside St. Nicholas, Dr. Theodore Walser, one of the three Quarantine physicians, encountered Tompkins and pleaded with him to stop the mayhem. "Some of our patients are very ill," he said. "Shall they have nothing but damp ground for a bed?"

Tompkins looked around and saw that the Female Hospital had not yet been set on fire. "Take the patients there," he told Walser. "I pledge to you that the building will not be touched." Then he hurried off to post a guard by it.

Outside the brick wall, about two hundred more towns-people gathered to cheer the arsonists on. Several of them fired muskets into the air, adding to the growing panic inside. Walser heard an insistent pounding. Someone was trying to break through the Quarantine's main gate. He and McCabe grabbed firearms from a storeroom and ran toward the sound.

As they approached, the gate burst open. Through it came Thomas Burns and the men of Neptune Fire Engine Company Number 9, some of them lugging hoses and others dragging their steam-powered pumper truck. To Walser, this was not a welcome sight. Burns was one of the most vocal opponents of the Quarantine.

"I know you, Mr. Burns!" Walser shouted. "We don't want you here!"

Burns and his men moved forward. Walser and McCabe pointed their muskets at them. "Stand back!" Walser ordered. "We will put out the fire ourselves."

But now, the mob that had gathered behind the wall pressed through the gate. Some of them had guns too. Walser and McCabe were hopelessly outnumbered. Reluctantly, they stood aside. The entering mob rushed off to set more fires.

The firemen set down their burdens, sat in the grass, and

watched the hospital burn. "Should have brought sausages for roasting," one of them said.

A boat docked at one of the Quarantine's wharves and disgorged a squad of Harbor Police. Their arrival had been delayed a quarter-hour by a 150-pound sturgeon that leaped into the boat. Its thrashing had threatened to break a hole in the hull, but the beast was finally wrestled overboard. As the squad debarked, it was met with hoots, howls, and a barrage of rocks. Most of its members retreated, but two of them joined the mob and rushed off to set fires.

Flames reached the roof of St. Nicholas Hospital now. In minutes, it collapsed. The statue of a sailor that had long stood on its peak toppled into the rubble. Inside, the floors gave way. One hundred iron beds crashed through them into the basement.

From his library window, Dr. Hollick watched the fires burn all night.

At dawn, smoke curled from the rubble. Hospital staff herded ambulatory patients onto the *Cinderella* for transport to makeshift quarters on Wards Island. Those too sick to be moved crowded the two floors of the Female Hospital. Remarkably, no patients had died in the fires; the stevedores and orderlies, with help from a few members of the mob, had managed to get them all out. But overnight, a yellow fever patient had perished from his disease. His body lay on the grass, covered by a blanket.

A stevedore was dead, a musket ball buried in his back. Perhaps he had been struck by a random shot fired over the wall. Perhaps one of the mob had killed him deliberately. But Dr. Walser suspected another stevedore had done it, perhaps taking advantage of the panic to avenge an old grudge about a woman.

That morning, handbills were distributed in Tompkins-ville and the neighboring villages, inviting all to a community meeting at Nautilus Hall to celebrate the destruction of the Quarantine. At seven thirty that evening, two hundred people crowded into Burns's hotel. There, amid much drinking of beer and hard liquor, they unanimously passed a resolution affirming the right of the people of Staten Island to rid themselves of the hazardous facility.

At ten p.m., Tompkins and a local hothead named Tom Garrett led celebrants out of the hotel. They crossed the street, pushed through the Quarantine's shattered front gate, and at-tacked the handful of buildings that had been spared the night before. They wrenched shutters and porch rails from Dr. Wals-er's and Dr. Bissell's residences, piled them inside, doused them with camphene, and set them alight. Then they swept across the grounds, burning the coffin house and several cottages where the boatmen lived. When that was done, they burned the wharves.

They surrounded the Female Hospital and gave the staff fifteen minutes to get the patients out. After the sick had been placed on the grass beside the brick wall, the building was torched. It went up like a bonfire.

At the wall, hot cinders fell on the prostrate patients, and the heat from the fires grew unbearable. Quarantine staff poured buckets of water on the sick to cool them.

Around midnight, as the mob straggled out of the gate, it began to rain.

The next day, Tompkinsville's saloons were packed with revil-ers. A thousand members of the Metropolitan Police arrived from Manhattan to restore order. The following week, the 8th Regiment of the state militia set up in the foothills outside the village to discourage any further disturbances. Sixty US Marines were deployed to protect federal property in the area.

There proved to be little for any of them to do.

Local police, under pressure from state authorities, reluctantly rounded up a dozen members of the mob. They were promptly released, their bail paid with cash that Cornelius Vanderbilt sent over on the ferry. New York's favorite tycoon, it seems, had been born on Staten Island.

In the end, charges were brought only against Thompson and Tompkins.

New York City newspapers demanded retribution. The *New York Times* was especially relentless, branding the two ringleaders "diabolical," "savage," and "inhuman." The pair had been motivated not by fear of disease but by greed, the *Times* thundered. They had cared about nothing but the Quarantine's deleterious affect on the value of their property.

That fall, Thompson and Tompkins were tried before Judge Metcalf. Dr. Walser and Dr. Bissell testified about what they'd witnessed on the nights of the fires. So did the watchman, McCabe, and a host of others.

The defense, led by Attorney Atherton, disputed none of their testimony. Instead, they offered a string of witnesses, including Dr. Hollick, who testified to the sickness and death the Quarantine had long visited upon the people of Staten Island. And they entered into evidence the Castleton Board of Health's resolutions as proof that the townspeople were justified in taking action "to abate a nuisance."

At the conclusion of the three-week proceeding, Atherton rose to make his closing statement: "I demand their immediate release on the grounds that they have committed no crime, but have simply done their duty as citizens and men. Here among their fellow citizens and neighbors, they will be looked upon as men of noble hearts who have acted fearlessly and zealously for the public good."

Judge Metcalf issued his ruling without delay: "Undoubtedly, the city of New York is entitled to all the protection in the matter that the state can give, consistent with the health of others. She has no right to more. Her great advantages are attended by corresponding inconveniences; her great public works by great expenditures; her great foreign commerce by the infection it brings. But the legislature can no more apportion upon the surrounding communities her dangers than her expenses; no more compel them to do her dying than to pay her taxes. Neither can be done."

And so he set Thompson and Tompkins free.

The decision surprised no one. The judge's sympathies were well known. His house was located just a quarter-mile from the Quarantine. And a decade earlier, he had attended his own brother, caressing his brow with cloths dipped in ice water and changing the sweat-drenched bedding three times daily, in the week that it took him to die of yellow fever.

PAYING THE TAB

BY MICHAEL LARGO

Four Corners

E ddie Lynch had opened the doors every afternoon at two since 1980. Even when his mother died, he came back in his funeral suit to fill the bins with long necks and dump them over with pails of ice. He wiped out the speed racks, dipped the glasses in the first sink of soap, and the two others for rinse. The day he bought the Sunnyside Lounge from old man Sully he promised not to change a thing, and he hadn't. The same wood panels painted black, L-shaped mahogany bar with a pipe for a foot rail, and swivel stools with red seat pads. He had reskinned the pool table in the back room many times, but always in red felt the way Sully said a bar pool table should be.

"Character," Sully had said. "Bars take on their own—and you can tell it by its aromas, if you let them fester. If I hear you add hanging ferns or make this shithole fancy, I'll come back from my urn and burn you alive."

Eddie knew that Sully was selling it to him for less, and not giving it to Sully's daughter like she wanted, because of his name: Eddie Lynch, the onetime famous local kid who had his name stolen as an alias by one of the greatest banker robbers of the twentieth century.

"Every busted nose, clogged toilet, and last-call puke lives in the walls." Sully wanted Eddie to know what he was getting into. Eddie remembered that day, looking at the small hexagonal floor tiles, and came to know that no matter the mopping of ammonia, Sully was right.

Today, Eddie left the front door unlocked while he stocked. He knew the soda gun guys were coming, wanting their cut, once again raising their fees. He saw the wedge of bright daylight slice in when the inner doors opened and thought it was them. But it was the first customer of the day, a man in a suit carrying a long-stemmed rose. When he took the stool that was normally Max's, he asked for a glass of water, bourbon in a rock glass, and a glass of red wine.

Eddie served him what he wanted and figured he'd have plenty of time to hear the winded BS of why the man was putting a flower in a water glass—since they all had their stories. That was what bars were for: telling your side of life's injustices to the captured bartender. But Eddie went outside to see if they had picked up the black trash bags piling ever higher on top of the dumpster. He'd start getting fines from the health department soon. Eddie refused to pay the rate hike on trash pickup and could get no new service to break waste removal routes and territories, all of that racket long established and divvied up.

Eddie went out the back door and surveyed like he always did before he opened for business. The bar's sign was white script letters painted on dark blue glass-paneled siding. The plate glass windows that ran on the Manor Road side were so dark he saw only a reflection of himself when he passed.

The last month or so, especially now with the garbage problem and the soda gun guys, he realized he was getting too old for this. He thought he saw Sully's face, the big cigar in his mouth, never lit and soaked at the end like a soggy dipstick, instead of his own reflection. Sully was laughing at him, giving him his classic nod that he gave to the parade of the misguided who sat on the swivel stools waiting for the bartender's verdict: *Now you did it, you went too far.*

"Everybody thinks owning a bar is easy, but it's a rock in your shoe, and a revolving hand in your pocket," Sully had told him.

It had been a dive, the Sunnyside, and would remain as such as long as Eddie could manage to keep its "character." But he was starting to understand how Sully one day said yes, and took Eddie's bag of cash, signing over his license. Red-faced Sully, with his permanent six-months-pregnant beer belly, never did make it to Florida like he planned, and died during a bypass in the hospital. No sunshine for Sully, and the curse of the Sunnyside got Eddie too, just as Sully predicted.

Eddie had been famous when he was a kid. Everyone knew the story of how the legendary gentleman bank robber, Willie Sutton, a.k.a. Willie the Actor, stole his name. There was a yellow newspaper clipping framed and hanging near the register to prove it. "You'll add a splash of character to the joint," Sully had said.

Continuing his daily outside survey, Eddie turned the corner onto Victory Boulevard. The street was empty, not a car up or down, like it was four a.m. Sunday, but the sun was out. Eddie stopped. There was a body on the sidewalk. A chubby guy, looking to be maybe twenty, dressed in a 1950s suit and overcoat. He was sprawled in that odd way only the dead can land, one leg out, one hand turned sideways. His fedora resting neatly two feet away, while a pool of blood slowly ran from the crotch of his trousers. His eye sockets were pockets of red, filled to the brim and dribbling down the sides of the head. Eddie knew it was the kid who'd spotted Willie Sutton on a bus in Brooklyn and then went and told the cops. It was the classic snitch shooting, with the first bullet dropping him to his knees and the eyes telling you to keep what you see to yourself. Eddie backed away and hurried along the Manor Road side and into the rear door of the bar.

"What the . . . ?"

The man with the rose pushed his rock glass forward and tapped the side. Eddie reached for the bottle and poured more by reflex, though he wondered what the hell was happening to his mind. He had seen that sprawled body a hundred times in his dreams, but never while he was working. Why were there no cars?

"You," the man knocked back the drink in one gulp and pushed the glass forward for another. "You're the owner, right?" He took the rose from the water glass and smelled it.

Eddie put on his reading glasses and looked for the numbers of services the bar used, and found the one for garbage pickup taped to the side of the ice machine. He'd call the trashmen and agree to pay most of the rate hike if they'd come and empty the dumpster today. It was the stress, he knew, and before he called, Eddie broke his own rule by pouring himself a scotch, which he never—almost never—took until after midnight. "You got to keep an eye in the back of your head," Sully had warned, "or they'll steal the shoes off your feet while you're walking."

"Sutton broke out of a Philadelphia prison. He tunneled, didn't he, like in a movie, in 1947," the man said as he put his rose back in the glass. "Another." He pushed the rock glass forward again, but left the wine untouched.

The trash number was a busy signal. "Listen, pal, I'm not even opened yet," Eddie said. "Drink, relax. I see your hundred there on the bar, so you can drink until you tell me to call you a cab. But—" Eddie dialed again and it was still busy, "I got business."

The man took out a pouch of tobacco and began to hand roll a cigarette.

"No smoking. You know the laws."

"You ain't open, *pal*," the man said, mimicking Eddie. He reached into his suit jacket pocket and pulled out a wad of cash in a bank wrapper, placing it on the bar. "That's ten thousand dollars, unmarked. I'm gonna smoke and you're gonna stay closed until I tell you."

Eddie looked closer at the man and he seemed familiar, but Eddie couldn't place him. He paused, then picked up the bundle of cash and fanned through the bills. "Never take their money," Sully had said, "or then they will really own you." Eddie poured the man another drink and put the money next to the rose.

"This is for?"

"So I can smoke. No strings. Take it." The man looked around the bar. "The floor is filthy. You haven't mopped and the tables are filled with bottles and glasses. You're a long way from opening, anyway."

Eddie always cleaned the bar after last call, turned on the bright lights, switched the setting on the back of the juke and played whatever while he got rid of the bulk of the night's mess. He never liked to close the doors and deal with it the next day, when the stench of yesterday's drinking was even too much for him. Eddie couldn't remember why he didn't clean up last night.

"You were, what, ten?" the man said. "And the story goes that Willie Sutton bought a newspaper from you and asked you what your name was."

Eddie was going to pull down the framed article, like he'd done a thousand times, to show new customers the history he had, describing how the bank robber used Eddie Lynch as his alias while laying low in Staten Island. But the garbage line was busy, and there were no cars on Victory. He never left bottles on the table from the night before.

"Sutton worked in the Farm Colony for almost three years." The man lit his rolled-up cigarette. "It was an old folks' home, near Seaview Hospital. He worked as a janitor, with everybody calling him Eddie Lynch."

Eddie put down the phone and looked at the man closer. "You. Who are you?"

"Sutton's time at the Farm Colony was the best, where he took care of the old ladies." The man closed his eyes and rubbed his forehead like something pained him.

"He lived a few blocks from here on Kimball Avenue, while he was hiding out on Staten Island. I know all about Sutton," Eddie said.

"No you don't. It really broke his heart, the way they sat there in their wheelchairs with nothing but memories, waiting for their kids who never came. Or when they did visit—what do you think they brought their mothers who wiped their tears and bandaged their cuts? A bag a candy or a five-cent comb. Like that was enough, all that was needed for the payback."

"I might take that money," Eddie said. "I should get out of this business. Do something different. You want to buy this place?"

The man rolled another cigarette. "We waste so much time, don't we? Everybody does. There's no way around it. Robbed banks for thirty years, bagging more than two million, when a million was something. But half of the time in the joint, for what? For the money, I guess, but—" The man let out a deep breath. "It don't matter now."

Eddie poured the guy another drink and another for himself. He picked up the bundle of cash. He peered closer at the man's face. "You look like . . ."

"You still didn't figure it out yet, did you?"

"The body on the sidewalk. No cars."

"Take the cash, if it makes you feel better. You don't need it anymore, but take it. It took me some time to understand how it all works too," the man said, "why I wasn't going."

"Going where?"

"I don't know exactly. But where we all go. Where Sully went. Where the poor guy on the sidewalk outside went. Where you'll go. You got to clear the slate, pay off everything before you go. This I finally got."

"Willie."

"That's why I'm here with the dough, kid. I caused you a lot of bad dreams. Who knew dreams had a price? They do, though, so try to remember who you give bad dreams to and you'll go faster." The man stood, glanced at the wine, but didn't drink it. "That was for my landlady Mary, over there on Kimball. And the rose is for when I see her. She's gone; I know she is, since I never saw her waiting around like us."

"I'm not going anywhere," Eddie said. "I'm not waiting."

"Kid, you already are." The man took the rose from the water glass. "Now we're square, ain't we, Eddie?" He left the bar.

When the health department citations piled up and no more could fit stuck in the front door, that's when they found Eddie. The Sunnyside hadn't opened for a week and the regulars banged on the door, tried to peer through the thick plate glass, could see the bottles on the dirty tables. They figured Eddie had just closed and run off like he always said he would. That's when they broke open the locks and found him on the floor behind the bar. The cops covered their mouths with handkerchiefs.

"One in the back of the head," a cop said. "And shot in both hands."

"That's it," the other cop said. "He owed somebody."

"Yeah," the older cop said. "Garbage or soda. Look at the tickets from HD. He was stingy, not paying up, or he just got tired of playing by the rules."

ASSISTANT PROFESSOR LODGE

BY BINNIE KIRSHENBAUM

Grymes Hill

I t was autumn. Late October. Evening, early evening, but the sky was midnight dark and the moon cast a silver glow; the air, crisp like a red apple, was redolent of autumns past: dried leaves, pumpkins, ghost stories, all manner of things Halloween-related. It was that kind of autumn evening. I buttoned my coat for the walk across the campus from Parker Hall to the Grymes Hill bus stop.

Parker Hall, neo-Gothic, lugubrious such as it was, inspired the whisperings of a dark history, but the story that it had once been a Dickensian orphanage where terrible things happened simply wasn't true. There are always stories. Another Wagner College legend, the one about Edward Albee, that he taught here in the early 1960s and that Wagner College was the setting for *Who's Afraid of Virginia Woolf*, that wasn't true either but, unlike the Parker Hall story, it was rooted in fact. In the early 1960s, Albee did participate in a summer literary conference at Wagner College that was organized by a friend of his who was a professor in the English Department. It was common knowledge that this mess of a professor and his spectacularly boozy wife were the inspiration for Albee's gin-soaked brawling love birds, but the setting for *Virginia Woolf* was Trinity College in Connecticut. Not Staten Island.

But just how Parker Hall *looked* as if it had been an orphanage, I'll say this: the Wagner campus looked spot-on right for the part in Albee's play.

There was definitely that bucolic New England-y small college thing about the place. It photographed well, like Williams or Bennington, it made for a nice brochure. The Main Hall was, as was Parker Hall, early-twentieth-century Gothic. Both buildings were ivy-covered and shrouded by trees. Evergreens mostly, and there were lots of squirrels around. Even a few of those all-black squirrels, which are rare. The lawn for playing frisbee was oval-shaped. Eponymous Cunard Hall was originally the Cunard family mansion and its guest cottages were once faculty housing, but now one of the cottages was the chapel; the other was the admissions office.

Never before had I been on campus in the evening. True, this was largely a commuter school, but that not one other person was out and around was curious, until I realized why I was, seemingly, all alone. The student union, the cafeteria, the dormitories, the library, all the buildings busy at this hour were the newer ones. Cement and plasterboard institutional-ugly, they were constructed out of view.

I was there late because I was with a student. It wasn't often that students wanted to meet with their professors, but this one was in the throes of discovering literature and he had that kind of enthusiasm going, the naïve kind, unaware that there were professors out there who couldn't wait to piss on his earnestness, to jade his sincerity, to mock his wearing white T-shirts with the cuffs of the short sleeves rolled up in homage to Jack Kerouac. But that wouldn't happen for years to come.

The previous spring, he took Comp and Lit with me. Last fall semester, I taught three sections of Composition without the Lit, the same as this fall. Required courses for freshmen. Students who had so much as a crumb of interest in literature were fewer in number than the black squirrels, which should not have come as a surprise to me. They were eighteen years old. A lot of the girls looked like beauty pageant contestants, and it seemed like all of them were majoring in Education with the intent to teach kindergarten or first grade until having families of their own. These girls appeared to me to be without rebellion, and they elicited not my anger exactly, but an impatience, a lack of generosity. I wanted to shake them and say, *There's a world out there!* The way I remember the boys, they were business majors, their intended careers were vague. The boys—party boys, fraternity boys, athletes. In the end, I felt sadder for the boys. They were not, as I saw them, young men of promise.

Although I am not generally inclined to indulge in psychobabble, at this point in time, as I am looking back, it occurs to me that my perceptions of the students, the *what seemed likes* and the *as I remembers*, could well have been my projection. I might well have been reflecting my own fear of the future outward onto them. My fear that this was it. Not all, but some of my colleagues, once dreamed of grand places in academia. They saw themselves as professors at Harvard or Stanford, but that didn't happen. Their dreams denied caused them to turn bitter and mean and petty. Despite how their dreams were not my dreams and how this was only the start of my second year here, I feared getting stuck like a mastodon in a tar pit. I feared becoming one of them.

I wasn't off about the beauty pageants, though. Two years in a row one of the students was crowned Miss Staten Island. Not the same one twice. *Two* different Miss Staten Islands, back to back.

The student who came to my office that afternoon took off his varsity jacket—he was on the baseball team—draping it over the back of a chair which he then turned around and straddled. His arms were crossed and he leaned forward as if he were in an acting class. Method acting. He told me that he'd

BINNIE KIRSHENBAUM // 143

been reading the Beat poets. This semester he was taking Survey of American Lit I—Whitman and Dickinson. "Professor Lodge suggested I read some of the contemporary poets."

"John Lodge? You're in John's class?"

"Yeah, he's great. He said I had to read John Ashbery and Seamus Heaney. What do you think of them?"

"Definitely worth reading," I said. "Who else did he recommend?"

"That's it for now. But he's going to give me copies of his books. His books of poetry. Ones he wrote."

"You know what I really think?" I said. "I think you should transfer to some other school."

Professor John Lodge. No, no relation to the fancy-schmancy Lodges, but oh, please, if only you assumed he was, he'd be afforded a moment's pride. It wasn't that he wanted to be rich. What he wanted was to be a snob, or at least have some excuse to be a snob. His books of poetry—his books of poetry were not books. They were xeroxed copies of maybe twenty poems or so laid out two on the front and two on the back of five or six sheets of regular paper. Regular paper folded in half and three staples made the spine along the crease. Also, there were cover pages: an illustration set between the title and the *by John P. Lodge,* an epigraph or two or three epigraphs, a notation of copyright which was too sad to consider, and a page devoted to a dedication of *this book* to his wife. His emaciated wife, with a clavicle that would snap like a wishbone, had an emphatic nervous twitch that put me in mind of Bette Davis smoking a cigarette, although entirely unlike Bette Davis, John's wife had no juice. John aspired to be a snob, but his wife succeeded because she believed that to be painfully thin and in possession of one very good suit entitled her to be condescending to others.

John wrote a new "book," on average, every six weeks.

He'd leave a copy of this "most recent volume" in my mailbox where I'd find it with a Post-It affixed on the front asking me to *Enjoy!* Or beseeching *If you have time*, causing my heart to twist like a wet washcloth wringing out that last drop of pity. Pity that, after a while, turned to resentment because of the responsibility of it. What was I supposed to say to him about his "books" of poems? Never mind the sorrow of book form. Each poem, individually, judged on its own merits, stunk. Seriously stunk. Mostly they were about gin and alienation. The very worst ones were about sex. If the author of these poems were a student and not a professor, I'd have been less embarrassed by them but I would not have encouraged them, either.

It wasn't possible to avoid John. The department was small. We both often took the 4:20 ferry home to Manhattan, and he urgently wanted to be my friend. I didn't dislike the guy. Wagner College was no different from any other college when it came to the professorial pecking order. As the newest member of the faculty, I was expected to prove myself somehow, and until I did, I was to be excluded from the circle. For that first year, John was the only member of the faculty who was at all nice to me, which I sort of appreciated.

One morning, near the end of the last term, I found yet another of John's "books" in my otherwise empty mailbox. I took it to my office where I was intending to spend the twenty minutes before class whipping up that day's lesson plan. John's "book" I tossed in the previously empty wastebasket where it landed with an appropriately dull *flump*. Flipping the pages of my legal pad past the to-do lists and doodles, I reached a page that was pristine and on the top line I wrote: *Compare and Contrast*. That's as far as I'd gotten when John interrupted me. He had a Styrofoam cup in each hand. "Coffee," he set one cup on my desk. "Black, right?"

I nodded and thanked him, which he took as an invitation to pull up a seat. "Did you get the book I left for you?" he asked.

"Yes. Thank you. I haven't had a chance to look at it yet, but I will."

"You don't have to read it now, but I just want to see you open it."

Sure, I could've looked under my notepad and fished through my briefcase, pretending I'd misplaced the damn thing—except, as guilty as the cat with the canary in its mouth, my gaze went like a laser beam, a straight line of light from my eyes to the wastebasket, and John too saw his book discarded. After an extremely uncomfortable pause, he said, "Don't worry about it."

As if I didn't already feel like four pieces of crap, it was dedicated to me: A new friend, but a valued one.

I apologized of course. More than apologized. I apologized in writing. I wrote him a letter of apology about how my own writing of stories wasn't going well and how I'd had a fit of envy over how prolific he is and how it was a rude tantrum for which I am ashamed, and I thanked him profusely for the honor of the dedication. All of which I thought was remarkably kind of me, self-sacrificing, in the way that allowed me to think I was a good person.

My apology was accepted, and everything was the same as it was before with John and me, which amounted to chatting for a few minutes before classes began, and some days sitting together on the ferry going home. And let me not forget the time John was able to cajole me into joining him for a four o'clock cocktail in the back room of the chapel which had been turned over to the faculty, a designated place for them to gather for lunch or a drink at the end of the day. I would've gone there a second time if ever I needed a reason to kill myself.

The Kerouac-enthralled student sitting in my office told me, because I'd asked, what led him to choose to come to Wagner. He was not from Staten Island, and he lived in the dormitories. "The photographs," he said. "The old buildings, the lawn, people carrying books. It was how I imagined college would be."

Along with a list of contemporary poets, I gave him a list of some other schools where the buildings were old and the students carried books and where there was no John Lodge teaching in the English Department. And no me either, for that matter.

On his way out I called the student back and said, "Read those poets first. You can read Professor Lodge's poems later. After you have a foundation."

When he left, I stayed for a while longer in my office. A fairly long while, just thinking. That's how I came to be there in the evening, and I was glad of it. The quiet reverberated in the dark. Quiet, this kind of quiet, did that: it reverberated like a pulse of a heart until the wind picked up and brought with it another kind of quiet.

Evenly spaced lampposts illuminated the footpath.

The leaves rustled.

The Trautmann Square Clock Tower, a four-sided clock showing the time no matter where you stood, was lit.

That night, when the hour seemed much later than it was and the clouds, the incandescent night clouds, moved across the sky, and the dried leaves swept along the path, for a fleeting moment, I considered the notion that teaching forever at a small school set on a bucolic campus might be a good life for me after all.

The footpath narrowed. The trees were more dense. If this were a movie, here's the part where the heroine would get that creepy feeling, a sense that maybe she was not alone. She'd pause to listen. And of course the sicko following her would also pause because he might be a sicko, but he's not stupid. But this wasn't a movie, and I stopped only because I was no longer in a hurry.

It was then that I knew for certain that I would not return the following semester. And with the decision not to return absolute, I was overcome by cheap sentiment for a place where my connection was slight. Cheap sentiment that manifested as longing, a reluctance to part when the parting was inevitable, which was why I lingered there to experience the cottages deep in the shadows of a perfect autumnal night.

I was maybe twenty feet away at most, looking head-on at the smaller cottage. A halo softened the light above the door, and even though I knew for a fact that Albee's play was meant to be set at Trinity College and not Wagner College, this cottage, in the dark, evoked the very essence of the house where George and Martha tormented each other and their guests.

Yet, it was from the porch of the larger cottage, the chapel, that the noiselessness broke like a glass when I heard a woman say—no, no, that's wrong, she didn't *say*, she enunciated. As if the words were scripted, she enunciated, "You. Disgust. Me. There. I've said it now. You. Disgust. Me."

I could not have recalled all of Martha's lines verbatim, but surely this had to have been one of them, and the voice, the woman's voice, also sounded familiar. I was trying to place it—a student or maybe that professor from the history department, the one who wore serapes and necklaces made from walnuts—when the man said, "Please. Don't do this." His voice I knew. John Lodge said, "You're upset."

John Lodge and his twitchy wife.

They were not directly under the porch light, but off to the side. Having no idea if they were able to see me or not, I stepped behind a maple tree where it was less likely I'd be spotted. I'm not proud myself. They thought they were alone, and I should've respected their privacy. I should have, but I didn't.

"I'm upset," she said, "and you are pathetic. Where does that leave us?"

"Let's go home."

In all likelihood they'd been in that makeshift faculty room hitting the hooch since the onset of happy hour or maybe lunchtime. John always struck me as one of those sad-sack drinkers, the sort who drink a lot and often but never get sloppy drunk or have any fun, either. And her? I'd have bet she hadn't seen a sober day since her Sweet Sixteen.

"Home? You dare call that a home? It's a closet. We live in a closet, a broom closet, but what choice do we have, on your salary, *Professor* Lodge? Oh, excuse me. *Assistant* Professor Lodge."

That explained the address. When the ferry docked in Manhattan, John and I would part company. We did not take the same subway line home, and I did wonder how he afforded that neighborhood, that address which declared, *I have old money. I am stuffy. I am not even the least bit hip.* His wife, I knew, did not work. Supposedly she was going for her PhD but the particulars of that were never clear.

"Claire, please. I'm tired," he said.

"Tired? You're not tired. You're dead. And boring. You are deadly boring."

She was right. He was boring, but it wasn't like she brought sparkle to a room either.

"Please," John said. "Please stop."

"A pathetic, boring loser and you are never going to be anything but—"

"Stop it. Please. Stop it."

"A boring loser. And if you think anyone is ever going to publish that drivel—"

"Please, Claire. Don't."

"That drivel you write—"

John let go with a groan, a groan that I would've associated with a spectacular orgasm except that it was impossible to think of John Lodge or Ms. Twitch in such a state. The groan was followed by a thud. Or a crack. A sound of some sort or another.

If I hurried, I could catch the 7:20 bus and make the 7:40 ferry.

The next day John's class waited the twenty minutes allowed a tardy professor. I can safely assume that some of the boys high-fived each other before all the students flooded from the room. A no-show professor was as good as a snow day.

The chairman called John at home. He called again. And again. No one had seen Professor Lodge or his wife since the day before when a lot of people saw her waiting in the hallway for his class to end, pacing as if she were anxious, nervous about something, which was a lead to nowhere. Anxious, nervous was her natural state. A professor from Romance Languages said that as he was going into Main Hall, they were walking out. Holding hands, he claimed. But after that—nothing. John Lodge and his wife seemed to have vanished. After two more days of calling, the department chairman gave up and hired someone to cover John's classes for the remainder of the semester.

Unless there is some sort of evidence to the contrary, the disappearance of a husband and wife does not constitute a crime, which means nothing in terms of rumors spreading and theories zinging around like electrons in an atom. Everyone had an idea as to what really happened: they were the victims of a psycho-killer, they'd been kidnapped and were being held for ransom, they joined up with a cult, they had a suicide pact, they moved to Paris on a whim, they were abducted by aliens, devoured by coyotes. I steered clear of the gossip. I accepted the fact that sometimes that's how it goes, that sometimes you'll never know what really happened.

After that semester's end, I did not return to Wagner College.

Time passed and I can't say that I gave John or his wife a whole lot of thought, but when I did, I wished for them a rosy scenario: that the light of the next morning brought clarity; realizing how perilously close they'd come to *being* George and Martha was sobering, so they decided to make a fresh start and move to a small town where he would teach school and write bad poems and she would be super-snooty to all the rubes and it would all turn out happy in the end. That's what I wished for them because—why not?

More time passed. Years. It was three years later when I got the envelope in the mail, a five-by-seven manila envelope, the return address a post office box in Maine. No name, but I recognized John's handwriting as surely as I had recognized his voice that night.

There was no Post-It affixed to this "book" but there was a letter paper clipped to the "cover," which read:

Dear M.,

I look back on our days at Wagner College with love. Yes, I loved teaching there. I loved having an office in Parker Hall (which, did you know, was once an orphanage), and I loved having you as my friend and colleague. I greatly valued our talks, our time on the ferry. I believed that you understood me, and I continue to believe that to this day. It is that very faith in our friendship that enables me to swal-

low my pride and tell you that, although I live modestly, I am not always able to find work. I now have found myself in difficult circumstances of a financial nature. It is terribly awkward to ask for money, and I am intending this request to be a loan, but on the chance that I can't pay you back, I will give you the publishing rights to my books. Please know how hard this is for me.

One thousand dollars would make a world of difference right now. I hope you are well.

Love,
John P. Lodge

p.s. I saw you hiding behind the tree. I know you were there.

PART III

BOROUGH OF BROKEN DREAMS

. . . spy verse spy . . .

BY TODD CRAIG

Park Hill

I don't understand how niggers do it to themselves, ya
know?" Officer Lillmann exclaimed in the middle of the
PS 57 community playground. Even Schmidt stepped back
and looked at him.

"I mean, better *they* do it to themselves than us, right? Seriously, say I woulda shot one of 'em . . ." Everyone looked.
Another officer on the scene grabbed at Lillmann's shoulder as
if to say, *Quit while you're ahead.*

Detective Schmidt grimaced and mumbled under his
breath, "Are you kidding? You *do* realize we're in the middle of
a crime scene surrounded by hundreds of black people? At a
Troy Davis rally sponsored by Wu-Tang? *Really?*"

But Lillmann was a standard-issue blue wall dirty cop. "If I
did this, it'd be a whole big thing," he bellowed. "And I'd get off
at the end of it all, cuz that's how we work, but good it's one of
their own that did it. So now, no big deal. Badda-boom-badda-
bing. What do they call it, black-on-black crime? What a waste
of bullets!"

Lillmann jeered, sawing sugar away from his mouth with
the back of his wrist. They called him D2 in Park Hill . . . he
spent more time in Dunkin' Donuts on break than on patrol or
on duty. The whole Killer Hill loathed Lillmann. But D2 was
po-lice, so what could they do? One thing was for sure, though
. . . in the midst of the Raekwon and RZA–sponsored Free Troy

Davis rally, tolerance for police foolishness was little to nil, especially for Lillmann's racist politricks.

Mease sat in the car, waiting. He looked around, getting pissed at his brother's constant lateness, which was happening again. While waiting, all he could do was constantly check his cell phone to see if the newest text message had arrived. While Mease scanned the street on the left, he suddenly heard on his right:

Click-CLICK . . . SLAM!!!

"GOGOGOGOGO!!!"

Sy's shouts shot Mease right out his yin and into the thick of all yang. Without even looking, Mease slammed the tranny into drive, swerved out of his parking spot and into the street. Sy guarded the rearview, while it took everything Mease had to swerve back. Mease and Sy leaned hard left. Then Mease swerved back right, away from oncoming Manhattan traffic, and back into his lane.

The only thing they seemed to avoid was death, as a redheaded woman stopped running, flipped open her cell, and started dialing.

"Hahahahahahaha!!!! You shoulda seen ya fuckin' face, sun!" Sy squawked. Mease realized his brother was not only late, but joking with antics Mease hated with a passion.

"Yo, is you fuckin' crazy? I almost killed people, almost killed us!"

Sy giggled at his brother's reaction to impending death, but he could tell Mease had been pushed beyond the edge.

"Word to mother, I should pull over and take your stupid ass out myself! Where you goin', sun? Cuz I'ma drop ya crazy ass off e-mediate-ly!" Mease proclaimed.

"I'ma go uptown real quick and git right."

"Yeah, a'ight," Mease said as he switched lanes, speed-balling up the West Side Highway, hoping no police had seen his jeep or license plate. Little did Mease know that po-lice would be the least of his worries.

The brisk winter wind blew party fliers across the windshield. Sy jumped, coughing up chronic smoke. Mease slowly turned his head. They were sitting in the jeep a couple blocks away from The Tunnel. A few blocks off the West Side Highway—and the water—it was no wonder the wind curled in the quick of this night. It was cool, though . . . all Mease had to do was push the button on the dashboard to adjust the climate control, and all indications of frío in the Land Cruiser were nil. Problem was, Mease was so damn high and that button was so damn far away . . . when he reached for it, he could hear the ticking sound like when the Six Million Dollar Man flexed his bionic muscles to make some superhuman physical movement.

"Damn, sun . . . that shit . . . took a lot," Mease said, fi-nally lowering his arm after pressing the button to increase the blower speed.

"Oh, you fucked up, B. You only turned the heat up, it's *that* deep?" Sy snickered.

To Mease, it had been ten minutes . . . in real life, a twenty-second motion, the longest twenty seconds of his life.

"I told you, sun!!! I got the Billy Joel, cuzzin!"

Mease couldn't front on Sy for this one. He didn't even want Sy to pass it back to him. As far as their peoples were con-cerned, his younger brother was his twin. Only a year younger, Sy stuck to Mease like glue; thus, their street names: Symease Twins. They were sneaky, moving with a stealth unlike any other two-man crime team. Where you saw Sy, you always saw Mease.

Sy held the eL below the window and turned toward Mease as two people walked past the blood-maroon Land Cruiser that Mease had bought with straight cash. Out the corner of his eye, Sy saw this dude's coat: a bubble leather bomber, the identical color as the Land Cruiser.

They didn't even have to go in The Tunnel anymore. After all, why pay forty dollars–plus when you could do laps around the block with liquor and weed in the car and have your own party? Since it was Sunday night, Hot97 broadcasted Funk Flex live from The Tunnel. And everybody knew the system in Mease's car—it was legendary in his hood, you could hear it clear all up and down Vanderbilt Avenue. And that made it harder to understand how these two moved in absolute silence.

But The Tunnel wasn't their modus operandi tonight. This was a business trip—and they sat and smoked, waiting for Quentin to return so they could take flight back to Shaolin.

"You know you're a dickhead?!? Who's gon' believe that *you*, of *all* people, got Billy Joel's weed connect? Better yet, who the fuck's gon' believe Billy Joel even smokes weed?" Mease's words slid off his tongue like molasses. He couldn't even begin to conceal his highness.

"Nah, sun, fuck that . . . If these fools don't believe me, fuck'em—I just won't sell them shit! Dudes on these streets'll *have* to respect my pedigree after this one!" Sy took another pull, but coughed his lungs up. After he found oxygen again, he said, "That's my word! Kids that don't believe me don't need to be fuckin' with me anyway, strictly because they not acknowledging how gangsta I am with this shit, yo, word up."

Mease shook his head. He tried real hard to make it fast, but everything was slow. Mease dreaded the moment when Sy would pass the eL . . . and that was when Sy extended his arm, pinching it in his fingers. Mease turned his whole body away, toward the driver's-side window. Even blinking his eyes to focus became hard as all hell.

"*BA-uuuh-Bah-Bah-Battle anybody, I don't care you TELL!*" Funkmaster Flex blared through the Land Cruiser system. They sat there listening to Flex scratching double copies of "Rock the Bells." Mease finally focused in the mirror to observe a redheaded woman on the phone. As quickly as she noticed Mease through the mirror, she turned and scurried off. Mease didn't even really *see* this woman . . . but she most certainly saw him and Sy.

Mease was too stuck in perpetual tortoise trots—his mind felt like it had just stopped moving. He looked back over at Sy, a task that felt like a short moment in forever.

Sy started laughing. "Damn, sun, it got you like that? I told you."

Mease couldn't even argue.

As Sy opened the ashtray and outted the eL, he said, "Besides, look at the dude—mufucka's just like us, yo! You ever listen to that 'Uptown Girl' joint he made? You ever see the video? That mufucka's a broke-ass mechanic tryin' to get wit the high-siddity rich bitch . . . Man, that nigguh just like us, and we *smokes* weed!"

Mease started giggling, and knew once he started he'd be laughing entirely too hard for the next ten minutes. They were each other's other side. Mease was always so serious, he needed to laugh. And his comedic younger twin was known for splitting stomachs, stitches, and tear ducts with his sharp tongue.

"Homie bleeds just like us, and I'm sure he choke just like us on this shit too!!! That's what I'ma do: put this shit out on the streets and tell nigguhs I got that Uptown Girl . . . better yet, I got that BJ!"

Mease was trying with all he had to stop laughing. As he finally caught his breath, he said to his brother, "You really think people gon' buy yo shit? They gon' think you got that blowjob, stupid mufucka!"

Sy screwfaced his brother. Mease always shot down his get-rich-quick schemes. Mease always felt Sy should let him do the thinking . . . all little bro had to do was follow. But Sy wouldn't let Mease's reality-based pessimism take the glimmer out of his eye, which he felt was clearly on the prize.

"Nah, dude, it's the BJ . . . it's that Bomb Joint from Billy Joel's connect. They gon' feel me on this one. Just taste that shit, it's crazy . . . I'ma have the hood fucked up like the guy on the couch in *Half Baked*, sun! Watch me . . . I may even sell this shit as doobies on some real old-school shit. They ain't gittin' no chronic like this in the whole tri-state fam."

"Yeah," Mease jeered, "there's one thing you do got right about this shit . . ."

Unable to moderate himself, Mease reached into the ashtray, lit the eL, and took another pull, inhaling then pressing chronic steam out his spout just before he choked. Pounding with a closed fist, hoping to thump the cough outta his chest cavity, he pulled in enough air to say, "This some good-ass shit! Nigguhs in the hood ain't smoking nuffin' like this. Shiiiiit, you could call it the flying chocolate-dookie-smellin' bombazy and mufuckas gon' buy it. And if they don't come back, they fools!"

Mease put the eL back in the ashtray; he couldn't take anymore of the pure bubonic goodness. He looked at Sy and shook his head. For the first time, Mease really felt his brother was onto something. He reached over and gave Sy a pound. "I can't even front—this might just work."

Sy's eyes immediately brightened. "I told you, sun, what I tell you?!" Sy couldn't contain his happiness. He'd reached his long-awaited goal—his older brother's approval on his street-corner operations. Normally, Sy stayed getting shut down by

Mease. His schemes were always missing something. But this time, Sy got it right.

Mease looked at him and said, "Tomorrow we'll get up, I'll use some of this paper Quent's gittin' right now, and we'll cop a couple pounds of that shit. I can't believe I'm financing the fuckin' Billy Joel."

Sy started bouncing up and down in his seat.

Mease immediately sobered up. "A'ight, sun, chill—yo, chill!!! I just got the leather detailed, yo, be easy on that shit!"

As Sy calmed down, Mease began to settle back into his seat, remembering why they were parked there in the first place.

"Where's Quentin?" he asked, as he glanced past the rear-view mirror. "Damn, dude's coat is ill, that shit matches my car."

Mease sank into his seat, not really paying attention to the motions of the coat . . . and the three other dudes with the wearer of the coat. As he closed his eyes and opened them again, he leaned over and his vision lazily landed on the driver's-side mirror. When he focused, he realized the wording was indeed true . . . *Caution: Objects In Mirror Are Closer Than They Appear.*

Now Mease could not only see the blood-maroon leather bubble, he could also make out the mask and the all-too-familiar hand motions. Neither Sy nor Mease were unidentifiable, and this was part of the problem. And Sy didn't realize this. He'd meant to tell his brother about the robbery he did earlier in the day, on his way to cop the Billy Joel sample. Sy's blooper session was a joke, but every joke contains an ounce of truth. Normally they always filled each other in on the solo dirt they did. Yet Sy was so high, he'd forgotten about this particular ounce he owed Mease.

But dude who walked past the car had confirmation that

the dude sitting next to the dude was starring as the dude who had robbed him earlier in the day, who now played the role of the dude playin' Big Willie, suckin' down ganja smoke. He thought it was luck. Sy thought it was Billy Joel. Mease thought it could never happen, but now it was.

"Oh shit, sun—move, git down!!!"

Mease wasn't quick enough to put the car in reverse and navigate out the parking spot this time. Bullets riddled the car. Mease and Sy yelled to each other between the cannons blasting at them. Innocent bystanders ran for cover. Mease and Sy balled up in the foot panels as they heard shots whizzing around them.

Pingpingpingpingpingping . . .

Everything was slow motion like empty shells hitting the concrete in *The Matrix*. Mease couldn't see Sy, but heard him screaming. Sy couldn't see Mease, but even the voice of his older brother didn't slow the sparks where metal ripped through metal, where hollow points pointed at their target. Who was it? And how had this happened? Normally, a shootout this close to The Tunnel made squad car sirens light up and wail.

Four and a half clips worth of slugs later, all that could be heard were screams, blaring car alarms, and the footsteps of people fleeing in every direction. As quick as it started, as long as it lasted, it came to a screeching halt.

Mease slowly lifted his head, and banged it on the steering wheel. It all happened so fast, neither he nor Sy had a chance to reach into the glove box and handle their own business with the Desert Eagles. They weren't usually that slow.

As Mease eased his way up the seat, he checked himself to make sure he wasn't hit.

"Fuck was that shit? Yo, Sy . . . yo, sun . . ."

Mease quickly got up to see his only brother slumped in

his seat. Blood oozed from Sy's body, which was peppered with gunshots.

"Yo, Sy . . . no . . . NOOOOOOOOO!"

Mease slapped his brother's face, trying to wake him up.

"C'mon, Sy, stay with me, stay with me, yo!!!"

With what little life he had left in him, Sy coughed up blood, then slowly whispered to his brother, "My fault . . . I meant to tell you . . . on the way to git the Billy Joel, I robbed thi—"

"Yo, Sy . . . Sy!"

Mease cupped his brother's face as Sy's life slid through his fingers. Mease had always been his brother's keeper. What would he keep now? He kissed his brother's forehead.

Mease stepped out of the truck and gave himself a thorough looking over. Not a drop of blood, no trace of gunshot residue. The cold didn't even bother him. He was in a daze, high off his brother's death, and sober to the Billy Joel. Now he looked at the bullet holes that splattered the back door of the truck. Still dazed from what happened, Mease saw the blue and white lights approaching as he walked over to the other side of the truck.

The blood-maroon Land Cruiser was bullet-riddled on the passenger side too, just like Sy. But Mease was not even scratched.

"How the fuck?"

Mease was in awe. And for a split second, what locked his brain wasn't the fact that his brother was slain, but that he was still standing there in one piece.

"MEEEEEEEEEEASE!"

Quentin, with gat in hand, screamed at his man from the opposite corner. He tucked the weapon between his jeans and hipbone, and ran over. "What the fuck is this, sun?"

Mease stood in utter shock. "Yo . . . I really don't know—"

"C'mon, sun, we gotta motivate! Them boys is on the way!" Quentin could see Mease wasn't moving, and the people who had fled the street were starting to return. He leaned through the shot-out window to grab Mease's coat, then went to the side of the truck to pull Mease away from the scene of the crime.

"My broth—"

"We gotta fly, Mease. If they catch us here, we finished! We gon' find out who did this, but right now, we gotta motivate!" Quent pulled a shell-shocked Mease away from the horrific sight while trying to force him into his coat.

In a moment of clarity, Mease broke away, leaned back into the truck, reached into the ashtray, and took the only memento left from his brother. They quickly skated around the block, into the entirely too long Tunnel line, then blended into the night on their way to the subway.

"License and registration."

Damn, Mease thought, heeding the words of Officer Lillmann. *How the hell did the parking lot turn into a checkpoint?* He was fine until he'd turned off Jersey Street to park, where he saw the usual routine—barricades with one of the po-lice looking and the other one pointing. Of course, Mease got pointed before he could straighten the nose of the Lexus and keep it moving. He'd made it all the way here—now he saw Quentin walking past. Mease knew not to drive the solo car alone. But he was gonna be hard today . . . hardheaded. And they told him not to sniff nothing, but he was *coooool*, he could make it. And he almost had. But then he remembered that factoid— most fatal car accidents happen within a one-mile radius of the driver's home.

Here he was, skeed out his mind, about to be hemmed up by po-lice in the dirty car with three gats: one four-pound, one nine, and one Tec. All that *and* the half-kilo of coke . . . with his boss witnessing this spectacle.

Mease tried to slyly wipe the white powder away from his nostrils while po-lice checked his vitals. "Damn, I was just tryin' to git to my fuckin' son," he said in the empty car. Clearly the coke was getting to him—so much, in fact, he didn't even notice Lillmann back at his window.

"Well, all your info is fine, but here's a ticket . . . Put that in the visor so ya don't lose it."

"What's this for, I wasn't doin nuffin'!?"

"Nothin' except for ridin' with a passenger that looks like a half-ounce of that Pet Shop 'dro from uptown."

Mease looked to his right. Sure enough, he was so worried about the coke, he'd forgotten all about the bright-green bag of Mary Jane he'd copped for the crew to burn down during their cook-up session.

This was why Quent specifically told Mease not to get high.

"Don't worry, me and my old lady'll—how do you fools say it?—*burn it down*, right? Yeah, me and the old lady will burn it down in your honor! As for you, get outta the car slow. I been *waitin'* for this moment! And don't worry—I'll have a cruiser pick up Sy so you ain't too lonely. How 'bout those apples?"

Mease woke up in a cold sweat, drenched and so scared that he'd pissed on himself. Mease wasn't scared of po-lice, but had a pinch of fear when it came to Lillmann, because D2 had the power to take his freedom. He'd done it before to other dudes in Stapleton, Park Hill, Richmond Terrace, and every other hood on the Rock. But since Mease had nothing to care for anymore and no one to keep, he figured he'd body a cop before going to jail.

"Shit . . ." was all he could say when he realized he'd just

166 // STATEN ISLAND NOIR

awakened from a nightmare. He rolled over toward the window, saw that daybreak wasn't yet approaching. He could hear *American Splendor* on the TV, the part when Harvey is diagnosed with cancer and tells his wife, "I can't do it . . . I'm too scared and not strong enough to fight it."

Mease responded: "I feel you, homie."

Shit. Mease was pissed because he pissed, but couldn't really flip. Instead, he collected the soiled sheets and made moves from the Richmond Terrace apartment he'd acquired from an old customer just before crack got her evicted. Richmond Terrace was ideal—the hilly concrete terrain enclosed a murky urban underbrush perfect for the movements Mease needed to make. He hopped in the whip with the saturated laundry bag and skated from the Terrace over to CNB Laundromat—the twenty-four-hour spot—at three thirty a.m.

Mease watched the sudsy clothes and sheets spin through the glass window while reflecting on his dream. Every day was hard since he lost Sy, no doubt about it. And somewhere along the way, he'd lost it all . . . and not by bad decisions, but simply by choice. Without Sy around to balance him out, Mease quickly fell—from crime boss controlling the majority of illegal operations in Killer Hill to low-level crime flunky. He now commuted from Richmond Terrace to finish jobs for Quentin, who had been one of his workers and at one point had owed Mease money. He couldn't care less, though. Without Sy, he did the bare minimum to survive. No more smart maneuvering, no more planning and calculating. Mease would go in, kill you, drop the gun at the crime scene *with* his prints, and dare you to detain him.

Now, six years after Sy had been shot, Detective Schmidt was frantically searching for Mease, always just a step behind. But Mease's whole existence resembled the motion of the soiled fabrics in the washer. He watched as his pissy shit got clean.

Then Schmidt's worst nightmare materialized. The Troy Davis rally was pretty tame—Shallah Raekwon made sure the word throughout Park Hill was "PEACEFUL," even toward po-lice. Two years before the miscarriage of justice that led to Troy Davis's 2007 execution date, Rae had approached the man known as The Abbott of the Wu-Tang Clan. He coerced RZA to couple some of that Quentin Tarantino *Pulp Fiction* Hollywood clout with his hip-hop pull to fund the rally supporting the wrongly accused black man. But no one could've anticipated this move.

While Schmidt tried to secure the crime scene in the area between Hubert H. Humphrey School and Targee Street, things began to spiral out of control. He asked, "What's the victim's name?"

"Quentin Montgomery," Lillmann snickered. "That asshole finally got his just desserts!"

Schmidt's face turned sheet-white. He looked at Quentin's body—no open casket for him. "Forty-five-caliber hollow tip wounds? You can't be serious!" Schmidt knew the work of this hollow-tip Desert Eagle executioner.

"I need you to put out a BOLO on—"

"On who, Schmiddy? Every nigger in the projects? We really gonna waste that much manpower on these savages?"

"Cut the shit, Lillmann!" Schmidt screamed, but it was entirely too late. In the lull between the chants of "Free Troy Davis!" someone turned the tide. The onlookers, overseeing the po-lice's treatment of Quentin's body, were already disgusted with Lillmann's foolishness. All it took was one "FUCK the PO-LICE!!!"

"Nah, FUCK D2, yo!"

"Yay-yea-yeah!!!"

Before he knew it, Schmidt was witnessing a riot unfold. The rustling amongst the people focused, becoming unified.

"Yeah, FUCK D2!"

Mease got off the bus on Tompkins Avenue clenching an aluminum briefcase. He began walking toward the hood. He kept an indiscreet hooptie in the parking lot; after losing his Land Cruiser, he had no desire for upscale luxury. "From point A to B" was Mease's vehicle motto now. He heard the project's heartbeat quicken as he walked through Stapleton Playground into the hood, and soon saw there was an outside event. A theater company was putting on an interactive play entitled *Bamboozled* for the kids in the projects.

"And that's exactly what it is," Mease murmured as he proceeded through a parking lot toward the interior of the projects. He passed familiar faces and landmarks like the teens with their pit bulls engulfed in blunt smoke.

Quick glares showered Mease, but no one thought twice about who he was. *I wish a mufucka would,* Mease thought, as he opened and closed each finger around the briefcase handle. He was blind to everything but his destination.

People knew Mease as the gangster gone wash-up. He was simply a lackey for Quentin, the dude who somehow usurped Mease's power once Sy was slain. Everyone knew Mease didn't care anymore. He was to Stapleton what Omar was to *The Wire*—when you saw him coming, you either ran, hid, or prepared to dodge slugs.

Mease followed the path into the double-sided building Stapleton was so well-known for. On the benches, another kiddie crew was drinking, smoking, selling crack, and clowning all the addicts who walked by. Spanky always sicced his pit on fiends who didn't look or smell right, which included damn near every customer. When Mease walked past the crew, they stopped talking until he made it to the lobby.

The Warren Street building was commandeered by Casper's crew for purposes beyond just family living. The lobby reeked like a Port Authority restroom. Mease made his way to the elevator, but couldn't enter because it was caught between the first and second floors, exposing the elevator shaft. He turned around and saw three more soldiers standing right behind him, guarding the building entrance and watching his every move. He took the stairs, and passed three-man crews on each landing.

He finally made it to the fourth floor. At the terrace entrance, Mease held his arms open, spread eagle, never letting the case go. He was patted down by two burly security guards, who then opened the door to "The Dub": two apartments connected by a wall removed. Mease and the briefcase were directed to the bathroom, which had been converted into a recording studio vocal booth. A small note taped to the mic read, *PUT THESE ON*. Mease set the briefcase down, stepped into the bathtub, stood in front of the mic, and slipped on the headphones.

He immediately heard Casper: "*I see you still remember your way to the hood, huh?*"

"Yeah, it's been awhile, but I made it," Mease replied.

Feeling awkward holding a conversation with a microphone, Mease scanned the room from floor to ceiling and located the camera posted on the wall above the mic, aimed at him.

"I see some things never change," Mease said, referencing Casper's anonymity. The crime boss had committed so much dirt in Stapleton that he had to remain nameless and faceless. And since there was already a Ghostface in Stapleton, he got stuck with the next best moniker.

Casper cackled through the headphones. "*No doubt. I called you out here for a reason, so lemme give you the details.*"

As he listened, Mease's face told it all.

"You really think that's gonna work? He's gonna be there for *that*?"

"*Fuck you think you talking to, nigguh? Look, I understand you outta the hood now, and I can even sympathize with the reason behind it. But you ain't been here, so don't question how I make moves. You here for a fuckin' job, so do as you told! Leave all the thinking to me, ya heard?*"

"A'ight . . . I got it . . . and you got me, right?" Mease countered.

Casper let out a deep sigh. "*Yeah, nigguh, I got you! You know the whole hood asking why you sleeping with the enemy? You ever think of that?*"

Mease looked puzzled.

"*I'ma put you outta this misery, cuz I know you really want out. And given what you been through, I'ma hook you up. One of my mans just ripped this jump-off he met in Manhattan. What's bugged is she talkin' 'bout how she messed with Harvey and was delivering paper for him. She told my dude that one time she got robbed by a kid from Killer Hill that Harvey's brother bodied.*"

Mease's brain began to move again. It hadn't in a very long time. "And . . ."

"*And my man said shorty was brunette up top . . . but was fire-engine-red down below.*"

Mease's face blanked. He couldn't believe it.

"*Yeah, believe it, fam. Don't never say I ain't do nuffin' for you, homie. Leave the case in the bathtub and break north. Do my job—that'll be your last. Then do what you need to, and don't fuck it up! Make sure you git it right, yo! Now get the fuck out my hood 'fore I sic some killuhs on that ass! You've been warned, ya heard?*"

"No . . . no doubt," Mease stuttered, puzzling the pieces together.

He took off the headphones, placed them back on the mic, stepped out the tub, and sat the briefcase where he once stood. When he opened the bathroom door, an identical briefcase was sitting in his path. Mease quickly picked it up and left.

It was starting to make sense to Mease. Harvey was Quentin's brother. They were both from QB and acted like they hated each other. Problem was, it was all game—all for show in the hood so they could extort info from people. This dude might tell Harvey about some bullshit Quentin did. Meanwhile, Quentin found out from someone else why they were scheming on Harvey. They had it down to a science.

No wonder Quentin never had my money that night, Mease thought. Sy did a robbery. He robbed the fire-engine redhead Mease remembered from that night . . . Harvey's girl. And now Mease woke up.

He proceeded to his usual escape route; after sliding the briefcase into a duffel bag slung across his back, he moved briskly across the terrace to the adjoining building and noticed the uniforms running into the other entrance.

And at the back of the pack was Officer Lillmann. As Detective Schmidt cautiously hopped up the stairs, gun drawn, to the fourth floor, Mease was already on the other side of the building. When he reached the far end of the terrace, he hopped the enclosure gate and climbed down. Mease was tall enough to hang from the outside of the terrace fence and plant his feet on the top of the third-floor fence.

Maneuvering onto the third-floor terrace, Mease opened the apartment window from outside. Casper's instructions were good, and Mease darted through the apartment to the far wall, opened the window, and climbed onto the cemented air conditioner. From there, he sprang down to the curved lamppost jutting from the building. He let go, landing on his feet.

Mease was track-star status to his hooptie in the parking lot. While he was pulling outta Stapleton Houses, Schmidt and the po-lice brigade knocked down the door to find the apartment empty, except for the mic and headphones in the bathroom.

Mease knew Schmidt would be pissed that he had just missed him . . . again. But Mease was awake now, and back to his Harry Houdini when it came to Schmidt's pursuit—always a step ahead.

"FUCK D2 . . . FUCK D2!"

Schmidt slapped his palm against his forehead. For the first time, Lillmann looked at Schmidt helplessly, his eyes opened wide, irises big as saucers with hole-punched black spots in the center.

"FUCK D2 . . . FUCK D2!"

The other officers on the scene approached the crowd tentatively, trying to calm them down. Lillmann walked up to Schmidt.

"Schmiddy, what are we gon—"

Schmidt saw Lillmann's eyes pop out of his head in slow motion. A spatter of red liquid hovered in the air like late-July humidity. Schmidt didn't recognize what was happening. Then he gasped as Lillmann's face was pulled from his head.

"What the . . . ?" Schmidt tried lifting his hand toward Lillmann, but the gesture took a lifetime. And then it all resumed in real time.

The thud of Lillmann's body bouncing against the concrete echoed in Schmidt's ears. The angry mob screamed, swaying in various directions. Po-lice on the scene ducked, squawking like pigeons, searching for the assailant's angle. But Schmidt stood erect, scanning with his eyes. He'd been told Mease was working on a big job for Casper that would allow him to exit the game. At first, he figured it was Quentin; but then it dawned on him that was Mease's thing—the job was a hit on the most hated officer in Park Hill history.

As the crowd dispersed, the remaining residents saw that Lillmann had been hit.

"DAMN—they shot D2 in the face!!!"

"Rude bwoy . . . bo-bo-BO!!!"

"YEAH . . . FUCK D2 . . . FUCK D2!"

A few po-lice grabbed their walkie-talkies, calling for backup, the riot squad, any extra manpower to contain and control a steaming hood crowd. Schmidt was still, craning his neck, surveying the landscape for the culprit.

Just then, a black Lincoln livery cab turned the corner from Park Hill Avenue onto Palma Drive. While everything seemed slow to Schmidt once again, this cab existed in the same wrinkle of time he now occupied. His head and eyes stopped, locking in on the moving vehicle. The driver was unrecognizable—until he pulled the black bandanna off his face and the black hood off his head.

"Mease," Schmidt whimpered.

Mease winked at the detective who'd been following him since Sy's death. "This one's on me, Schmiddy!"

Focused on his getaway route, Mease's fingers stumbled through the ashtray. He'd killed Lillmann for Casper . . . Shit, he'd killed D2 for the whole hood! But Quentin was responsible for the death of his baby brother Sy. Finally, his fingers fell on their target. He picked up the small clip left from that night's eL. He put it to his lips and lit up. He had kept this clip for a long time, and promised himself he'd dead it when he deaded his brother's murderer.

When Mease turned onto Targee with the hood in an absolute frenzy, he cracked the window and let the smoke fly as he choked on his last few pulls of that Uptown Girl named Billy Joel.

[Editor's Note: all characters in this story—even those based on real people—are fictional or used in a fictional context.]

BEFORE IT HARDENS

BY EDDIE JOYCE

Annadale

His parents called it his graduation barbecue but Mikey knew better. This was their party, their chance to show off their oldest son. So he stood there, in the tiny fenced-in backyard, and answered the same questions over and over. Yes, he was glad that school was over. Yes, he was excited to go up to LeMoyne. No, it wasn't a full scholarship, just half. Baseball was different than basketball. The coach only has a dozen scholarships to divide among twenty-five players. He wasn't sure what he would major in. No, he probably wouldn't start freshmen year.

After a few minutes, his cheeks started to ache.

When they were done congratulating Mikey, the well-wishers—neighbors, old friends, twice-a-year cousins—walked over to his father, cooking burgers at the grill, and slapped his back, or they sidled up to his mother, standing on the small brick patio drinking Chardonnay, and kissed her cheek. They all said something and then glanced back at Mikey. Something like *Good job* or *Great kid*, like it was all his parents' doing, like Mikey had played no role at all. His graduation party. Right.

Sure, Pete and Benny were there. Jenny, of course. And Jenny's best friend Amy. But that was it, as far as his friends went. Mikey didn't even mind because these were the only people he might actually stay in touch with when he went away to college. At graduation, all the kids around him were crying and hugging, promising to hang out this summer, swearing they would keep in touch. But Mikey just smiled and shook hands and wished them good luck. His life, his real life, was in front of him, not behind him, and he saw little sense pretending otherwise.

As soon as he could, Mikey retreated to the picnic table in the back of the yard.

"Dude, how long do we have to stay here? This is boring as balls."

"Benny, do you have to use 'balls' in every sentence?"

"Yes, Amy, I swear on my hairy balls that I do."

Amy stuck her tongue out at Benny, who gave her the finger in response. They'd been flirting all year; nothing had happened. Mikey sat down, picked at a plate of pasta salad. He looked back toward the patio and saw his uncle Tommy letting himself in through the chain-link gate at the side of the house. His uncle—squat, mustachioed, and grim, raising three kids on his own—was wearing construction clothes. He'd come straight from a job, on a Saturday.

Tommy plucked two tall boys of Bud from the enormous white cooler stationed near the grill and walked over to their table. Every stiff-legged, achy stride pushed a wince across his face. He handed Mikey one of the cans and took a long, foamy pull on his own.

"Congrats, Mikey." Tommy brought his beer can down, knocked it into the one he'd put in Mikey's hand. He looked around the table at the others. "Having fun?"

Mikey cracked his beer, took a surreptitious sip.

"Yeah, I am now."

Tommy laughed. "Good. Well, enjoy your day. Enjoy your day."

He turned away and then turned back, a quick pirouette

that caught Mikey in the middle of rolling his eyes at Jenny.

"Because a week from Monday, you come to work with me. Gonna teach you a little something about hard work before you head up to that country club."

He walked over to the other adults huddled on the patio. Benny started to laugh. Mikey told him to shut up.

"Sorry, bro. That sucks. That really sucks."

Pete shrugged his shoulders. "At least he gave you a beer."

The next morning, Mikey got up early and went down to the kitchen. His mother was cooking bacon and eggs. A white box from Galluccio's bakery peeked open on the kitchen table, the red and white twining already cut. He walked up beside his mom and kissed her cheek. He glanced out the window above the sink to the backyard. Already clean. The chairs folded, the trash collected in four tidy white bags.

"Mom, you should have waited. I would have helped you clean up."

"It was nothing. Took no time at all."

With her spatula, she lifted a few pieces of bacon out of the hissing pan and dropped them on a plate covered with a paper towel. Mikey grabbed a piece of bacon and put it in his mouth.

"Christ, Michael, at least wait for it to cool off." She laughed. "You know, I saw that beer Uncle Tommy gave you yesterday. I let it slide but don't get used to it. You're still living under my roof."

"Jesus, Mom, it was one beer."

"I don't know what my brother is thinking sometimes."

Mikey reached for another piece of bacon from the plate. His mother put the last of the bacon in the fat-filled pan and it crackled before fading into an agitated sizzle.

"Yeah, Mom, about Uncle Tommy, I don't know about this

construction job. I thought I'd work at the CYO camp again."

"Michael, the pay is great. You'll make three times what you did at the camp. You'll have some pocket money at school."

"I don't need money for school, Mom. I have a scholarship."

"That doesn't cover everything. You want a bike to get to class? Or some CDs? Or what if Jenny comes to visit, you want to take her out to dinner? These things cost money." She pointed the grease-coated end of the spatula at him to accentuate each point.

"But Coach Whelan said I need to gain weight this summer. He said I need to gain ten to fifteen pounds of muscle."

"This job will help. You'll be lifting things all day."

Mikey knew he wouldn't win. He retreated to the kitchen table and flopped into one of the chairs.

His mother talked at him over her shoulder, her voice raised so he'd hear her above the frying bacon. "Michael, you know how things are right now. Money is tight. This will really help."

She turned off the burner, brought the plate of bacon over to the table. She sat down next to him.

"And look, you have a week before you start. Go and have some fun. No moping."

Mikey's pout eased into a reluctant smile. He knew he was being selfish but he couldn't help it. He'd worked hard for four years. He hadn't slacked off his senior year like most of his friends. He'd kept his grades up even though it didn't come easy, had never come easy. He'd busted his ass, in the classroom, in the batting cage, on the field. He'd earned that scholarship. He figured he was due a breezy summer.

Mikey's dad walked into the kitchen, took a crumb bun out of the bakery box. He'd probably overheard their conversation and waited things out in the living room. Left all the heavy lifting to Mom. As usual. He stood there for a minute, taking small bites out of the crumb bun. He'd been on furlough for four months. Not sure when it would end. Money *was* tight.

"Tommy told me that you'll be working out at Shea Stadium. That'll be cool, right?" Powdered sugar stuck in the corners of his father's mustache. He said this seriously, like it made up for the fact that Mikey's summer was ruined.

Mikey stood up, put on his baseball cap, and stared straight at his father. He was already a few inches taller and now he was actually taking his father's place, bringing in money for the family. He pointed to the emblem on his cap, filled his voice with sarcasm. "Yeah, it'll be cool. Except for the fact that I'm a Yankees fan and except for the fact that Shea is a fucking dump."

Mikey didn't wait around to be reprimanded. He walked out the side door into the bright morning sun. He didn't see his father turn to his mother for an explanation, didn't see his mother shrug her shoulders in response.

Mikey did what his mother suggested: he tried to squeeze a whole summer into one week. Went down the shore with Pete to his parents' house for a few nights. Took the 4 train up to the stadium and caught a Yankees game with Benny. Bought a twelve-pack of condoms and made his way through them with Jenny. Picked her up from work in the afternoon, went straight to her house, up to her bedroom, her parents still at work.

One night, he took Jenny into Little Italy for dinner. Mikey ordered a carafe of red wine. The waiter didn't react, didn't give him the once-over or ask for ID. He just brought over two glasses and a full carafe. They giggled at their good fortune. Mikey poured some for each of them and made a toast, like a big shot.

On the ferry back, they sat outside looking at the long, graceful span of the Verrazano, lit up against the night. Jenny's head was on his shoulder, her hand rubbing his leg, just above his knee. Her fingers were tucked inside his shorts, touching the inside of his thigh, the spot that drove him nuts. His face felt hot, flush with wine.

"Mikey, have you thought at all about what we're going to do when we go away to college?"

He hadn't. Not really. They'd be dating for six months. He really liked Jenny, maybe even loved her. He wasn't sure. How could he know? He loved it when they were alone together, the way she made him feel. And he got pissed when he thought about her with another guy. Not just kinda pissed. Rip-your-head-off pissed. Can't-hold-a-thought-in-your-head pissed. Maybe it was love. It was definitely intense.

He still thought about other girls. Wanted to do with them what he did with Jenny. But that was normal. Everyone had thoughts like that.

When he'd started dating Jenny, he asked his dad what he thought of her. They had just picked up bagels at the Annadale Deli and they were back in the car, his father driving.

"She's nice, Mike, she's really nice. Cute girl."

That had made Michael happy, his father liking Jenny, approving of her. And then, a few minutes later, the car parked in their driveway, his dad had ruined it. He turned to Mikey.

"You're young, Mikey, you're very young. And just remember: even if you're banging Miss America, you still wanna bang the runner-up." He got out of the car quickly, embarrassed by what he'd said.

Mikey was furious. Just like his dad to taint something good. But that's what he thought of now, with Jenny's hand on his thigh and the question about their future hanging there, unanswered. He thought about his dad's stupid advice and the fact that he was gonna be in Syracuse and Jenny would be three hours away in Albany.

"Yeah, kinda."

"Well, what were you thinking?"

"I thought, like, that we'd stay together but also, you know, see other people. Still be together but be allowed to see other people."

Jenny didn't respond for a little while. Her fingers kept massaging his thigh.

"Why? What were you thinking?"

"I mean, I don't really want to see anyone else. I just want to be with you."

The warm feeling from Mikey's face crept down into his chest. He felt bad and he was pissed that he felt bad. He didn't want to talk about this now. He didn't want to explain. He was about to say something when Jenny continued.

"But I guess that makes sense. I guess."

That was enough for Mikey. He didn't think about it again, not on the ferry, not on the train, and not when they got back to Jenny's house and used the last of the condoms on the couch in her basement while her parents snored two floors up.

The week drew to a close. On the Sunday before he started working, Mikey went with Jenny to Amy's house. It was hot and muggy; Amy had a pool, a small above-ground number, but it did the trick. They took dips then dried themselves in the sun on the small wooden deck next to the pool. Jenny wore a one-piece blue swimsuit that accentuated her compact figure; she had small, pert breasts and a pleasantly thick rear. Amy wore a halter top green bikini, displaying a voluptuousness Mikey hadn't realized was there. His eyes kept wandering to Amy's hips, her bare stomach, her large breasts. He hoped Jenny didn't notice.

When Jenny went inside to call her parents, Amy turned her entire body to face Mikey. She brought one hand above her temple to shield her eyes from the sun. She'd gotten out of the pool just a few minutes earlier. Droplets of water trickled across the goose bump–covered flesh of her stomach.

"When do you head up to school, Mikey?"

"Week before Labor Day."

"Oh, that's late, right? Isn't Jenny leaving in the middle of August?"

Mikey nodded, a slow, uncertain movement. Amy wasn't going away to school. She was staying home, going to CSI.

"We should hang out. If you want to come over and jump in the pool or something. You know, after Jenny goes away."

Mikey couldn't see Amy's eyes under the cup of her hand. He nodded again, less uncertain. He raised his right knee and shifted his towel over his groin. With his left hand, he guided his developing erection flat against his thigh. He tried to keep his gaze on Amy's forehead.

He heard the porch door slide open, then the pad of Jenny's bare feet on the deck. She sat down on her lounger, her sunglasses perched on her head.

Amy completed her rotation onto her stomach, her face turned away from Mikey. "What did your parents say?"

Her voice was a lazy slur. "Nothing. Same old stuff."

Mikey stood up and slipped into the pool in one quick motion. He turned back to Jenny, pushing himself right up against the side of the pool to stifle his erection. He felt it bow against the wall of the pool and slowly recede.

"My father said good luck tomorrow. Ame, his uncle is picking him up at four thirty in the morning. Can you believe that?"

Mikey smiled. He'd managed to keep the job out his head most of the week, even though it popped in here and there.

"How bad can it be?" he said. Then he bent his knees and dropped his head below the water's surface.

The next morning, Mikey waited outside his parents' house in the predawn blue. Per Tommy's instructions, he wore jeans, boots, and a long-sleeve T-shirt. He stood there half-asleep until his uncle's battered gray van turned onto the block and cruised to a stop in front of him. They drove in silence to a deli near the expressway. Mikey ordered a ham and egg sandwich on a sesame bagel. His uncle paid the tab, handed Mikey a tall coffee as they walked back to the van.

"Thanks, Tommy, but I don't drink coffee."

The driver's door creaked open, slammed shut. Mikey could hear the words before his uncle opened his mouth.

"You will."

Tommy was so predictable.

The highway was empty. They flew across the island, the complaints of sports fanatics drifting out of the radio. The Yankees had blown two games in the ninth inning over the weekend. The callers were apoplectic; they wanted a new closer, a new manager, a new owner. Mikey took a few sips of coffee. It wasn't terrible but he'd rather have a Coke. Or a Snapple. Something cool.

As they ascended the upper level of the Verrazano, the sun crept into the sky. A soft yellow haze spilled out over the whole city. Mikey could see the rides out on Coney Island, the skyscrapers at the base of Manhattan, a pair of yellow ferries passing in the harbor.

Mikey let out a long, silent yawn that pushed his chin down to his chest.

"You should sleep now."

The van descended into Brooklyn and the highway thickened with cars, buses, and trucks. The callers had moved on from the Yankees; they were decrying the Knicks' latest draft pick.

Mikey closed his eyes and nodded off.

"What do you think, has the kid gotten a taste?"

"I don't know. Ask him. Kid, you gotten your first taste yet?"

"He hasn't gotten a taste. Look at him. He's all skin and bones."

"Kid, stick out your tongue. Let us see if you've gotten a taste."

"Nicky, take a look at the kid's tongue. Tell us what you think."

Big Nicky strode over to Mikey. He was huge, a colossus.

"Let me see your tongue, kid."

Mikey stuck his tongue out. He already knew that you didn't say no to Nicky, even for something this stupid. Nicky leaned down and inspected Mikey's tongue. He took his time, rotating his head so he could examine the sides. He stared down Mikey's throat. The other guys were laughing, enjoying the performance. Mikey felt ridiculous, standing there, tongue extended, but he couldn't show it. Nicky lifted his hands from his knees, delivered the verdict.

"This kid has definitely gotten a taste."

The others broke into hysterics. A few even cheered. Nicky thudded a hand on Mikey's shoulder, lowered his voice.

"Kid, young pussy is the best fucking thing in the world. Enjoy it while you can."

His uncle piped up, ending the party: "All right, all right, you've had your fun. Enough fucking around. Back to work."

The guys shuffled off, their bodies tilted one way or the other by the pails of concrete they carried. Nicky reached down and lifted two of them with ease, one in each hand, like they were cans of soup. He walked down the ramp and winked at Mikey as he passed. Mikey retrieved another bag of dry cement and carried it over to the mixer.

His uncle slapped him on the back. "Having fun yet?"

Mikey tore the bag open. A chalky gray mist rose into his nose and then down to his lungs. He coughed; the spasm knocked a dose of sweat off his face. He felt an ache in his lower back, in a spot he never knew existed. He glanced at his watch. It was just past nine. The day wasn't even half over.

At the end of the shift, Mikey was whipped. He'd spent the whole day mixing cement. Eight hours. A rushed half-hour for lunch. His hair was caked with tiny flecks of concrete and his jeans and long-sleeved T-shirt were heavy with sweat. His forearms throbbed and his legs hummed with nascent cramps. Two oysters of ache lay tucked behind his shoulder blades. He sat on the asphalt of the enormous parking lot and waited for his uncle. The other guys split into groups of three or four and piled into cars, except for the handful of Mexicans who just walked out of the lot into the bustle of Queens. Mikey closed his eyes, fell into a grimy half sleep.

Tommy flicked Mikey's ear, waking him. Mikey pushed himself up and lurched toward the passenger door of his uncle's van. Tommy laughed and tossed him a set of keys.

"You slept on the way in."

Then Tommy climbed into the emptied-out back of the van and laid down. He was asleep before the van left the parking lot. Mikey was terrified. He'd never driven in traffic like this. It was chaos, every man for himself, stop-and-go speeding up to a harried group crawl before reverting back to stillness. Sudden explosions of movement, cars swerving across two lanes, the noses of yellow cabs butting in everywhere.

And Mikey's eyes were shutting on him, despite the fact that it wasn't even three o'clock and the van was beset on all sides by hostile, honking drivers. When the van settled into line for the toll on the Verrazano Bridge, Mikey engaged the cigarette lighter. He pulled it out, and when the concentric circles had faded from orange to brown, he singed his left forearm. The pain jolted him awake and he drove the rest of the way home watching a blister form where the lighter had touched his skin.

His house was empty. He took a quick shower, turned on the fan in his bedroom, and slipped under the sheet. He'd just rest for a half-hour, an hour at most, and then he'd go the gym and lift or take some swings in the backyard. The phone rang but he didn't have the energy to get it.

Mikey heard his mother calling him. He opened his eyes, looked at the clock. It was almost eight. He'd been sleeping for three hours. He was still sore. He threw on shorts and a T-shirt and staggered downstairs. His mother and his brother were waiting for him at the kitchen table. He gorged himself on chicken cutlets and rice for twenty minutes and then excused himself and went back upstairs to sleep.

Later, he heard his mother yell something up to him but he didn't answer. He just rolled over and went back to sleep. When the alarm clock sounded at four a.m., he sprung awake, reinvigorated but miserable, astonished that people actually lived like this.

The week took forever. Every day was a marathon of dust and toil. Mikey stopped showering in the morning, slept the whole way in. He started putting names with faces. A few of the guys were all right. They joked around, they made him feel welcome. A few of the guys were assholes. They didn't like him, could never like him. This was their life; he was just visiting.

The Mexicans didn't joke or judge. They just worked.

On the drive home every day, he stopped at a deli near Shea and bought a liter of Coke. It kept him awake but overfilled his bladder. One day, he pissed right into the empty Coke bottle as the van sat in traffic on the West Shore Expressway. The sound woke his uncle, who peered in from the back, laughed, and went back to sleep. It wasn't ideal but it beat the cigarette lighter.

At the end of his first week, Jenny offered to cook him dinner. He hadn't seen her all week. He'd been too tired to do anything but sleep, eat, and watch television. Her parents were away for the weekend. Tommy dropped him off at her house.

He was going to take a shower and then maybe a nap but within two minutes, he was on the floor bare-assed and Jenny had him in her mouth. He was in ecstasy, the job a distant memory, when she said she wanted to feel him inside of her. She told him it was safe because she had just finished her period. She crawled up his torso and lowered herself onto him, slick and easy. It was different with nothing between them, primordial and elemental, the mystery finally revealed. He felt out of time, alone in the world with Jenny. After a few minutes of euphoric thrusting, they came together. She collapsed onto his chest, breathless.

He fell asleep right there on the hardwood floor with his shirt off and his jeans and underwear clustered at his ankles. When he woke up, Jenny was setting the table and the air was thick with the smell of homemade tomato sauce.

Mikey took a quick shower. A bolt of anxiety rippled through him as he loosened the grains of concrete in his hair. They were always careful; they'd always used condoms before. He hadn't even used the "pull and pray" method that Pete joked about. Jenny had just slid down on him, hadn't even really asked. Sure, it was fantastic, but it was too risky. She shouldn't have done that. He shouldn't have let her. He wouldn't let it happen again.

When he got out of the shower, dinner was ready. Spaghetti and meatballs with her grandmother's gravy, a simple salad, a fresh loaf of bread from Galluccio's. Jenny stood at one end of the table, a kitchen apron around her midsection, a satisfied smile on her face. In that light, in that pose, she looked like her mother. Mikey sat down. Jenny brought the platter of food over to his plate and loaded it with pasta and meatballs.

"Isn't this nice?"

Mikey didn't answer. He ushered a large meatball into his mouth and tried to ignore the dry aftertaste of cement that lingered in the back of his throat.

The summer droned on. July was brutal but fair; blistering heat but no humidity. The sun baked them in the still air of the empty stadium. Mikey understood why they started work so early: the mornings were bearable, the afternoons hellacious. After lunch, time hit the brakes. Mikey's legs grew sluggish and his stomach swelled with bread and meat from lunch. The air stung like lava. Nothing to rush the day. A nerve-wracking drive home on the horizon.

Most days, Mikey worked by himself, mixing load after load of cement. The other guys would arrive in groups. There'd be a few minutes of companionship as he shoveled concrete into their pails. *Fucking brutal today. See the Yanks last night? Look at Mikey, his tongue's hanging down to his chin. Mikey, you up all night eating pussy again?* Mikey didn't mind. He'd stick his tongue out, reach it up to his nose, wink at Nicky. *I can still taste it,* he'd say, and the guys would laugh. The same jokes every day. Jokes you could lean on.

He tried out his Spanish on the Mexican guys, all the dirty words he knew. *Coño. Pendejo. Tengo grande pene.* They laughed, maybe with him, maybe at him. He didn't care. It passed the time. A few minutes of fun in the soup. A flutter of camaraderie. Then he'd be alone again, for an hour at least, maybe longer.

When he was alone, his mind drifted to the Sunday before he started working. Jenny and Amy lying by the pool in Amy's backyard; Mikey nestled on the lounger between them. He thought about his conversation with Amy, what she'd said to him about Jenny leaving for school early. He thought about some of the looks Amy had given him. Looks that said all things were possible. He thought about her green bikini, all the flesh it covered and all the flesh it didn't. He thought about these things until his groin stirred, until he felt half alive again in the scalding gray haze.

Jenny called him every night, complaining that they weren't spending any time together. When he hung out with one of his buddies or tried to slip in some batting practice or a lift, she protested, whining into the phone that she was leaving in a month, in three weeks, in two weeks. Did he even care? While she pestered him, he cursed her silently. He cursed his parents for making him take this job. He cursed his uncle for making him drive home every day.

And he cursed the weather because his uncle had told him they couldn't work if it rained and it hadn't rained a single fucking drop the whole summer.

In August, the weather turned diabolical. A humid front squatted over the city. The air swelled thick. Every night, the weath-ermen predicted thunderstorms and downpours that never came. The sweat came off Mikey in sheets. It was too hot to even laugh. Even the Mexicans slowed.

Mikey barely saw his parents or his brother. He woke be-fore them, got home before them, went to bed before them. When he did see them, he floated past, a ghost stuck between two lives, not fully there but not yet at college. He counted the days. Just a few more weeks. Then he'd never mix cement again.

One day, a week before Jenny left for school, his uncle sent him and one of the Mexicans, Renny, to knock out some cement in the ceiling above the concourse. They had to stand on a plat-form and use a mini-jackhammer. The motion was awkward and painful; Mikey had to switch shoulders every few minutes.

Renny was the hardest-working and happiest guy in the whole crew. He spoke no English. He smiled constantly. They fell into an easy rhythm. A few minutes of attacking clatter, thirty seconds of rest. The same exchange filled every silence.

"Renny, yo quiero muchas cervezas? Coño-faced."

"Coño-faced?"

"Yeah, coño-faced. Shit-faced. Borracho."

A big laugh from Renny. Then back to the jackhammers.

One time, Mikey pulled the trigger a second too early, while he was still looking at Renny. The jackhammer's blade spurted to life, found something metal, recoiled, and popped him be-low his left eye. Mikey stumbled back and his feet slipped off the platform. He had a moment of complete terror, like drop-ping into a dark cave, until his right ankle found the ground and buckled. The rest of his body followed, pain reverberating through him as his right knee, elbow, and shoulder impacted.

He flopped over onto his back, throbbing everywhere. Ten feet above, Renny looked down, surprise and concern on his face.

Mikey closed his eyes, tried to assess what hurt the most. His ankle was screaming; the bone below his eye felt like it had been pushed back into his mouth.

He heard Renny climb down from the platform, heard the scamper of his boots on the concrete, and heard his uncle name's being yelled in a panicked Mexican accent.

His uncle drove home, annoyance slowly losing out to compassion. Mikey wasn't really hurt. No permanent damage. He had a sprained ankle, a skinned knee, and an ugly black eye; his ribs and back were tender and sore, but he was otherwise fine. An ice pack dangled over his bare ankle. He held another up to his eye.

"Renny thought you were dead."

"I did too."

Tommy chuckled. "I'm glad you're not. Your mother would've killed me." He glanced over, gave Mikey a tight smile.

He does this every day, Mikey thought. *Then he goes home to three kids.*

They drove the rest of the way without talking. The incessant heat had sapped the whole city of energy. Even the callers on sports radio could only register mild complaints; their quibbles were swatted away by an aggravated host.

Hot air rushed in through the open windows of the van. Mikey peered out on the highway and watched the blurry lines of heat rise. Every bump renewed the pain in his joints; still, his eyes fell shut.

A gentle flick on the ear woke him.

"Keep icing your ankle, Mikey, though I don't think we'll be working the rest of the week."

Mikey was still groggy, didn't understand. He followed his uncle's gaze until he saw a fat drop of rain land on the front windshield of the van. The sky had darkened during his snooze. The temperature had dropped a few degrees. Mikey hobbled out into a sudden downpour, feeling better than he had all summer.

The house was empty. Mikey checked the weather report. Rain for the rest of week and through the weekend, bringing much-needed water to the drought-plagued tri-state area. He felt renewed, alive for the first time in many weeks, despite the pain all over his body. His thoughts turned to Jenny. He wanted to be with her right now, wanted her to fawn over his wounded, tired body.

She answered on the second ring. She sounded like she'd been sleeping.

"Hey, it's me."

"Hey."

"Looks like I won't have to work tomorrow or Friday. Maybe we can go to Denino's tonight, stop at Ralph's afterward. We can hang out all day tomorrow."

"I'm sick, Mikey. I've been nauseous all day. I didn't even go into work today." She sounded awful.

"All right. Well, I'll come over then and we can just hang out in your room, watch a movie or something."

"Right. Or something. I don't feel good, Mikey. Maybe I'll feel better tomorrow."

This was bullshit. She'd whined all summer that he wasn't spending any time with her and now she was too sick to hang out? A nasty thought popped in his head.

"Okay, Jenny, maybe tomorrow." He softened his voice, tried to sound spontaneous. "Hey, do you know if Amy's around?"

He could just imagine the look on her face. He waited.

"What do you mean?"

"No, I just figured if you're not feeling great, maybe Amy would be up for some pizza."

"What do you mean?"

He'd hit his target. He could hear it in her voice.

"Well, I've been so busy all summer, I haven't seen anyone. I just thought maybe I'd—"

"Why would you say that?"

"Forget it, Jenny. I was only asking."

"Why would you say that?"

"Jenny, just forget it."

He heard her start to cry. A dose of guilt shot through him. Then he felt something fierce and explosive, an anger that shook his hands. He screamed into the receiver.

"You're not the only one who had a shitty day, Jenny!" His face was burning. "My whole summer sucked. And all you did was make it worse!"

Jenny was sobbing. Mikey wasn't even sure whether she'd heard him. He repeated himself.

"All you did was make it worse!"

Then he hung up.

He wasn't serious about calling Amy. Sure, after he had a shower, he took out his address book and turned it to the page that held her number. He looked at it for a long time, imagined how the conversation would go, and thought about what would happen if she said yes. But he wasn't really serious. He just wanted to try it out in his head. He ended up calling Benny, who he hadn't seen in weeks.

Mikey'd heard about the place. It was a few miles over the Outerbridge in Jersey. Benny had gone a few weeks earlier with his older brother. He described it to Mikey on the drive over.

They had split a six-pack in the basement of Benny's house and were feeling pretty good

"What if they don't let us in?"

"Relax, Mikey. They don't care. They just want your money."

"Shit, I hope we get in."

"We will. Wait till you see these chicks, bro. Wait."

The big neon sign out front read, *Molly's*. The lot only had a few cars in it. Benny parked near the entrance. The rain had thinned to a drizzle.

The doorman, a hulking figure in gray sweatpants and a black T-shirt, didn't even want to see ID. He just took their twenties and waved them in.

Inside, a few customers sat at a rectangular bar that surrounded a stage. Soft light filtered through the room, dying in the corners. At either end of the stage, a scantily clad stripper was wrapped around a pole. The woman nearest Mikey was topless. She titled back, hands around the pole, bare legs stretched up to the ceiling. Her breasts hung back toward her face. Blond curls of hair dangled down to the stage floor. She flashed Mikey an upside-down smile.

The bartender—an older woman, all business—interrupted their reverie. "Boys, what are you having?"

Benny stepped forward, put a crinkled ten on the bar. "Two Buds."

The bartender put two bottles on the bar, flicked them open. "Try not to fall in love."

Mikey had never been inside a strip club. He was overwhelmed; his eyes flitted around the room, trying to take it all in. There was flesh, a cavalcade of it: curved rears, hardened nipples, bruised thighs, lithe necks. It was all on display and you were supposed to look. The dancers wanted you to ogle them, to desire them. They cavorted and gyrated and contorted. They took the stage and stripped down until only a sliver of fabric remained between their legs. They pulled and tugged at that fabric until what was behind swelled into relief.

After they danced, the strippers walked straight up to you, unabashed, and pulled their tits apart so you could place a dollar bill between them. Most of them weren't beautiful, most weren't even cute, but it didn't matter; their appeal was primordial.

After a few hours, it was time to leave. They'd had their fun, slipped a single between the tits of every dancer in the place three times over.

Mikey was drunk; all the beer had dulled the pain in his ankle and the soreness everywhere else. He took a difficult piss in the bathroom and when he came back to the bar, the blond dancer was seated on his stool and Benny was whispering in her ear. Mikey saw Benny slide a twenty into her hand. She was wearing a see-through white teddy and she extended her hand. Mikey shook it.

"I'm Mandy. Looks like you had a rough day."

She brought a soft finger to the cheek below his left eye. She was younger than the other dancers. Less worn out. She had a pretty face that was somewhat familiar; she looked like a friend's older sister, someone you once pined for. She scooted from the stool and took his hand.

"Well, you are certainly tall and long. Bet you're long in all the right places."

No one had ever talked to him like this. This was the talk of porno movies. This wasn't real. Benny was leaning onto the bar, a sleepy grin on his face.

"Your friend wants to give you a little going-away present."

She led him over to a little side lounge, darker than the

bar area and separated by a sheer black curtain. He was unsteady on his feet, a mixture of the beer and his swollen ankle. She pushed him down on the couch and removed her teddy. She started dancing, brushing her bare tits across his face. She smelled like perfume and sweat. She placed Mikey's hands on her hips. She turned, grinding her bare ass into his groin.

This was a real woman with full tits and an ass you could mount. Jenny might be like this some day but she wasn't yet. Mikey was excited and embarrassed and trying to hold himself back. After a few minutes with her ass rubbing against him, he was ready to go. He tried even harder to hold back. But when Mandy turned again and slid her legs over his hips and lowered herself onto him, the whole throbbing bit of him, he came right in his boxers.

Mandy relaxed in his lap as she felt him retreating. The euphoric feeling faded and left Mikey feeling hollow. Mandy smiled and kissed his forehead. He thought he might vomit.

The next morning, Mikey woke to the sound of rain pounding outside his window. The end of the night was a blur, just vague unconnected bits: a hasty exit from Molly's, Benny's car drifting across the narrow Outerbridge, Benny faking sobriety at the toll, Mikey sneaking under the covers as his alarm clock pulsed 2:57.

His head throbbed. His body ached. At least he didn't have to work. He could sleep for a few more hours. He looked over at the alarm clock. Just after nine. The hostile red digits reminded him of the sign in the strip club's parking lot. He tried to ignore the guilt that was gathering in the back of his head. Better to sleep it off. It was just harmless fun.

The door to his bedroom creaked open and his mother peered into the grayness, concerned. "Michael?"

"Yeah, Mom, what's up?" He didn't open his eyes, hoped his nonchalance would throw her off.

"Tommy called. He wanted to see if you were feeling okay. Why didn't you tell me about the accident?"

"It was nothing, Mom. Just a sprained ankle and a black eye. It happens."

He could tell she wanted to come in, to inspect him and confirm that he was fine.

"Are you sure you don't need a doctor?"

"Mom, I'm fine. I just need some rest. Can I just get some rest?"

"Okay, Mikey." But she didn't leave. A thin slice of light from the hallway lingered on the bed. "Jenny's downstairs."

"I'll be right down."

He swung out of bed and gingerly placed his swollen ankle on the floor. It was twice its normal size and bluish streaks were visible on the swell. He threw on a T-shirt and the jeans he'd worn the night before and hobbled downstairs.

Jenny sat at the kitchen table, still wearing her yellow rain slicker. His mother was at the sink, washing dishes but attentive. Jenny stood and he could tell that she had been crying. She looked like a little girl lost in a mall; she couldn't contain the panic on her face.

He knew right then, knew before they left the house without a word, before she drove a few blocks away and pulled the car over. He knew before she started to cry, before the crying turned into great heaving sobs. When he reached over to comfort her, she blurted it out.

"I'm pregnant, Mikey. I think I'm pregnant. I missed my period and I feel sick in the mornings. Mikey, what are we going to do?"

Now it was solid, in the world. It was spoken fact. Desperation flooded through Mikey. LeMoyne was a million miles away, its campus sliding away in the rain. He saw his future harden into something ugly, something clichéd. The summer and its miseries had smothered the memory. A few thrusts on a hard wooden floor. One time. It wasn't possible. He started to cry.

They drove to a pharmacy and Mikey bought a pregnancy test. They chose a sleepy diner on Hylan as the place for her to take it. Mikey's skin hummed, his stomach churned. This would not happen. He would will it not to happen.

No, it would. He was powerless to stop it. His life was ruined. He was soaked to the bone, shivering despite the month. Jenny was a zombie, gliding through the streets, all cried out.

They parked the car across from the diner and Jenny dashed inside. Mikey waited in the car, making promises to God if He would only let Mikey escape this. He could not shake the image of Mandy on top of him the night before, smiling at him; his jeans were still seeped with that betrayal. This was punishment.

No, this was Jenny's fault. She wanted to trap him.

Fifteen minutes ticked by, an eternity.

Mikey left the car and hobbled into the diner. An older man was mopping behind the counter and there was a solitary customer reading the paper at the far end of it. The customer looked at Mikey and then pointed to the bathroom door.

Mikey heard Jenny sobbing. He opened the door to find her sitting on the floor, wedged between the toilet and the wall. The test was facedown on the mopped linoleum, a few inches away from her splayed feet. Jenny reached for Mikey. He reached for the test.

A single pink line. Negative. He tucked it into his rear pocket. He helped Jenny to her feet and they floated out of the diner into the rain. He checked the test again as they crossed the street. Negative. He placed her in the passenger seat. He didn't care about the rain. He was floating. He was free.

When he got into the car, Jenny was still crying. She reached over and hugged him. She said she knew he hated her, she knew she'd lost him. She asked Mikey whether he loved her. Rain pounded onto the car.

Mikey said that he did love her, that he would always love her. He said it because it didn't matter, because she was already in his past. The whole miserable summer was just concrete that had already hardened and he had somehow escaped it and he would never let it touch him again.

THE FLY-ASS PUERTO RICAN GIRL FROM THE STAPLETON PROJECTS

BY LINDA NIEVES-POWELL

Stapleton

S he was last seen sitting on the front steps of PS14, on the Tompkins Avenue side, across the street from the New York Foundling, the place that finds homes for unwanted or abused children. The day before the Fourth of July. The old church lady with the crooked brown wig and thick glasses, who lived close enough to the Foundling to volunteer from time to time, saw her sitting there. Waiting.

The Fly-Ass Puerto Rican Girl lived in the Stapleton projects with an elderly grandmother who was always too tired, too ill, too medicated, too unlucky to hit the numbers, too stuck in her novellas to keep track of her granddaughter's whereabouts. So she had no idea that the Fly-Ass Puerto Rican Girl was the most hated girl in the hood. Unlike her daughter, her granddaughter was too perfect to live in the Stapleton projects. She was nothing like the rest of them who lived or hung around in the hood. She was different. She was like the star of that *Twilight Zone* episode where the lone gorgeous female is considered a freak among monsters.

They wanted a piece of her. And more. Dudes wanted bragging rights. "Yeah, I fucked that bitch. Hard."

Common-law wives wanted to kick her ass far out of the projects: "I will slice that bitch's throat if my man even sniffs the air around her pussy."

Little did they know that you can't break a bitch if she's already been broken. Inside.

But he and everyone else saw perfection. Outside.

That made him crazy. That made them all crazy.

He swept the grounds, unraveled the twisted swings, made sure the community pool was safe and nontoxic, tried to teach the hood kids how to use the chess tables the right way. They tried to convince him that "Boogie Nights" was on the flip side of "Always and Forever," a steal. He collected three hundred a week for eight weeks. Easy summer job. Even if he had to cover for his boss who used the Parks & Recreation uniform to impress prepubescent females who were easily impressed by any man in a uniform, no matter the rank.

No one messed with him. Everyone, including his father, seemed to know this.

"You coulda had a job workin' for Esposito, organizing shit. Instead you want to work in the fucking jungle, with the monkeys? I dare you to bring home a monkey. I dare you. I fucking dare you. Monkey-lovin' fuck."

He had just turned seventeen, like her.

So many, like his father, had it out for her. Wives, girlfriends, and ex-boyfriends stayed up at night hoping that the Fly-Ass Puerto Rican Girl from the projects would step on a needle, get hit by a Cadillac Seville, or walk into the wrong neighborhood at the wrong time. For the following reasons:

Hair too bouncy, too soft, too straight, too manageable. Skin unblemished, olive, more European than Latina. Taller than the average tall girl. The space between a set of perfect thighs, a perfect view. Her heart-shaped ass. Heart-shaped face. Full ruby-colored lips, not too plump, not too thin, like her nose that was always buried in a library book. Curves and narrow hips, more in line with Patti Hansen, the Tottenville supermodel who married a Rolling Stoner, than Iris Chacon, the big broad on Spanish television.

And she spoke English. Well.

Who the hell she think she is? She ain't better than nobody. Why she don't talk like the rest of them Puerto Ricans talk? Like Jesenia, the one with the cottage cheese thighs, the pockmarked sister who talks all half Spanish and shit. Calls dudes *papito*, says *coño* every two seconds, and eats plantains like she's making money on every one she swallows. Or Mary Poseur or Mariposa, whatever the fuck that girl's name is, who lives in 2B, or not 2B. Why she don't act like Mariposa? Mariposa talks like a real bitch talks, she blows real good, she almost black. That's how a real Stapleton bitch talks. That's how a real Staten Island bitch walks. Hunched. She walk like she got a stick up her ass. Too straight. Too white. Who the fuck she think she is?

The old woman told the detective that a white car had picked up the Fly-Ass Puerto Rican Girl from the projects. All white. White tire rims. White interior. White paint. White.

"So you're telling me you saw nothing but white?" the detective asked.

"Sir, I saw what I saw."

"Those glasses are really thick."

"But I knows what I see."

"You knows the difference between a German and Jew?"

She glanced at his badge. Esposito. She'd run into a few Espositos on Staten Island. There was Esposito's Bakery.

Esposito's Car Wash.

Esposito's Pizzeria.

Esposito's Salumeria.

Esposito's Bagel Shop.

Esposito's Car Service.

Esposito's Dry Cleaners.

Esposito's Liquor Store.

Esposito's Nursery School.

Esposito's Hardware Store.

"No sir, I don't, but I think he be Eyetalian."

"Eyetalian? You mean Italian."

"You Eyetalian?"

"It's none of your business."

"Okay, well, he looked like he could be you."

She wanted to lick her index finger to gauge the temperature in the space between them, hoping that the frigid air was biting enough to make him leave. But he pushed her down into her armchair. Accidentally. She felt a loose spring stab her in her back. Pain. Always by the hand of a man.

Mostly always white.

"Oh, I'm sorry. Let me help you." He reached out his hand.

She ignored it.

"Well, thank you for your time. If you can make it down to the precinct, we'd like for you to look at a couple of mugshots to see if you recognize anyone. Oh, wait." He flashed a mugshot he conveniently had in his pocket of a young black boy, no more than eighteen years old. "Is this him, the boy you saw?"

She shook her head.

"You sure?"

She nodded.

"Hmm, okay. Looks like you might need a new pair of glasses."

He left the front door open on his way out.

She wished that he'd trip, fall, and twist his ankle on the open cracks on the concrete steps.

When the news broke out, about how the Fly-Ass Puerto Rican Girl from the Stapleton projects was missing, most folks in the hood thought that the young nickel-bag seller had something to do with it. Everyone knew that although he and the Fly-Ass Puerto Rican Girl were kind of together, he hated the thought of a smarter, better-looking brother tapping that ass. The thought just fucked with him.

She had that kind of ass, though. The kind that once he hit it, it made him cry and he knew no other ass would ever compare. No matter how many other fly-ass girls he tapped. They were all imitations, forgeries. Her ass made a brother take a trip back to the cocoon. It was safe, warm, nurturing. No fear of pain. No fear of being rejected. No fear of having to prove his worth. It was a place where knives, guns, drugs, poverty, welfare cheese, and absent parents were as real as unicorns.

The brothers in the hood called it electromagnetic pussy vibes. But what it really was, what it really really was, was love.

That is what she threatened all of them with.

She made him fear the warmth he didn't know he yearned for. If he let go, she could undo his carefully constructed defense mechanism, his brick wall, his chip on his shoulder. Could make a brother weak. Gotta be smarter than a bitch. Tighten up. Hurt a bitch, before she hurt you.

Lucky for him, though, one of his other, not-so-fly girls assured the detective that he'd been with her the night the Fly-Ass Puerto Rican Girl from the projects disappeared.

"You don't believe me? I got a Beta tape, a little nasty, but all the evidence you need to see."

Her grandmother called the police forty-eight hours in. Not because she had been worrying. But because the gossip had landed at her dirty sandaled feet while she washed her clothes at the neighborhood laundromat.

They found the Fly-Ass Puerto Rican Girl's size-eight sandals from Kinney's in the wooded area behind Greenfield Avenue near the A&P, under the high concrete arch, the entryway to Rosebank, better known as *No Niggerland*.

Those words were painted on the highest point of the arch. In black.

A few weeks earlier, he boarded the R104 bus with some of his teammates from the Curtis High School football team, a.k.a. the offspring of the Rosebank Boys, whose reputation was equivalent to that of the KKK—sans the burning cross, since they were all devout followers of Jesus. He sat in the back of the bus. Slid the window open, stuck his hand out, and flipped the bird to the quarterback waiting for the bus to Grasmere, the town on the right side of the Staten Island Expressway. In return, he got a flip and a glob of spit on the window. That's when he saw her black hair blowing in the wind. He tapped Esposito's arm so he, too, could glimpse the girl standing on the corner. Esposito checked her out, then violently snapped his head. "You fuckin' kiddin' me, douche bag. She's a spic."

"I know, stupid. I was just playing."

"Don't fuckin' play like that. You know I heard she fucks teachers, old men, and homeless dudes for money."

"Right."

"You a nigger lover?"

"Joking, stupid."

"Yeah, well, don't say shit like that. It's bad enough your hair looks like fucking Brillo."

His father hated his hair.

"Now that's a hot babe right there!"

Esposito was pointing at Liberty. Talk about whores. Between Liberty's legs was a neon sign that read: *Enter, 24 hours a day, at your own risk*. But he wasn't one to play follow-the-leader, even if Liberty did have a bodacious rack. He wasn't interested in what Liberty had to offer.

He'd invited her into the woods, a few feet beyond the arch, the midway point, because that's where you went when you wanted to experience that thing, that thing, that thing. It would eventually become the place that would be known as the scene of the crime.

She went anyway, knowing the danger, but trusting his pretty green eyes.

He grabbed her hand and pulled her into the sharp brush. He scratched his arm trying to stop the branches from poking her eyes out or, worse, ruining her perfect skin. Finally he found the dirt path, the one that lead to the wide tree stump where young couples had carved and revised their love for one another.

She turned a full 360, taking in the dense, almost impenetrable brush, and sat next to him on the wide tree stump.

He said, "If you didn't know that there was advanced civilization just fifty feet away, you'd think you'd just stepped—"

"Onto an island," she said.

"Yeah. If you listen carefully, you can hear the ocean."

"Really?"

"Close your eyes. Use your imagination. Do you hear it? Do you hear the waves hitting the shore?"

He stared at her perfect face, moving closer to it, looking for something wrong with it. Anything to not want her.

"Not really."

"You have to listen, shhh. And keep your eyes closed."

"I hear it."

"You do?"

"Yes. I can hear ships in the distance."

"You hear ships?"

"Yes, I can see them now. Oh my god, it's the *Niña*, the *Pinta*, and the *Santa María*."

She opened one eye and waited for his laugh.

"Funny."

A rustling sounded in the bushes. He jumped up. Then stood still. Dusk had set in.

Squirrels ran past their feet and up into a tree. "Aww, how cute. We scared them," she said.

"We scared them?"

They laughed.

He'd never gotten this close to a girl like her before.

"So, how can someone as beautiful as you not have a boyfriend?" He stroked her hair and watched the strands of black silk fall between his fingers.

"I don't know."

"Can I ask you a question?"

"Why do people ask permission when they're going to say or do what they want anyway?"

He chuckled. "Why did you come here, with me?"

She rolled her eyes. "You invited me."

"That's the only reason?"

"I like you. You're different."

She took her hair back. He watched as she twirled a thick strand around her finger.

A rustling sounded in the bushes again, but this time they ignored it. As he moved in closer to her, three intruders crashed through the brush. His older brother and two others, all bored and angry, all high, circled around them. He and the Fly-Ass Puerto Rican Girl jumped up.

"What the fuck, dude? Are you fucking serious? You do know that Dad will beat your ass if he finds out about her? Come on, get your ass home now."

"I'll be home later."

"I said come home now."

"I said I'll be home later."

When his younger brother didn't follow him, he moved closer to the Fly-Ass Puerto Rican Girl, circled around her, and asked, "You live in the Stapleton projects, don't you?"

But before she could answer, his younger brother squeezed between them.

"Does Dad know you're still smoking pot?"

"*Does Dad know you're still smoking pot?*" mimicked the older brother.

The friends laughed.

"It doesn't matter, we know how to find her."

He spat at his little brother's feet. She felt some hit her open toes.

"You're dead."

The three intruders walked out of the brush and disappeared into the darkness.

"Meet me tomorrow in front of PS14," he told her.

"Okay."

"I'll pick you up. We'll take a ride and talk."

"Okay."

They walked out of the woods together, holding hands. But outside they let go. She walked north, head up high. He walked south, head down.

It was the day before the Fourth of July. Most folks were off from work and school was out. The firecrackers were going off full force in the baseball field nearby and the neighborhood deejay had successfully cold-lamped the streetlight, giving juice to his ones and twos. Everyone was in the baseball field celebrating America's birthday a few hours early. The rest of the neighborhood was empty except for the corner near PS14.

He pulled up in a Sedan DeVille. All white. He called her over. She hesitated.

The old woman with the crooked wig was across the street at the Foundling, picking up her reading glasses that she'd forgotten to take with her the last time she was there. She stood on the hill, waiting for her item to be brought to her. That's when she noticed the Fly-Ass Puerto Rican Girl sitting, then standing, then hesitating before walking toward the white car.

"Little girl walked, then she stopped. She peeked inside the car. But then she looked up. Over at me. That's the thing that always stabs me in my heart when I think about that girl. The way she looked up at me. Like she was asking if it was okay to leave. Why she get in the damn car if she wasn't sure? I wanted to yell out, *Baby girl, don't trust it!* But it was like it was meant for her to leave cause I sure couldn't do nothing for her from where I was standing."

That's what the old woman told her pastor, over and over again.

Thirty years later, he came back. Leaving his apartment outside of New York, he connected to the R train toward South Ferry to attend his father's funeral. He hadn't been on the island since leaving for college, then joining the service, then opening up his software business.

Though he had a car, he took the ferry. He knew that he would never come back and he wanted to see everything for the last time, in the way he had remembered, by bus.

He boarded what was now the S52 bus with the other Saturday-morning riders. First stop, the bus shelter in St. George.

When the doors opened, three teens boarded. Maybe two

were Ecuadorian, possibly Honduran or Peruvian, the other blond, maybe Albanian, maybe Russian, but definitely not Italian. One was wearing a red, white, and blue T-shirt of an African-American presidential hopeful. Another boy was holding a skateboard, talking about a professional skateboard champion, the son of a Mexican comedian who beat the hell out of the white boy. They all spoke English.

Well.

A conversation like that, thirty years ago, could have cost you your life. Now it was small talk.

He watched the neighborhoods morph into hoods, then back into neighborhoods, then back into hoods. What was once a Burger King was now a variety of places to eat, a Sri Lankan restaurant, a Dominican luncheonette, a West African coffee shop. As the bus made its way closer to Stapleton, he took in all that was there and all that had changed. The small post office across from the train station was gone, the Genovese was now a Rite Aid, C-Town was now Western Beef, and the White Castle that sprung out of nothing, in the middle of nowhere, had moved closer to the motorcycle shop. New African-owned shops replaced some of the old African-American-owned shops and the Paramount Theater was still standing strong. Steckman's, the place that made him his number 76 football uniform, was no longer in business.

The bus turned the corner near the best pizza on the North Shore and the three boys started talking about girls. In the distance he could see PS14. He put his head down, holding onto the cold silver bar, and waited for the nausea to pass.

Her body was never found. On days he felt nostalgic, he would search for her name on the Internet, just to see what he could find. But what he found were similar names living different lives.

"Yo, check it out."

"What?"

One of the boys pointed outside the window.

He looked out and saw a beautiful girl, very familiar, not your average pretty, sitting alone on the steps.

Waiting.

"Who is she?"

"I don't know her name but isn't she that fly-ass Mexican girl from the Stapleton projects?"

He glanced at the girl again, then closed his eyes for a few stops, trying to stop the images of his past from flooding his mind.

The bus continued south on Tompkins Avenue, past the arch—the old midway point. He got up, rang the bell, and turned back to glance at the young teens taunting each other as they played video game battles on their cell phones, before he exited the bus. He stood on the corner of St. Mary's and Tompkins Avenue watching as the bus drove the boys toward the right side of the Staten Island Expressway.

Time had changed some things. But the memory of her would haunt him forever.

TEENAGE WASTELAND

BY ASHLEY DAWSON

Tottenville

The crowd started throwing shit at the stage when the band lit into "Heart of Glass." Angry chants of "Disco sucks!" bounced off the low roof, cutting through the percolating synth rhythms and lush purr of Blondie. Sunny hopped up and down, bouncing in time to the music and catching glimpses of Debbie Harry and her band dodging gum, spit, bottles, and various other projectiles. What was the band thinking, she wondered, performing this disco version of their song at CBGB's, the mothership of punk music in NYC?

The crowd surged ominously toward the stage. Sunny felt the song's beat all the way down in her stomach, felt its rhythms transporting her through the skyscraper jungle of Manhattan like an elevated subway on speed, but she realized how sacrilegious the band was being with this new, amped-up version of "Heart of Glass." Her magic Manhattan carpet ride got bumpy as she collided in midair with Totò, her cousin, who was bouncing even higher than her and yelling through the din at Jimmy Destri. Blondie's keyboard player, Destri was one of the prime movers steering the band toward the electro-sound that was shaking their bones silly.

Sunny and Totò had grown up running into the older Destri, whose given name was James Mollica, on hot summer days in Brooklyn. Standing onstage with his hair coiffed in a Beatlesesque New Wave mop, he didn't look much like the

Jimmy Mollica she'd seen drenched in sweat, hauling the towering Giglio statue of the Madonna of Mt. Carmel through the streets of Williamsburg with a hundred or so other guys, but she still felt some kind of loyalty to him. Besides, there were Totò's feelings to consider. Pogoing there beside her, he was all smiles. Who really cared whether Blondie was playing punk or disco? All that mattered was that she and Totò were dancing together at CBGB's, in the heart of the East Village. At seventeen, they were finally making it out of Staten Island, just like Jimmy Destri had escaped from Brooklyn. Fleeing the island's claustrophobic suburbs, messed-up families, and time-capsule fashion sense. About time, Sunny thought.

Later, as the ferry carried them home across the dark waters of the harbor, Totò's enthusiasm for the band's new direction bubbled over.

"Ain't Jimmy's new synth cool? Sounds just like Kraftwerk!"

"Yeah, I guess," Sunny replied, "but I kinda miss the anger."

"Whad'ya mean, the anger? There's loads of anger in stuff like 'Heart of Glass.' It's all about being screwed by a boyfriend."

"I know, but Debbie Harry don't exactly sound angry," Sunny said. "She sings like she's a freaky robot or something."

"Yeah, okay, but that's the whole point, ain't it? I mean, she's been screwed over so much that she's kinda hollow inside."

"Maybe, but I figure Blondie is just trying to cash in. Next thing they're gonna be singing 'Stayin' Alive.'"

"That's total bull. Besides, disco gets a bad rap. It's not all about dickheads like Tony Manero . . ."

"Yeah, the other night I saw the Corleones at Studio 54."

"Oh, fuck you," Totò said with a grin, "you can't swallow all that Hollywood crap. There's a whole lot going on that those assholes don't know nuthin' about."

"You're only saying that cuz ya got a crush on Jimmy Destri."

Totò made a grab for Sunny, who was already convulsed with giggles. She slid quickly down the graffiti-scarred wooden bench, leaving Totò pummeling the air. Overcome with laughter, the two splayed out on the hard seats of the sparsely populated night ferry. Totò's laugh suddenly turned into a sputtering cough, which shifted into a wracking paroxysm.

"What the fuck, Totò, what's the matter with you?" Sunny gasped.

Too convulsed to reply, Totò staggered toward the bathroom. Sunny caught up with him and stuck her head under his arm to offer support. The two lurched into one of the open stalls of the men's room; Totò put his head down and started puking.

"Fuckin' kids these days," a wino pissing in an adjoining stall groused.

"Eat me, asshole!" Sunny yelled back, as she held Totò's head over the filthy john.

Gradually the shudders that had wracked Totò's body died down. When he'd recovered enough to stand up in front of a sink and splash cold water on his face, Sunny turned on him.

"What the hell's the matter with you, Totò?"

"I dunno. I ain't been feeling so hot lately. But it ain't what you think. Ever since Vito died, I swear I been off the stuff."

"You better not be lying to me, Totò."

"No, I swear, it's something else, like I can't breathe. Maybe I shouldn't go in the clubs no more, but I swear I can't smell nothing in there, cigarettes or anything, my nostrils been so eaten up by the shit smell waftin' off the dump."

Just then, a crackling metallic voice announced that the ferry was about to dock at Staten Island.

"Yeah," Sunny replied, "it's a bitch livin' in the city's asshole."

* * *

The next morning, Sunny's dad pounded loudly on her bedroom door.

"Annunziata Cacciatore, you get your ass up outta bed. I don't care if you stayed up all night, you still gotta come to mass. Jesus Christ, it's Pasqua!"

"Va fan' culo, Dad. It's too friggin' early!"

"Jesus! If it weren't Easter I'd smack you upside your head so hard. You get your ass outta bed and get some clothes on, Annunziata. And I don't want you wearing no dog collar, neither! Get some decent clothes on for a change."

Sunny dragged herself out of bed and over to her closet. There wasn't much in there that wasn't black or leather. Her dad would flip out if she wore any of her street clothes to church, but she wasn't about to go dressed like she was heading to her First Communion. Or, on second thought, maybe that was exactly the look she wanted.

Sunny pulled her old communion dress out of her closet and over her head. Not half bad, she thought, looking in the mirror. The white lace trim on her dress suggested a virgin innocence completely at odds with her tightly sheathed body. I like to keep them on their toes, she thought, without really thinking who the *them* was.

Sunny was lithe and tall like a boy, and scared off most Staten Island guys with her ripped-up clothes and Dr. Martens. She teased her black hair up into a billowing Siouxsie Sioux coif, layered white foundation over her face, and finished things off with a thick smear of coal-dark eyeliner.

Her dad was just finishing his breakfast when Sunny came down the stairs. His mouth dropped open.

"Madonna! There's no way you're going to church like that, young lady."

"Whaaat! But Dad, it's my communion dress."

"I know, but that was four years ago. You're busting out all over it."

Sunny gnashed her teeth. Her dad was getting more conservative every year. It was as if he wanted to take all his anger at the counterculture of the last ten years out on his daughter, grinding her down into a Catholic schoolgirl Barbie doll. Life with him was becoming impossible.

Seeing Sunny smoldering, her dad called for backup: "Toni, get a load a this!"

Sunny's mom stuck her head into the kitchen. "O Dio!" she blurted out. "You look ridiculous. But we don't have any more time. We gotta hurry up or we'll miss the procession."

"No way. I'm not taking my daughter out looking like that."

"We don't have time to argue, Pippo. Senti, we gotta go now or we won't make it."

"Non mi frega, Toni, there's no way in hell we're gonna take Annunziata to church dressed like some kinda puttana."

He grew more and more red in the face as he argued with his wife. Sunny was left standing in the middle of the room while the two of them argued backward and forward, their voices rising and their vocabulary veering toward scatological Italian. In the middle of a tirade about his honor as a father that involved multiple references to his dick, Pippo suddenly choked and began coughing. Hacks wracking his body, he lurched toward the bathroom.

"Che cazzo, Pippo?" Sunny's mom yelled. "What the hell's da matta with you? This is the third time this week. Get your ass outta that bathroom."

"What's going on, Mom?"

"I don't know, Sunny, he's been coughing and getting sick for a few weeks now. You know him, though, of course he's trying to act like it ain't nuthin'."

"Wow, that's exactly the same thing that happened last night to Totò."

"Your cousin Totò is into some bad stuff. I'm not surprised he's sick."

"That's not fair, Mom. Totò doesn't do that anymore. Besides, last night he said he thought it might have something to do with the stink off the dump. Maybe dad got sick from the same smell."

"Look, Sunny, that's ridiculous. Your dad puts on a mask every time he goes to work. He couldn't smell a raw onion if you held it right in front of his nose. Besides, I'm gonna kill Pippo long before the Fresh Kills cough gets 'im. Pippo," she yelled, "you get your ass outta that bathroom! We're gonna miss communion at this rate and I ain't gonna burn in hell cuz of you!"

Around midnight, Sunny woke to a rain of pebbles on her window. She pulled on a leather jacket, slid down a drainpipe, and followed Totò into the dark alleyway behind her house.

In a heavy whisper, Totò told her the news: "My dad said he heard something's going on over at Fresh Kills. When I tol' him I been feeling bad lately, he said lots of other people been sick too. But I couldn't get him to say anythin' else, he just got real sad and stared off into space an' shit. I say we check the place out. You in?"

Sunny still remembered how confused she'd been as a young girl when Totò's dad Enzo started growing his hair out long. Enzo went over to Vietnam a year after his older brother, but he came back earlier and even more messed up in the head than her dad. Sunny's dad and Enzo had long shouting matches about 'Nam. Eventually, they stopped talking to one another entirely.

When Totò and his brother Vito were younger, their dad

would often be gone, traveling around the country protesting the war. After the troops came home, Enzo still wouldn't settle down. He kept his hair long and refused to take a job working for the city like her dad and so many other men on Staten Island. He was unemployed for a long time, his wife left him, and Totò and Vito spent a lot of time with their grandparents. Totò went through a rough patch, and his brother Vito went completely off the rails. But now Enzo owned a small guitar shop and was trying to make things right with Totò.

"Yeah, sure, I'm in," she said.

It was a chilly night, winter not yet having loosed its grip on the city. The moon was scudding between clouds, casting a silver light on the leafless trees. It looked like a thin coat of snow had just fallen on the island. Totò and Sunny walked away from her pale blue two-story house in Tottenville, down Lighthouse Avenue, and then cut off the road and headed across the Jewish cemetery toward Fresh Kills Landfill.

Sunny's dad had worked for the Department of Sanitation for years, so she knew something about the history of garbage on the island. Fresh Kills was opened after World War II. It was only supposed to stay open for twenty years, but dumping is a hard habit to kick. Fresh Kills was still accepting hundreds of tons of garbage every day. It seemed like her dad had a job for life at the dump.

As they climbed through the jagged teeth of the chain-link fence that surrounded the place, Sunny whispered to Totò, "Ya gotta watch your ass. There's packs of wild dogs on the hunt at night in here."

"Yeah, lots of fresh-killed meat around here, I guess."

"No, wise-ass, that name means the place was filled with fresh creeks."

"Ain't too fresh no more."

"No shit, Sherlock."

"Oh man, it stinks!"

"Yeah, shit buried in Fresh Kills don't stay underground for very long," Sunny said.

"Hey, I think I hear something."

As they climbed over a rise in the rolling landscape created by decades of accumulated garbage, Sunny and Totò were blinded by a half-moon of arc lights. When their eyes had adjusted, they saw a couple of huge yellow bulldozers moving across the reeking piles of waste like giant prehistoric insects. The stench was overwhelming, hitting like a swift kick to the head.

"What're they doin' workin' here at night?" Sunny whispered.

"Looks to me like they're digging holes."

"Oh yeah, you're right, but what the hell for?"

Sunny and Totò crouched and looked down into the garbage valley until their legs as well as their lungs were ready to give. Just as they were about to walk back down toward the fenced-off perimeter of the dump, a truck came rumbling up the access road, its running lights a piercing red in the near total darkness. It pulled off the road and headed toward the brilliant circle of light where the bulldozers were at work. Sunny and Totò held their breath as the truck pulled up alongside one of the holes dug by the bulldozers. The bed of the truck cantilevered slowly into the air, and some sort of dense liquid began pouring out into the hole. The acrid smell of garbage, which had begun to recede as their senses grew accustomed to the reek, became overpowering. It was as if someone had flung acid into their faces.

After the truck had emptied all its foul liquid into the hole, one of the bulldozers pulled up with a jerky motion and began to push piles of garbage into the hole, gradually burying the sludge under a mountain of junk. All evidence of the truck's dark contents was soon obliterated.

Communicating with hand gestures, Totò and Sunny turned away from the infernal scene and headed back toward the hole in the fence through which they'd entered Fresh Kills. As they walked back across the cemetery, their lungs filled with relatively clean air.

"What the fuck's going on, Sunny?"

"I dunno. I don't get why they're dumping shit at night, and why they're bringing it in trucks. Usually all the garbage comes in on barges during the day."

"Whatever that shit was, it stank even worse than the rest of the dump."

"Yeah, that's the truth. Must be some evil stuff."

"Just thinking about it makes me wanna start pukin' again."

"My dad's been coughing too."

"What're we gonna do about this, Sunny?"

"I dunno, Totò, I dunno. You think I should talk to my dad?"

"Well, he works at the dump, right? Perhaps he knows about what's going on at night."

"Yeah, and even if he don't, maybe he can find something out. Okay, I'll talk to him."

The next morning, Sunny crawled out of bed at what felt like the crack of dawn. Her dad was busy putting on his heavy overalls when she stuck her head into her parents' bedroom. Sensing her presence, Pippo stopped dressing and turned toward his daughter.

"You going to school today dressed in your pajamas or what?" he said, an amused glint in his eye.

"Nah, Dad, I still gotta get ready for school. I wanted to talk to you about something."

"O Dio! Don't tell me you're pregnant."

"Naah, course I ain't pregnant! I wanted to talk to you about Fresh Kills. Some kids told me that they heard weird noises coming from the dump at night. And it's been stinking even worse than usual recently. You know about something strange going on there?"

Pippo's dark eyes flashed, all signs of amusement suddenly draining out of his face.

"Sit down, Annunziata."

Oh shit, Sunny thought. Now I'm really gonna get it. He's gonna take out all his shit on me, as usual. Don't dress that way, don't listen to that crap music, don't cut Sunday school.

It was worse than the Ten Commandments. Ever since her dad came back from Vietnam, he'd been obsessed with how he and his buddies who stayed to fight the gooks had been betrayed by the hippies and his sack-of-shit brother. He lashed out at anyone who questioned the hell he'd gone through and the sacrifices he'd made. Now that Sunny was no longer a cute little innocent kid, he was starting to see her as in league with the Great Betrayal as well.

"No, there's nothing strange going on at the dump," Pippo said. "I been working there for twenty years, and the place reeks worse every year. After a while, though, you don't smell it too much. So don't worry about me or Fresh Kills."

"Yeah, but Dad, it's not just you that's sick. Totò and a bunch of other people are getting sick. Shouldn't we do something if the dump is leaking poison into the neighborhood?"

"Listen, Annunziata: I don't want you nosing around there, okay? It's not just that the place stinks. Fresh Kills is like an iceberg. There's a lot more to it than meets the eye. You don't want to start digging up trouble. That's an order. Stai zitta, capisci?"

"Okay, Dad, I hear you," Sunny replied. She did her best to put on a sweet smile as she stood up to walk out of the bedroom. I shoulda known it's no use talking to him, she thought. Never question authority—that should be her dad's motto. He's just like all the other idiots on this island, Sunny thought. A buncha sheep. 'Cept he's worse: he probably knows how fucked up the situation is, but he's too chicken to do anything about it.

"Wha'd he say?" Totò asked when Sunny arrived at the playground, where they and the other students of Tottenville High waited before the first bell rang, summoning them to morning assembly. He, Sunny, and the rest of the punks always hung out in a corner of the playground as far away as possible from the other kids, with their elaborately blow-dried Farrah Fawcett and Leif Garrett hairstyles, their atrocious leisure clothes, and their spine-chilling love of the Bee Gees.

"He told me to shut up about Fresh Kills."

"Wha?"

"Yeah, he said there wasn't anything funny going on there, and that I should stop talking about it."

"No way. But what about his cough?"

"I get the feeling he's scared of something. It's like he knows something's up, but he don't wanna let on."

"I hate to say this, Sunny, but maybe there's a reason he ain't talking. Maybe he ain't scared. Maybe he's on the take."

"What're you talking about, Totò?"

"I mean, don't get offended or nothing, but we both know that the garbage biz is pretty mobbed up."

"No, Totò, he can't be a part of that."

"Look, I ain't saying he's a made man. I mean, you know how things work around here. You wanna keep your job or your business, you gotta learn to be a little cooperative. Sometimes you gotta learn to look the other way, or to take a little kick-back that makes you part of the whole thing. You get dirty once, and you can't never get clean."

"I can't fucking believe it. If he did that, then he's even more of a jerk than I figured he was."

Maybe this was the explanation for the glint of fear she'd seen in her dad's eyes. Maybe he was terrified of what was going on at Fresh Kills, but also part of it. While the thought didn't make her feel much more sympathetic toward her dad, it did make her really angry. Who, she wanted to know, was screwing around with her dad? Whoever it was, they were victimizing not just her dad, not just her family, but Totò and the rest of the people living near Fresh Kills too.

"Listen, Totò, I wanna find out what the fuck's going on at Fresh Kills. I don't care what my dad says. Can you meet me again tonight?"

"Sure thing, Sunny."

"What about a car? Can you get us a car?"

"Yeah, I think my dad will probably lend me his. But we better not fuck it up. He'll fucking kill me. He don't give a shit about most things, but he really loves his Camaro. We ain't gonna take it into Fresh Kills, are we?"

"No, Totò, we ain't going driving through the dump. I wanna find out where those trucks are coming from."

That night, Totò parked his dad's Camaro on a dark stretch of Arthur Kill Road near one of the main feeder roads to the dump. He and Sunny slumped down in the seats and waited for something to happen.

"Hey, Starsky," Sunny said eventually, wiping some of the fog that was accumulating on the windows off with her sleeve, "it's starting to get cold in this fuckin' jalopy of yours."

"Yeah, I don't know 'bout you, Huggy Bear, but I'm getting cold *and* sleepy."

"We been sitting here for hours. Detective work ain't all it's cracked up to be."

"Right on, I'm bored stiff."

"Yeah, me too."

They sat for another hour or so, their shivers the only thing keeping them from drifting off to sleep. Suddenly, Totò snapped awake.

"Hey, Sunny, wake up, I see some headlights."

"Oh shit, you're right. It's one of the trucks. Start the fucking car. No, wait, don't start it. Wait until the truck goes by."

"Make up your mind, why don'cha?"

Totò turned the ignition key but kept the Camaro's lights off. The truck pulled out of the feeder road and onto Arthur Kill Road. Totò turned the lights on and drove off after the truck, which was headed toward the expressway.

"Don't get too close to them, okay, Totò?"

"Course not. Hey, check it out, they've got outta-state plates."

"Holy shit, you're right. So whatever they've been dumping, it ain't from around here."

"Jesus."

"Yeah, looks like we're not just the asshole of New York City. Looks like someone else is shitting on us too."

As Totò followed the truck up onto the narrow steel span of the Goethals Bridge, the industrial landscape of northeastern New Jersey rolled out before their eyes. A fairyland of glinting white lights sprang up in front of them as they sped toward the oil refineries and tank farms clustered along the shoreline of Elizabeth. Driving down the far side of the bridge, they could make out a forest of snaking pipes running for miles through the refineries, illuminated by twinkling lights strung along every inch of them, as if to demonstrate to the heavens how much energy they could pump out. Above it all hung many tongues of blue flame, burning off waste gases and belching fire and smoke into the atmosphere.

"Holy crap, looks like Christmas in hell," Sunny whispered.

"Amen, sister."

"I had no idea that we lived near all this shit."

"Me neither."

The truck barreled along the densely intertwined roads leading to the New Jersey Turnpike. Just before hitting the highway, it took a sharp right and drove down a small backstreet near the entrance to the sprawling port. The truck turned into a large lot surrounded by a high fence, to which were affixed neat white signs emblazoned with blue letters: *Refinement International*.

"Whadda we do now?" Totò asked as he pulled the car over down the block from the lot.

"I say we try to find out more about what they been dumping," Sunny replied.

"You crazy or what?"

"Well, you just wanna go home after we came all this way?"

"Okay, okay, but don't tell me I didn't warn ya."

They got out of the car and walked along the fence. It was impossible to see through the canvas that covered the wire mesh. There was a gate at the entrance through which the truck had driven; it was still open. There, on the other side of the lot, was the truck. Sunny and Totò looked around the yard but couldn't see anybody. After watching awhile, they decided that the driver must have gone into the office building, which stood on the opposite side of the yard.

After a quick whispered consultation, Sunny and Totò headed over to the truck. Totò went around to peek into the cab while Sunny looked into the back of it. They had just met up on the far side of the truck and were about to head back out of the lot when a loud voice stopped them in their tracks.

"Who the fuck are you and what're you doing here?"

Two men were moving fast toward them from the office building. The one who had spoken was big and burly, and was dressed in a suit.

"We ain't doing nothing, mister," Totò blurted out. "We was just looking for a place to be alone."

"*Just looking for a place to be alone*, huh? You planning on getting some action tonight, huh? Well, let's take a look at your girlfriend."

The two men were now standing right in front of them. The suit walked up to within a foot of Sunny while his partner, a short guy dressed in jeans and a nylon jacket, hung back.

"Oh man, she's pretty weird looking. What's with the spiky hair? You put your finger in an electric socket or something, sweetheart? And why're you dressed like a boy? Not very attractive, I must say, but I bet your pussy is still sweet. Say, my friend, I'm sure you wouldn't mind sharing some of that sweet poontang, now, would you? What you think, Joe, shall we sample this funky thing's merchandise?"

"Sure thing, boss," the short guy said, "even if she is kinda scrawny."

Totò lost it and made a run at the suit, who saw him coming and punched him hard in the stomach. Totò reeled backward, into the arms of the suit's partner, who grabbed him from behind, threw him onto the ground, and started delivering a series of thudding punches to his head.

"Now, where was I before I was so rudely interrupted?" the

suit said, as he advanced toward Sunny. "Oh yes, I was speaking admiringly of your pussy. I'm sure you don't want to disappoint my great expectations, do you now? So, let's get down to business, shall we?"

Sunny stood still, paralyzed by fear. But just as he reached her, she yelled "Stronzo!" with eardrum-popping volume and swung her steel-capped Dr. Marten–clad foot up into his knee-cap. The suit screamed out in pain and toppled over. Sunny stepped back and delivered another carefully aimed kick to his stomach. The suit's high-pitch screeching turned into a deep groan.

Sunny wheeled around just in time to see Totò leap onto the back of the short guy, who had stopped punching him and was coming over to help his boss. Totò couldn't see much since his eyes were already swelling up from the punches, but he did momentarily distract the guy. Sunny cocked her leg back and delivered one more kick, this one straight to the man's groin. He howled and crumpled to the ground.

Sunny grabbed Totò by the hand and dragged him out of the yard and down the street. As they approached the Camaro, she grabbed the keys out of his pocket, pushed Totò into the passenger seat, climbed in, and gunned the car's engine. They took off back toward Staten Island in a screech of burning tires.

"Oh fuck, they sure kicked the shit outta me," Totò moaned as they flew back across the Goethals Bridge. "But I gotta hand it to you, you really saved my ass."

"Don't mention it. Those assholes really had it coming to 'em. They didn't even know what we was doing and they still wanted to fuck us up!"

"Fuck *you* up, more like it."

"Well, they won't be trying that stunt again anytime soon."

"Yeah, you were so cool! They really picked the wrong

chick to fuck with. Watch out, muthafuckas: she's got DMs and she ain't afraid to use 'em. So cool! Oh shit, I'm bleeding all over my dad's car. He's gonna fuck me up even worse than those guys did."

"Don't sweat it, Totò. I'll explain to him. I have proof that we weren't just fuckin' around. Check this out!"

Sunny took a small plastic container out of her jacket.

"What the fuck's that? You gonna show him that you been eating yogurt for your diet or something?" Totò quipped, and groaned as his joke brought a painful smile to his face.

"No, dipshit, I scooped some of the liquid from the back of that truck into this yogurt container. This is all the evidence we need to bust those sons a bitches."

"Jesus! Nice move, Sunny, but get that shit away from me."

Two days later, Sunny was standing in the usual corner of the playground waiting for the morning assembly bell to ring. Today she was alone. She didn't feel like shooting the bull with the other kids. Debate about the merits of Patti Smith's collaboration with Springsteen on *Easter* or even about the death of Sid Vicious, so significant just a week ago, seemed pretty tame in comparison with what she'd been going through. Like a giant toxic whirlpool, Staten Island had sucked Sunny back in, but it left her even more alienated from everyone around her than before.

And Totò was still out of school. His dad had been pretty cool about the blood in his car when they explained what they'd found at the dump. Turned out he was actually pretty worried about Totò's cough, and angry at the authorities for not doing anything. Typical fucked-up way they treat people, he'd said. Then he started railing at the government for dropping Agent Orange on the Vietnamese and dumping heroin and other shit here in the States. Damn, he really is like the complete opposite of my dad, Sunny thought. But Enzo didn't have any good ideas about who to turn to. And Totò wouldn't be back in circulation for a week or so while the bruises on his face healed.

Sunny's fear that the suit from Jersey would track her down somehow was starting to fade, but she was still feeling really jumpy. She had all the evidence that she needed to bust Refinement International, or whoever was behind it, but she didn't have any way to figure out what was really in that yogurt container, which she'd been keeping at the back of the fridge, hoping none of her family would accidentally eat it. And even if she could figure out what that pungent black liquid was, who could she tell about it? Even if her dad wasn't involved in any way, Totò was probably right that the local authorities in the Department of Sanitation were on the take. Despite having come so far in such a short time, Sunny felt totally stuck.

The assembly bell rang and Sunny started toward the school auditorium for another day of mindless tedium. She hadn't gone more than a few steps, though, when she felt a tap on her shoulder. She turned and found a man in a dark suit and tie standing a few feet away from her. No, not the same suit, not the same guy, she thought. The man smiled at her.

"Hello, Annunziata. I'm a friend of your dad's. I and my associates would like you to talk to you about what you've been up to lately."

"Do I have any choice?"

"No, mi dispiace, cara, you don't."

Sunny walked slowly over toward the black car indicated by her dad's "friend."

The two got in and drove in silence for about fifteen minutes. Sunny tried to sit like a statue as her mind flipped backward and forward between white-hot rage and blind terror.

Come what may, she wasn't going to let this asshole see what was going on inside her.

After the car pulled up outside a place called Joe and Pat's Pizzeria, the guy in the black suit took her into the joint and led her over to a table near the window, where another man, also wearing a suit, was sitting. He pulled out a chair for her and asked if she'd like something to eat or drink. Sunny declined and sat waiting to hear some sort of explanation. The driver strolled out of the store.

The man who'd been waiting for her in the pizzeria began: "Hello, Annunziata. My name's Rocco. I'm a friend of your dad's. You don't need to know anything more about me. But I want to know more about you. I hear you've been doing some investigations at the dump recently?"

"Did my dad tell you about this?" Sunny asked, her anger barely in check.

"No, but we have our ways of getting information about matters in the community."

"Okay," Sunny said, knowing that it wouldn't make much sense to lie about the basics, "I found out that a lot of people in my neighborhood were getting sick. I figured it might be related to Fresh Kills somehow, so I checked it out one night. What's it to you?"

"I'm askin' the questions for now, Annunziata. What did you find during your investigation?"

"I saw some trucks dumping stuff."

"That's all you know?"

"Yeah, that's all I know at the moment, Rocco. Why do you care?"

"Let's just say that it's a matter of territorial integrity, Annunziata."

"What?"

"My associates and I like to take care of the people who take care of us. We don't like anyone else comin' in an' messin' with La Cosa Nostra, with our people and our business, if you understand me. We got wind recently that someone has been dumpin' somethin' at Fresh Kills. Bad stuff. Really bad stuff. Cyanide, naphthalene, and all kinds of other very unhealthy chemicals. Now, we like to think of Fresh Kills as part of *our* garden, even if the rest of New York City believes it belongs to them. We admit, there's a lot of unpleasant material in that garden of ours. But there are limits. And we like to make sure those limits are properly observed, you get me?"

"Sure," Sunny replied, "I get you."

"So we want to know who's behind this dumpin'. We don't know yet, but we heard that you might know. Is that true, Annunziata?"

Sunny's heart leaped into her throat. How much did these guys really know? Were they wise to her trip to Elizabeth? She decided to gamble.

"Well, I saw that the trucks had outta-state license plates."

"And that's all you know?"

"Yeah, that's all I know."

"Okay, but just in case you learn anything else, let me leave you my number. Remember, Annunziata, we're only trying to protect you and the other good people of this island."

"Thanks, Rocco. I'll be in touch if I find out anything else."

"Va bene, Annunziata. Ma stai attenta, be careful. Garbage is a dangerous business."

"So I've heard."

Rocco got up and sauntered out of the pizzeria, leaving Sunny staring at the opposite wall. What the hell was she going to do? Had her dad ratted her out because of some kind of twisted desire to protect her? Should she confide in these genteel thugs? The idea of turning to them to save the neighborhood from the shit at Fresh Kills was ludicrous. After all, they were the ones who helped make sure the place stayed open all these years in the first place. But where else could she turn?

As her thoughts became increasingly agitated, her eyes slowly came to focus on a headline in a copy of the *New York Times* lying on a nearby table: *Love Canal Is Extra Tough on Children*. She walked over to the table, sat down, and began to read. The article told the story of a toxic waste dump in upstate New York. Local authorities had built a school on top of land sold to them by a chemical company, and now kids from the community were starting to get sick. Local women were having miscarriages and giving birth to kids with horrible defects. The article talked about a housewife, Lois Gibbs, who'd demanded that the government pay for people to be relocated from homes built near the dump. When she got no response, she started organizing the community. Gibbs, the article said, had held government officials hostage, feeding them milk and cookies for days and demanding that they release information about the waste buried in the community. She'd even formed an organization to push for what she called environmental justice. She was a real fighter.

Sunny looked up from the paper. Her mind gradually settled. She knew where she was going to send her toxic waste.

LIGHTHOUSE

BY S.J. ROZAN

St. George

I t sucked to be him.

Paul huffed and wheezed up Lighthouse Avenue, pumping his bony legs and wiping sweat from his face. His thighs burned and his breath rasped but he knew better than to ask if he could stop. One more uphill block, he figured, then he'd turn and head back down. That would be okay. That would take him past the mark one more time, even though there wasn't much to see from the street. A wall with a couple of doors, a chain-link fence, raggedy bright flags curling in the autumn breeze. The building itself, the little museum, nestled into the hillside just below. Paul didn't really have to see it. He didn't have to do this run at all, truth be told. He'd been there a bunch of times, inside, in that square stone room. He used to go just to stand in the odd cool stillness, just to look at those peculiar statues with all their arms and their fierce eyes. Long time ago, of course, before The Guys came, but the place hadn't changed and he already knew all he had to know about it. Alarm, yes; dog, no. Most important, people in residence: no.

He kept climbing, closing in on the end of the block. Paul liked it here. Lighthouse Hill was easy pickings.

It always had been, back from when he was a kid. The first B&E he pulled, he boosted a laptop from the pink house on Edinboro. Years ago, but he remembered. The planning, the job, his slamming heart. The swag. Everything.

It was good he did, because The Guys liked to hear about it. While he was planning a job they liked to help, and then when it was done they liked to hear the story over and over. Even though they'd been there. They wanted him to compare each job to other jobs so they could point out dumb things he did, and stuff that went right. That used to piss Paul off, how they made him go over everything a million times. Turned out, though, it was pretty worthwhile to listen to them, even though in the beginning he'd wondered what a bunch of stupid aliens knew about running a B&E. He was right about Roman too. Roman really was stupid. He never knew anything about anything. Paul had to be careful when and where he said that, even just thought it, because if Roman was listening he could do that kick thing and give Paul one of those sonuvabitch headaches. There was a way he'd found where he could sometimes think about stuff, sort of sideways and not using words, and The Guys didn't notice. But the thing was, even if Roman did catch Paul thinking about how stupid he was, it didn't matter; it was still true.

Larry and Stoom, though, they were pretty sharp. "You mean, for aliens?" Stoom asked once, with that sneer he always had. Paul thought for sure he was curling his lip, like in a cartoon. That was how he knew they must have lips, because of Stoom's sneer. Stoom was the only one who still used his alien name, and he was the nastiest (but not as pig-eyed mean as Roman). He was always ragging on Paul, telling him what a loser he was.

"Then why'd you pick me?" Paul yelled back once, a long time ago. "I didn't invite you. Why don't you just go the fuck back where you came from?"

Stoom said it was none of his business and then *whammo*, the headache.

But as far as the sharp-for-aliens thing, Stoom and Larry were actually pretty sharp for anybody. It was Larry who suggested Paul do his preliminary reconnaissance ("Casing the joint!" Roman bawled. "Call it casing the joint!") in sweats, jogging past a place a couple of times, at different hours. That was good for a whole bunch of reasons. For one thing, Larry was right: no one noticed a jogger, except other joggers, who were only interested in sizing you up, figuring if they were better or you were better. If they could take you. Of course, if it came to it, any of them could take Paul and he knew it. Real runners were all muscle and sinew. Paul looked like them, lanky, with short hair and sunken cheeks, but his skinniness was blasted out of what he used to be, drained by junk. As though the needles in his arm had been day by day drawing something out instead of pumping it in.

But he still laced up his running shoes and made himself circle whatever neighborhood it was, every time he was ready to plan a job. Which was pretty much every time the rent was due or the skag ran out. Even if he had the whole job ready to go in his head and didn't need to, like now, he still ran the streets around it. For one thing, The Guys liked that he did it this way, and as awful as the wheezing and the fire in his legs were, the headaches when they got mad were always worse.

Another thing: suiting up and going by a couple times over a couple days stretched out the planning part. That was Paul's favorite. He liked to learn stuff about his marks: who they were, how they lived, what they liked to do.

"Oh, please," said Stoom, about that. He sounded like he was rolling his eyes, though Paul didn't know if they had eyes, either. He'd asked once, what they looked like, but that turned out to be another thing that was none of his business. "You're a crook," Stoom went on. "You're a junkie. You're a loser with aliens in your head. All you need to know about people is what they have and when they won't be home."

"Maybe he wants to write a book about them," Larry suggested, in a bored and mocking voice. "Maybe he's going to be a big best-selling author."

That had burned Paul up, because that was exactly what he'd wanted before The Guys showed up. He always had an imagination; he was going to grow up and be a writer.

He never talked about The Guys anymore. He had, at first. It took him awhile to figure out no one else could hear them and everyone thought he was nuts. "There are no aliens, Paul. It's all in your head. You need to get help." Stuff like that.

Well, that first point, that was completely wrong. Paul used to argue, say obvious things like, "You can't see time either, but no one says it isn't there." All people did was stare and back away, so he stopped saying anything.

The second point, though, was completely right. That's where The Guys lived: in Paul's head. Where they'd beamed when they came to earth on some kind of scouting mission, Paul didn't know what for. Or from where. They never did tell him why, but Stoom had told him from where. It's just, it was some planet he'd never heard of circling some star he'd never heard of in some galaxy really, *really* far away. *Magribke* was the closest Paul could come to pronouncing it. The Guys laughed at him when he said it that way, but they didn't tell him how to really say it. They didn't talk about their home planet much. Mostly, they just told Paul the Loser what to do.

They first showed up when he was fourteen. He supposed he'd been a peculiar kid—God knows his mom always thought so—but he wasn't a loser then. ("Oh, of course you were," Stoom said, but Paul knew he was wrong.) It was them, making him do weird shit, distracting him so he started flunking out, giving him those kick headaches—they were the ones who screwed him all up.

And the third point, get help? He'd tried. What did people think, he liked it like this, these bastards giving him orders, making him hurt really bad when he didn't do what they said? When he was sixteen and he knew for sure The Guys weren't leaving, he went looking for someone who could tell him what to do. Somebody at NASA or something. But NASA didn't answer his e-mails and his mom dragged him to a shrink. The shrink said she believed Paul about The Guys, but she didn't. She gave him drugs to take but the drugs made the world all suffocating and gray, and they didn't make The Guys go away, it just made it so Paul couldn't hear them. They were still there, though, and he knew they were getting madder and madder, and when the drugs stopped working he'd be in bad trouble. So he stopped taking the drugs, and The Guys were so pleased he'd done it on his own that they only gave him a little kick headache, not even a whole day long.

What The Guys liked best was Paul breaking into places and boosting stuff, so that's what he started to do.

He didn't live at home anymore, not since he stopped seeing the shrink and taking her drugs. He knew his mom was relieved when he moved out, even though she pretended like she wanted him to stay. He still went home to see her sometimes. She acted all nervous when he was there, which she tried to hide, but he knew. She especially got nervous when he talked to The Guys. He'd asked them to just please shut up while he was with his mom, but of course they didn't. So he still went, but not so often.

He had a basement apartment in St. George. It had bugs and it smelled moldy but it was cheap and no one bothered him and it was easy to get to whatever neighborhood The Guys wanted him to hit next. It was also easy to get to his dealer, and it was a quiet, dark place to shoot up.

The first year after he moved out was the worst of his life. The Guys wouldn't shut up, and they were really into the head-aches that whole year. It was part of some experiment they were doing for their planet. Even sometimes when Paul did exactly what they told him, they'd just start kicking. Sometimes he thought they wanted to kick his brains out from the inside.

Sometimes he wished they would.

That year it especially sucked to be him—until he discovered heroin.

Damn, damn, damn, what a find! The only bad thing: he hadn't thought of it years ago. Shooting up wasn't like taking the shrink's drugs. The Guys liked it. A needle of black tar, and everyone just relaxed, got all laid back. Made him laugh the first time, the idea of a bunch of wasted aliens nodding out inside his head. He was a little afraid right after he laughed, but while they were high The Guys didn't care, didn't get mad, were so quiet they might as well not have been there at all.

It was the only time anymore that things were that way, the only time Paul could even pretend it was like it used to be before The Guys came, when he could do what he wanted and not what he was being told to do.

He reached the top of the hill and turned around. His long, loping strides down were such a relief after the pain of fighting his way up that he almost cried. He guessed that was another thing Larry was right about, though. If The Guys didn't make him do it this way, he'd be just another junkie passed out on a stinking mattress with a needle in his arm. He wouldn't be pull-ing B&E's, he'd be mugging old ladies when he got desperate for a few bucks to buy the next fix. The running kept him in some kind of shape, kept his muscles working, and cleared his head for planning his jobs.

"Well, sure. Glad to help. Because I don't think you really want to go to prison, do you?" Larry asked as Paul passed the bright line of flags again. Paul didn't answer. Larry's questions were never supposed to get answers. "There's no heroin in jail, you know."

Paul knew, and that was enough to make the idea terrifying. No skag, and for sure The Guys would come with him. How shitty would that be? If he thought they wouldn't, he'd let his ass get picked up in a New York minute, but no such luck and he knew it.

Though on his bad days—and what day wasn't bad, really?— he wondered how long he'd be able to stay out anyway. He had an arrest record, had been fingered twice for B&E's, but he was good ("*We're* good," Stoom said. "Whose idea was the surgical gloves?") and the cops were way overworked and no one had gotten hurt either time, so they cut him loose. But lately there was a new problem.

Lately, The Guys had started liking for people to get hurt.

The first time he'd hurt someone it was by accident. Well, all three times it was. But that first time, it was a year ago and fucked if Paul wasn't as scared as she was. He'd just slipped into the garage window of a square brick house in Huguenot, and like he knew it would be, the car was gone; and like he expected, the door to the kitchen had this cheesy old lock. ("Even you can pick that," Stoom said. Roman whined, "Oh, come on, kick it in," but Paul hadn't. He didn't have to do what Roman said if one of the others said something different.) The lady who lived there never came home before noon on Tuesdays. Paul wondered where she went, to the gym, to a class or something, and if it was a class, what did she like to learn about? The Guys jeered at that but no one kicked him, and he jiggled the credit card down the doorjamb and got in.

The girl at the kitchen counter dropped the coffee pot and screamed.

Paul almost pissed himself. He'd never seen her before. She didn't live there. Curly brown hair, brown eyes, she looked like the lady, maybe a sister or something, maybe visiting, shit, what did it matter? Good thing he was wearing the ski mask. He backed toward the door, was trying to run but she threw a plate, brained him, and he went down, slipping in all that spilled coffee. He thrashed around trying to get up and she whacked at him with the broom, so he had to grab it and pull at it and she wouldn't let go. He yanked really hard and she slipped too, went down with a thud, and then gave a loud moan and a lot of, "Ow-ow-ow!" Rolling around on the floor clutching her arm. Paul sped back through the window and ran down the street, ripping the mask and gloves off as he went, shoving them into a dumpster behind the bagel place, where he stopped and threw up.

As he was wiping his mouth he realized with a chill that The Guys were laughing.

Not at him; they did that all the time and he was used to it. But with each other, like he and his buddies used to (when he was a kid and had buddies) when they'd ring old lady Miller's doorbell and run away, or when they'd boost a couple of chocolate bars from Rifkin's. It wasn't the thing, the event itself: it was the rush. That's why they'd done it, and laughed like hell afterward, from the relief of not getting caught, and the rush. That's the kind of laughing The Guys were doing now.

"Glad you thought that was funny," he said, straightening up. "You like it that she clobbered me, huh?"

"Seriously? Who gives a shit?" Roman cracked up again.

"Did you hear her screaming? *Ow-ow-OW!* I bet you broke her arm!"

"I enjoyed that face she made," Larry said. "When she screamed. I didn't know people's mouths could open that wide. That was very interesting."

Even Stoom was chortling, though he didn't have anything to say. Paul couldn't wait to get home, get his works, shoot up.

It was more than six months after that before the next person got hurt because Paul was in their house. Another accident, same kind of thing, a man coming home early, Paul barely getting out, The Guys close to hysterics. The one after that, just last month: the same but not the same. Paul had a bad feeling that time. He liked the house, full of small, fenceable stuff, he liked the layout—lots of trees and shrubs, once you got to the back door you were seriously hidden—but the lady who lived there had this funny schedule, you couldn't trust her not to come home. He was thinking maybe he should look for somewhere else but then Larry chimed in. The Guys never had an opinion before on where he should hit—at least, they'd never expressed one—but this time Larry said Paul should just go ahead and do it. Paul wanted to explain why not, but Roman started chanting, "Do it! Do it! Do it!" and when Stoom said, "I think it's a good idea too," Paul knew he was sunk. He did everything he could to be sure the lady would be away, and she was when he broke in and she was while he emptied her jewelry box into his backpack and shoved a laptop in with it and a nice little picture from the wall that might bring a few bucks, but before he could go back down the hall toward the stairs he heard her car crunch gravel in the driveway. He flashed on different ideas—hide in the closet, go out the window—but they were all stupid and he slammed down the hallway and flew down the stairs hoping he could get out while she was still wide-eyed staring and thinking, *What the fuck?* He didn't, though. She was like the girl the first time, this lady, she came right at him, screaming and cursing, smashing at him with her handbag, her fists, she was like a crazy lady. "Just move!" he yelled at her. "Just let me out of here!" But she wouldn't, so he pushed her. She stumbled backward and fell, banged her head on the floor. She made a long, low, sad/angry sound, tried to get up, couldn't get up. She pushed at the floor and flopped back, just glaring at Paul with eyes full of hate. When she tried to get up and he thought she'd be able to, he grabbed for something from the coat rack, it was just an umbrella but it was a big heavy one, and he raised it over his head.

Two things happened.

One: the lady's eyes got wide, her face went white, and she froze like a lying-down statue.

And two: Larry said mildly, "Hit her."

Paul froze too. Two frozen statues staring at each other. He dropped the umbrella and backed away, stumbled past the lady, yanked open the door, and ran. The Guys started kicking him even before he got the ski mask off. By the time he arrived back at his place his whole head was pounding, even his nose and his cheeks, like they were trying to kick his face off. It was one of the worst headaches ever and it took a long time to go away, partly because it was so bad he could hardly see to light the match and melt his tar.

When the smack wore off The Guys kicked him some more—they were really mad Paul didn't do what Larry said—so he had to have another fix. After that one, though, they calmed down for a while. By nighttime Paul was able to move his shaky self out of the apartment, get a cup of coffee and a slice.

The next day he felt okay enough to do some business. The lady's jewelry pawned pretty well, and he sold the laptop for some nice bucks. The picture, it turned out, wasn't worth shit, but his fence gave him a little for the frame, and for a couple of weeks Paul could spend the days running, eating pizza and Chinese, and shooting up. The Guys stayed pretty mellow, not like they weren't there, but it was just a lot of bullshit ragging on him, no headaches, no stupid ideas like the time they told him to jump off the ferry and he had to squeeze the rail so hard he thought he'd break his fingers. That time, they finally told him okay, he didn't have to, and then they laughed and laughed. Nothing like that now, and he relaxed a little and got into a rhythm. He saw his mom, and things were as close to good as they ever were, since The Guys had come.

Eventually, though, it got to be time to plan another job.

Paul had this idea, thinking about it only in that no-words way so The Guys wouldn't catch on. The little museum on Lighthouse Avenue, the Tibetan Museum, it had a lot of art in it, small statues, some made of gold or silver, some even with jewels on them. He told The Guys about them, how easy they'd be to fence and how much he could get for them, as long as he took them into Manhattan. He knew The Guys would like that, they liked that trip, which sometimes Paul made for skag if his dealer was in jail or something. He told them about the skylight into the square room and the alarm that even if it went off—and he didn't think the skylight was wired up, but even if it was—no one lived there and the precinct was at least five minutes away. Paul could stuff half a dozen, maybe even more, of those strange statues into his backpack and be out the door and sliding down the overgrown hill out back before the cop car ever pulled up in front. The police would walk around for a while with their flashlights, anyway. They'd try the doors in the wall, and by the time someone came to let them in, Paul would be home stashing the statues under the bed and breaking out his works.

The best part of the plan was the part he wasn't thinking in words. No one lived at the museum. No one would stop him. There'd be no one for him to hurt.

Long ago some people used to live there. Long, *long* ago the lady who built the museum lived next door, and the gardens were connected and she'd have come running. But there was a wall there now and the people who lived in her house didn't even like the museum all that much. He wasn't worried about them. And in the hillside below there were two little caves, for monks and nuns to meditate in. When Paul was a kid and used to come here, sometimes there'd be one of them in a cave for a few days, just sitting and thinking with their eyes closed. They used to leave their doors open and Paul would tiptoe over and hide behind the bushes and peek at them. Once, one of the nuns opened her eyes and saw him and he thought she'd be mad but she just smiled at him, nodded like she was saying hi, like she knew him already, and closed her eyes again. The nuns didn't look like the ones he was used to. He'd never seen real monks, only in Robin Hood comics, but they didn't look like this either. These monks and nuns had shaved heads—all of them, the nuns too—and gray robes and big brown beads, like rosary beads but not. He liked the way they seemed so calm and peaceful, though. That's why he liked to watch them. Even when he was a kid, even before The Guys came, he'd never been calm and peaceful like that.

But that was a long time ago. No one had used those caves for ten years, maybe more. The museum stopped having monks and nuns come and no one was ever there when the place was closed, and thinking without words Paul knew this was a good idea.

Even though he also knew he didn't have a good idea for next time.

He wasn't worrying about that now, as he finished his run and swung onto a bus for St. George. He couldn't. He needed to go get himself together. He'd have loved to get high but there was no way he could shoot up now and still be able to do this job when it got dark. So he went back to his basement apartment, pushed some pizza boxes and takeout cartons out of the way to find his black shirt and pants. He took a shower, even though the clothes were filthy, and then lay down, rolled himself in his blanket, and slept. He hoped The Guys would give him a break; sometimes they liked to scream and yell and wake him just as he was falling asleep. He was braced for it but they didn't and he slipped away.

When he woke up it was just after sunset. Excellent. He took his black backpack and stuffed his ski mask and his gloves into it, plus a rope, and a hammer and a pry bar for the skylight. He stuck in a light-blue sweatshirt too, for afterward when they'd be looking for a guy all in black. If anyone saw him to describe him to the cops. But no one would see him; that was the beauty of this plan.

At the bodega he bought two coffees, lots of cream and sugar, and threw them both back before he got to the bus stop. Now he was buzzed; good. He took the bus up to the corner past the museum and walked down. It was dark, with yellow squares of light glowing in people's windows, the kind of people who had normal lives and no aliens in their heads. Except for one dogwalker, no one was out. The dogwalker had gone around the corner by the time Paul got to the fence. He climbed it easily, trying to avoid the flags. He didn't know much about them but they were called prayer flags so he thought it was probably bad to step on them. He slid a little on the wet leaves on the north side of the building but he was completely hidden there from both the street and the next house. Because the building was buried in the hillside he was only maybe ten feet be-low the roof, and the rope tossed around a vent pipe took care of that. ("Lucky you're a broken-down skinny-ass runt or that pipe would've busted," Stoom pointed out. Paul didn't answer.) The skylight, like he figured, was some kind of plastic, and the panels were even easier to pry loose than he'd hoped. He lifted a panel out, laid it aside, and waited. Right about that too: no alarm. He grabbed onto the edge, slipped over, and he was in.

He dropped lightly into the center of the square stone room, almost the same spot on the floor he used to sit on when he was a kid and came in just to stare. The lady who sold the tickets thought it was neat that a little kid kept coming around, and didn't make him pay anything. Sometimes if he'd boosted some candy bars he'd bring her one, and she always took it with a big smile and a thank you.

He slipped the headlamp on and turned slowly, watching the beam play over the room. The place hadn't changed much, maybe not at all. On the side built into the hill a couple of stone ledges stepped back. Most of the statues sat on them, lined up in rows. A bunch more were in cases against the other three walls. Two of the cases stood one on either side of the door out to the balcony. The space smelled cool and damp, like it was one of those caves where the nuns and monks used to stay. It was still and silent, but not the heavy silence of the shrink's drugs or the skag. Those made him feel like everything was still there, he was just shutting it out. This, it was a quiet like every-thing had stopped to rest.

"What a lovely little trip down Memory Lane," Larry said acidly. "Can we get to work now?"

Paul swung the backpack off, opened it, and stepped up to the shelves, leaning over each statue. He wanted them all, wanted to take them and put them in his basement room just to stare around at them, but that wasn't why he was here and no matter how many he took that wasn't what would happen to them. He reached out. This one, it was gold. He held it, let the headlamp glint off it. Then into the pack. That one was beautiful but it was iron. Leave it. The two there, with jewels and coral, into the pack. The silver one. That little candlestick, it too. That was all the best from the ledges. Now for the cases on the walls. Paul turned his head, sweeping the light around.

There she was.

Just like the first time, the girl in the kitchen, Paul almost pissed himself. A nun, in gray robes, big brown beads around her neck. She smiled softly and Paul's mouth fell open. It was the same nun, the one from the cave, smiling the same smile.

"You—you—you're still here?" he managed to stammer.

"I've always been here," she replied. Her eyes twinkled, and she stood with her hands folded in front of her. When she smiled she looked like the lady he used to give candy bars to. He'd never noticed that before, that they looked alike. "Paul," she said, "you know you can't take those."

His voice had rung oddly off the stone walls. Hers didn't disturb the sense that everything was resting.

"How do you know my name?" This time he whispered so he wouldn't get the same echo.

"You came here when you were a little boy."

He nodded. "I used to watch you sitting there. Meditating."

"I know. I thought perhaps you'd join me sometime."

"I—"

Larry interrupted him, barking, "Paul! Get back to work."

He said, "Just give me—"

"No!"

That was Roman. The kick was from him too. Paul's head

almost cracked. The pain was blinding, and he barely heard the nun calmly say, "Roman, stop that."

The kicking stopped instantly. Paul stared at the nun. "You can hear them?"

She smiled. "You don't have to do what they say, you know."

Paul swallowed. "Yes, I do."

"Yes, he does," Larry said.

"Yes! He does!" Roman yelled.

"No," said the nun.

"I can't get them to leave." Paul was suddenly ashamed of how forlorn he sounded. Like a real loser. He heard Larry snicker.

"Even so," she said.

He wasn't sure how to answer her, but he didn't get the chance. "Paul?" That was Stoom, sounding dark. When Stoom got mad it was really, really bad. "Do what you came for, and do it now. Remember, Paul: no swag, no skag." It was one of those times Paul could hear Stoom's sneer.

Paul looked at the nun, and then slowly around the room. The headlamp picked out fierce faces, jeweled eyes. "There's lots of places I could hit," he said to The Guys. "Doesn't have to be here. This was a dumb idea. You know, like my ideas always are. How about I just—"

"No," said Stoom.

"No," said Larry.

And Roman started kicking him, chanting, "No swag, no skag! No swag, no skag!" Then they were all three chanting and kicking, chanting and kicking.

Paul staggered forward, toward a statue of a person sitting cross-legged like the nun did. Pearls and coral studded its flowing gold robes. He reached for it but the nun moved smoothly in front of it. She said nothing, just smiled.

"No," Paul heard himself croak. "Please. You have to let me."

She shook her head.

"Paul!" Stoom snapped. "You moron loser. Push her out of the way."

"No. I'll get a different one."

"I want THAT one!" Roman whined.

Paul swung his head around. The headlamp picked out a glittering statue with lots of arms, over in a case by the door. He turned his back on the nun and lurched toward it. By the time he got there she was standing in front of it, hands folded, smiling. He hadn't seen her move.

"Paul," she said, "this life has been hard for you. I don't know why; I think, though, that the next turn of the wheel will be far better."

He didn't know what she was talking about. Wheel, what wheel? All three of The Guys were kicking him now, Roman the hardest, trying to pop his right eye out. "Please," he said. "Get out of the way."

She said nothing, just smiled the ticket lady's smile and stood there.

Paul took two steps over to the next cabinet.

There she was.

"Please!" he shouted at her. "Stop it!" His head pounded, the pain so searing he thought he might throw up. He could barely see but he knew she was still standing between him and the statues. "*Please!*"

"Hit her." That was Larry. Paul barely heard him through the pain. He tried to pretend he didn't hear him at all but Larry laughed. "Hit her. With a statue."

Paul's hands trembled as he reached into the backpack, took out the gold statue. "Please," he whispered to the nun–ticket lady. "Please move."

She just stood and smiled.

Paul lifted the statue way high. As he brought it down on her shaved head he realized he was screaming.

He felt the impact on her skull, felt it all the way up to his shoulders, his back. The nun crumpled to the floor without a sound. Blood flowed from the smashed-in place, started to pool under her face. Paul dropped the statue; it fell with a splash into the puddle of blood. "Oh my God," he whispered. "Oh my God oh my God oh my God."

"Oh my God is right!" Larry roared a grand, triumphant laugh. "You killed her!"

"Killed her! Killed her!" shrieked Roman.

"You know what happens now, don't you?" Larry said. "You go to jail. Prison, you loser, you go to prison where there's no smack and we go too! Oh, will that be fun!"

"No." Paul could barely get the word out. "I didn't. She's not dead."

"Really?" said Stoom. "Can you wake her up?"

Paul kneeled slowly, put out his hand, shook the nun gently. She still had that little smile, the ticket lady's smile, but she didn't respond at all.

"Look at all that blood," Stoom said. "You're stupid if you think anyone could be still alive with all their blood on the floor like that. You're stupid anyway, but she's dead and you killed her."

"Prison!" Roman bellowed. "Killed her! Prison!"

"No." Paul stood slowly, shaking his head. "No."

"Oh, yes, yes," Larry said. "Oh, yes."

Paul took one more look at the nun, then staggered toward the exit door. An alarm shrieked as he pushed it open. He ran across the terrace, slipping on the autumn leaves. When he got to the railing he stared down; the headlamp shone on branches and bushes growing out of the wall beneath him but couldn't reach all the way to the street below.

He grabbed the rail, ready to vault over.

"No," said Stoom in that very hard voice. "No, you're staying."

Paul felt his grip tighten on the rail, like The Guys were controlling his fingers. He heard a siren wail. That would be the cops, because of the door alarm. If he was still here when they came, he'd go to prison for sure.

"That's right," Larry said with satisfaction. "Prison for sure."

Paul took a slow, deep breath. "No," he whispered. "She told me I don't have to do what you say."

The Guys yelled, they bellowed and kicked, but Paul loosened his fingers one by one. He climbed over the railing, stood for a minute on the edge of the wall. Then he dove. His last thought was the hope that The Guys wouldn't have time to clear out of his head before he smashed it to bits on the pavement.

The impact, the thud of a body landing forty feet below, didn't penetrate very far into the square stone room. It barely disturbed the resting stillness, didn't echo at all past the golden Buddha in the middle of the floor. The statue lay on its side on a smooth dry stone tile, beside a backpack full of other statues. Except for the statue and the backpack, and the single panel removed from the skylight, nothing was out of place. The calm silence in the room continued, and would continue once the statues had been replaced in their proper spots by the museum's new director.

She would be pleased that something had scared off the thief, though greatly saddened that he'd fallen to his death over the railing at the terrace. As advised by the police, she'd add an alarm to the skylight. She had much to do, as she was all the staff the museum had. She guided visitors, and also sold the tickets, the ticket lady having retired years ago. She didn't mind the work. She was hoping, even, to soon reopen the meditation caves, to perhaps make the museum not just a serene spot, but a useful one, as it once had been: a beacon for poor souls with troubled minds.

ABOUT THE CONTRIBUTORS

TED ANTHONY, a longtime journalist, has reported from more than twenty countries and forty-seven US states. He has been a foreign correspondent in China and covered the aftermath of 9/11 in Pakistan and Afghanistan and the early months of the war in Iraq. He is the author of the cultural history *Chasing the Rising Sun: The Journey of an American Song.*

Ted Anthony

TODD CRAIG is a product of Ravenswood and Queensbridge Houses in Queens, New York. He is a writer, educator, and deejay. Straddling fiction, creative nonfiction, and poetry, Craig's texts paint vivid depictions of the urban lifestyle he experienced in his community. He currently teaches English at the College of Staten Island while completing his doctorate in English at St. John's University.

Rachel Crick

ASHLEY DAWSON is a professor of English at the City University of New York's Graduate Center and at the College of Staten Island. He is the author of *Mongrel Nation: Diasporic Culture and the Making of Postcolonial Britain* and *The Routledge Concise History of Twentieth-Century British Literature,* and coeditor of three essay collections, including *Democracy, States, and the Struggle for Global Justice* and *Dangerous Professors: Academic Freedom and the National Security Campus.*

Ashley Dawson

BRUCE DESILVA is the author of the hard-boiled Mulligan crime novels *Cliff Walk* and *Rogue Island,* with a third, *Providence Rag,* on the way. His fiction has won Edgar and Macavity awards and has been a finalist for the Anthony and Shamus awards. He worked as a journalist for forty years, most recently as a senior editor for the Associated Press. He reviews books for the Associated Press and is a master's thesis advisor at the Columbia University Graduate School of Journalism.

Patricia DeSilva

LOUISA ERMELINO is the reviews director at *Publishers Weekly.* She has worked at *People, Time,* and *Instyle,* and written three novels: *Joey Dee Gets Wise, The Black Madonna,* and *The Sisters Mallone.* Her family summered in Staten Island and it is the home of her husband's family and "the site of a large part of our courtship."

Carrie Tuby

Kerry Kehoe

EDDIE JOYCE was born and raised on Staten Island. He is working on his first novel. Before he started writing, he was a criminal defense attorney in Manhattan for ten years. He lives in Brooklyn with his wife and three daughters.

Marion Ettlinger

BINNIE KIRSHENBAUM is the author of two story collections, *Married Life* and *History on a Personal Note*, and six novels: *On Mermaid Avenue, A Disturbance in One Place, Pure Poetry, Hester Among the Ruins, An Almost Perfect Moment*, and *The Scenic Route*. She is a professor and currently serving as chair at Columbia University's MFA program. She taught at Staten Island's Wagner College twenty years ago.

Lisa Largo

MICHAEL LARGO has published three novels and four books of nonfiction. He won the Bram Stoker Award for *Final Exits: The Illustrated Encyclopedia of How We Die*. He was born on Staten Island and grew up a few blocks away from where Willie Sutton once lived. He attended the College of Staten Island and, among other things, once owned the St. Marks Bar & Grill in Manhattan.

Celeste Marshall

BILL LOEHFELM is the author of three novels, most recently *The Devil She Knows*, as well as *Fresh Kills*, winner of the first Amazon Breakthrough Novel Award, and *Bloodroot*. All three novels are set in Loehfelm's home borough of Staten Island. He grew up in Eltingville, and is a graduate of Monsignor Farrell High School. He currently lives in New Orleans' Garden District with his wife, A.C. Lambeth, a writer and yoga instructor, and their two dogs.

Matthew Powell

LINDA NIEVES-POWELL was selected as one of the 100 Most Influential Hispanics by *Hispanic Business* magazine. She is the author of the novel *Free Style*, and the writer and director of the award-winning plays *Yo Soy Latina!* and *Jose Can Speak,* and is the creator, cowriter, director, and producer of the comedic web series *Happy Cancer Chick*. She moved to Staten Island when she was thirteen, and still lives there today.

Meg Penncavage

MICHAEL PENNCAVAGE won a 2008 Derringer Award for his story "The Cost of Doing Business." He has been an associate editor for *Space and Time* magazine, as well as editor of the horror/suspense anthology *Tales from a Darker State.* He has been published in approximately eighty magazines and anthologies, and is a member of the Mystery Writers of America, the Horror Writers of America, and the Garden State Horror Writers.

Ashley Gilbertson

S.J. ROZAN is the author of thirteen novels and three dozen short stories. She has won Edgar, Shamus, Anthony, Nero, and Macavity awards, and was a recipient of the Japanese Maltese Falcon Award. She has served on the boards of Mystery Writers of America and Sisters in Crime, and as president of Private Eye Writers of America. Her latest book is *Ghost Hero.* Rozan set a large portion of her book *Absent Friends* on Staten Island.

Rachel Eliza Griffiths

PATRICIA SMITH is the author of six acclaimed poetry volumes, including *Shoulda Been Jimi Savannah; Blood Dazzler,* a finalist for the 2008 National Book Award; and *Teahouse of the Almighty,* a National Poetry Series selection. She is a professor at the College of Staten Island and serves on the faculties of the Stonecoast and Sierra Nevada College low-residency MFA programs.

Eric Lane

SHAY YOUNGBLOOD is the author of the novels *Black Girl in Paris* and *Soul Kiss* and a collection of short fiction, *The Big Mama Stories.* She is the recipient of numerous grants and awards, including a Pushcart Prize, a Lorraine Hansberry Playwriting Award, a 2004 New York Foundation for the Arts Sustained Achievement Award, and a 2011/2012 Japan-U.S. Friendship Commission Fellowship. Shay lived in Staten Island from 1995 to 2002.